On the beach is where it happened, Diary. I knew we shouldn't have gone there. I knew it was a bad idea. But I couldn't help myself. "I love walking on the beach at night," I said, dabbling a bare foot in the cool surf.

"Me too," Jeffrey said in a husky voice. "As long as I'm walking with you, Elizabeth."

He pulled me to his warm, strong chest and placed his lips against mine. Oh, Diary. It was the most incredible kiss I have ever had in my entire life. A romance-novel kiss. I was on fire with this delirious, uncontrollable happiness. But suddenly, the kiss changed. A shudder went through Jeffrey's body, and his hands tightened on my shoulders.

Jeffrey's eyes opened at the same time as mine. In them, I saw the sudden realization that the twin he was kissing was not Elizabeth.

We separated, and Jeffrey looked at me. Then he pulled me toward him again, and kissed me even more passionately.

We were wrong. We knew we were wrong, but we did it anyway.

JESSICA'S SECRET DIARY

Written by
Kate William

Created by
FRANCINE PASCAL

BANTAM BOOKS
NEW YORK · TORONTO · LONDON · SYDNEY · AUCKLAND

RL 6, age 12 and up

JESSICA'S SECRET DIARY
A Bantam Book / September 1994

Sweet Valley High® is a registered trademark of Francine Pascal
Conceived by Francine Pascal
Produced by Daniel Weiss Associates, Inc.
33 West 17th Street
New York, NY 10011
Cover art by Bruce Emmett

ISBN: 0-553-56659-8

Published simultaneously in the United States and Canada

Bantam Books are published by Bantam Books, a division of Bantam
Doubleday Dell Publishing Group, Inc. Its trademark, consisting of the
words "Bantam Books" and the portrayal of a rooster, is Registered in
U.S. Patent and Trademark Office and in other countries. Marca
Registrada. Bantam Books, 1540 Broadway, New York, New York 10036.

PRINTED IN THE UNITED STATES OF AMERICA

OPM   0 9 8 7 6 5 4 3 2 1

JUL 3 0 2005

155480

To Briana Ferris Adler

Prologue

I leaned on the redwood railing of the deck, looking at all that ocean and sand. I love the Pacific Ocean; on calm days it's exactly the same shade of blue-green as my eyes.

"I don't care if this place does belong to Bruce Patman and his stuck-up family!" I declared. "It is definitely the most gorgeous beach house in all of southern California."

"Jessica Wakefield, you exaggerate more than any person on earth," said my best friend, Lila Fowler, brushing an imaginary piece of lint off her expensive silk sarong. I know it was expensive because I was with her when she picked it out at Bibi's at the mall the other day. Besides, Lila is the daughter of a millionaire and would never be caught dead in an outfit that didn't cost about as much as my Jeep.

"Come on, Lila," Amy Sutton said, throwing me a let's-see-how-far-we-can-push-Lila glance. "Do you mean to say that you don't think this place is wonderful?"

Amy and I both love Lila like a sister—well, maybe I love her *more* than *my* sister lately. But it can be fun to bait her.

Don't get me wrong. Lila, Amy, and I will do just about anything for each other when the chips are really down. We've been inseparable for most of the school year—ever since Amy came back to town after living in the East for five years. And we've been even closer since our other good friend, Cara Walker, moved away. But we also compete with each other for pretty much everything. And we tend to take turns giving each other a hard time. At the moment it was Lila's turn to get ragged on.

"Oh, I suppose the Patmans' beach house is all right," Lila conceded.

I rolled my eyes at Amy. Lila was trying so hard to be low-key about the Patmans' luxurious beach cabana, but I knew she was green with envy—about the same color as her jade-green sarong. Bruce and his cousin Roger are the only kids at Sweet Valley High whose family is as wealthy as the Fowlers, and Lila hates to share her top billing in the Credit Card Hall of Fame.

Rich, handsome Bruce has the most awesome car in school, and an ego to match. Actually, he was almost human a few months back—even *nice*—while he was dating Regina Morrow. But by the time of his big beach party, he was back to being his usual self—in other words, an arrogant bore.

Amy gestured around the tiered deck. "This place

2

is a lot more than 'all right.' For a complete jerk, Bruce knows how to throw a fabulous party!"

Lila's brown eyes flashed.

"Of course," Amy added quickly, "the food and decorations don't have that Fowler flair." You can only push Lila so far, and Amy had hit on a dangerous subject. Everyone knows that Lila prides herself on giving the best parties in town. "But even *you* have to admit, Lila, that Bruce spared no expense for tonight!"

Lila finally gave in. "Well, he certainly could have done worse with the setting," she said, gazing out at the ocean. Her light-brown hair swayed in the breeze, shining softly with a hint of the rosy twilight that was fading from the sky.

Then Lila turned to me. "Not that *you* even noticed the setting, Jessica—until our dates went inside to get us something to drink. Whenever Jack Wayland is nearby, you are totally oblivious to everything else."

Amy nodded. "Admit it, Jess. You are head over heels for Jack! When he's around, the entire Sweet Valley High football team could prance across the beach stark naked, and you wouldn't even raise an eyebrow."

I laughed, though it wasn't a bad mental image. "All right. I admit it. I'm as crazy about Jack as he is about me."

"So is it true love?" Amy pressed, trying to squeeze some new gossip out of me. "Has he finally told you he can't live without you?"

"Well, not exactly," I admitted. "Jack is kind of shy

3

when it comes to talking about things like love. But he's almost ready to tell me he loves me. I'm sure of it. After all, how can he resist me?"

Lila raised her eyebrows. "This sounds serious."

"Of course it's serious," I said, annoyed. "I don't know why you both sound so skeptical. I'm officially in love. And I've been telling you so for days!"

"Yes, you have," Lila said. "But for most of the years I've known you, Jessica, you've fallen madly in love about twice a month. How am I supposed to know when you really mean it?"

Now, that wasn't fair. I always *think* I really mean it—at least until somebody better comes along. But this relationship was different. I was sure of it. "This time it's the real thing."

The big love of my life, Sam Woodruff, had died in a car accident a few months earlier. I'd been pretty messed up for a while after that. I'll never forget Sam, but I finally felt ready for another long-term relationship. And every time I looked into Jack's eyes, I knew I couldn't live without him.

"Jack is the best-looking, sexiest, funnest guy I know," I bragged, "not to mention the fact that he's a college man. And have you seen his eyes close up? They are the most amazing—"

"—the most amazing shade of deep brown, with golden sparkles in them," Lila finished for me. "You've told us at least six times a day for the last three weeks."

"You know, Jessica," Amy warned, "it can be dangerous to your self-esteem to place so much emphasis on a relationship, especially in the early stages—"

"OK!" I protested. "I'll stop talking about Jack's sexy eyes—but only if you stop with the Project Youth psychobabble. I swear, Amy, ever since you've been working at that hot line—"

"Unfortunately, I can't say that my own date tonight is as perfect as yours, Jessica," Lila admitted. She had a short attention span for any conversation that wasn't about herself. "Paul Sherwood is good-looking, of course. But I don't think I'll go out with him again. He's such a snob."

I stole a glance at Amy and tried not to laugh. Unfortunately, Lila noticed that glance and moved in for revenge.

"Actually, Jessica, I'm surprised you're even here tonight," she said in that acid tone she uses when she's ticked off. "Didn't you flunk the French test Ms. Dalton handed back today?"

"Hey, that's right!" Amy remembered. "I thought your parents said you'd be grounded for the rest of your life if you failed this one."

"I did," I admitted. "And I will be. But Mom and Dad went to Los Angeles for dinner and a show, and they're spending the night. They won't know I flunked Ms. Dalton's crummy test until they come home tomorrow. And if I'm getting grounded tomorrow, I might as well have a fantabulous time tonight!" I smiled, thinking about those gorgeous brown eyes with the golden flecks. "With Jack."

"Can't you just explain to your parents that the test was unfair?" Amy asked. "Maybe if they see that

5

no normal person could possibly have passed it . . ."

Suddenly I felt grumpy. "No chance. My brainy twin sister not only passed the test, but scored a perfect hundred! Isn't that disgusting?"

"Totally," Amy agreed. "Sometimes I think Elizabeth gets good grades just to show the rest of us up."

"I'm glad I'm an only child, Jess," Lila said. "It must be a drag, having someone as perfect as Liz around—especially someone who looks exactly like you."

She nodded toward the pool off the far edge of the deck, where Elizabeth and her boyfriend—tall, dark-haired, deadly dull Todd Wilkins—sprawled together on an enormous floating lounge chair.

I tried to appraise my sister objectively. Elizabeth is certainly beautiful—in fact, she looks like a mirror image of me. We're sixteen years old, with honey-gold hair, slim, athletic figures, and sparkling eyes. But everyone says the similarity is only skin deep.

The French test was typical. I really had meant to study for it. But I was just so busy all week doing more important things—going to cheerleading practice, shopping at the mall with Lila for new bathing suits and cover-ups for the party, gossiping on the phone with Amy, and, of course, seeing Jack and thinking about Jack and telling everybody all about Jack.

Elizabeth, naturally, had spent a half hour every night reviewing French verbs—even though she was busy, too, in her own way. Of course, Elizabeth's usual activities are so dull that studying French probably seems like a vacation. She spends her time writing for the school newspaper, tutoring people in English, organizing charity events, reading, and doing homework with her best friend, Enid Rollins—also known as the World's Most Boring Teenager.

So now Elizabeth had aced the French test, and I was left looking like an idiot in comparison. It just wasn't fair.

"I used to like being a twin," I said. "But you're right, Lila. Lately being one of a matched set is the pits! I wish Liz and I were just sisters. If we didn't look so much alike, people wouldn't be comparing us all the time."

The bad thing about being compared to Elizabeth is that she always seems to come out on top. Honestly, I was sick of hearing about Elizabeth's perfect grades and spotless room. Everybody loves my twin. Elizabeth is sweet and helpful and can keep a secret. And she's so darn good at everything. When Elizabeth cooks dinner at home, nobody ever gets food poisoning, as my family will never let me forget.

And, of course, being the perfect person she is, she's always on time. Elizabeth was born four minutes before I was, and I never seem to catch up, even when I try—though I have to admit that I don't try very often. In the grand scheme of life, a few minutes here and there isn't that big a deal. Is it?

For once I had Elizabeth beat, I realized with a grin. "She may be the perfect twin," I said, "but *I'm* the one who's dating the perfect guy!"

Amy pointed toward Elizabeth and Todd. "I don't know, Jess. You have to admit that Todd is one of the best-looking guys at Sweet Valley High—after Barry, of course," she added quickly, remembering her own steady boyfriend, Barry Rork.

"Oh, Todd's cute enough, but he's such a Goody Two-shoes," I said. "Face it—Liz has crummy taste in men!" I stopped, thinking of the one exception— Jeffrey French. Elizabeth had dated the blond soccer player for several months, when Todd's family moved away from Sweet Valley. But Todd had returned to town, and his relationship with Elizabeth was now as steady as a rock.

And just about as exciting.

"Todd is definitely a snooze of a boyfriend," I concluded. "He's not nearly as exciting as—"

"We know," Lila interrupted in a bored voice. She could have at least tried to *sound* supportive, for my sake. "He's not nearly as exciting as Jack."

"Exactly!" I said, ignoring her lack of interest.

"Speaking of Mr. Wonderful, he's on his way over here," Amy said, pointing. "With Barry and Paul. I wonder what took them so long with our sodas. I'm practically dying of thirst."

An hour later life was great. I swayed in Jack's arms to a slow ballad on the CD player. Jack was the perfect height to dance with. I always thought I liked really tall guys, but I was wrong. Jack was an inch shorter than six feet—tall enough to be gorgeous, but not so tall that my face got smashed against his chest when we danced. Of course, with shoulders as broad as Jack's, height didn't seem to make a bit of difference.

"Know what tonight is?" I whispered into his ear, making sure my lips were very close to his earlobe.

"Friday?" he asked.

"Besides that."

"I don't know. I give up."

I kissed him softly on the cheek. "It's our anniversary! It was just one month ago today when I walked into the reference room of the university library with my sister to research our stupid history papers. I reached for the J-through-L volume of the encyclopedia at the same time you did. And the rest is history."

I gazed into Jack's deep-brown eyes, and a delicious tingle ran through my body. Suddenly I felt very warm. I skated my fingers up his muscular arm, feeling the heat of his skin through his cotton sleeve. This was it, I decided. It was time. I took a deep breath and opened my mouth to tell Jack that I was in love with him.

Then I closed it again, afraid. How would he react? I wasn't used to making myself vulnerable with a boy. I'm one of the prettiest, most popular girls in the junior class; it's the guy who always declares *his* undying love for *me*. Then *I* get to decide whether to break his heart or make his day. But Jack was different. This was a guy who could break my heart, for real. And the thought scared me.

I leaned against his shoulder, breathing in the woodsy smell of his aftershave. Maybe I would wait a few minutes longer before telling him that I loved him. Or maybe I wouldn't have to. Maybe he would speak first.

Since our meeting in the library, Jack had come to the house again and again. He never actually asked me out. He was awfully shy. But he always agreed when I suggested we go to the Dairi Burger or a movie.

As we slow-danced, his muscular body sent little electric currents into me. *He wouldn't keep coming back to the house if he didn't really like me, would he?*

But did Jack *love* me? I couldn't be certain, but I thought he did. And he could hardly help but notice how much I liked him. My heart was pounding so hard as we danced that I was afraid Jack could feel it through the strapless, filmy dress I wore over my bathing suit.

"He's going to tell me tonight that he loves me," I whispered under my breath, crossing my fingers behind his back. Then I realized what the problem was. Someone as shy as Jack needed more privacy to make such a declaration. I decided I'd have to get him alone as soon as possible, away from the party. Then he would look down at me, his deep-brown eyes full of love, and he would say—

Suddenly a sharp impact knocked me against Jack. He steadied me in his strong arms.

"Oh, I'm so sorry," said a giggling voice. I turned to see a vaguely familiar sophomore couple. A fat, curly-haired girl was speaking. "We're still trying to get the hang of this dancing thing," she explained. "We didn't mean to crash into you like that, Elizabeth."

I clenched my jaw. *"I'm Jessica!"*

10

"Ooops, sorry!" the girl said, putting a hand over her mouth. "I'd heard she had a twin!" The fat little twerp shrugged, waved, and spiraled awkwardly away with her partner.

She called me Elizabeth! I fumed.

"Elizabeth," Jack murmured. "There are worse people to be mistaken for. Don't let it bother you so much."

"Don't let it bother me?" I stormed. "How can I not let it bother me?" Then I saw the stricken look on Jack's face and gave him a weak smile. I didn't want him to think I was mad at him. "Sorry. I guess I've been having kind of an identity-crisis thing, but I shouldn't take it out on you. It isn't your fault."

"Come on," he said as if he'd just reached some sort of decision. He steered me toward the steps that led to the beach. "Let's take a walk along the water, where we can be alone. There's something I want to talk to you about."

I held my breath. This was it. Jack *had* been waiting for a chance to slip away! Now he was going to tell me that he loved me. I wanted to skip and dance and shout. But I willed my feet, in my new silver sandals, to stroll slowly down the cool sand to the water's edge.

The moon lit a shimmering path on the rippled surface of the water, so bright that I felt I could walk on it. The sky was dotted with stars; the night was filled with the soft sound of waves brushing on the sand. And the salt smell of the ocean nearly overpowered the evergreen scent of Jack's aftershave.

11

"This is incredibly romantic," I breathed.

Jack cleared his throat, but then stared out at the water, obviously too shy to speak. If we were going to make our declarations of love tonight, I reasoned, I would have to be the one to start.

I took a deep breath and put my hands on Jack's shoulders, hoping my head was inclined at just the right angle so that the moonlight would shimmer like stardust in my hair.

"Jessica, you are so beautiful . . . ," Jack began in a whisper. He stopped, shaking his head.

I took a deep breath. "It's all right, Jack," I said. "You don't have to. I know what you're going to say. And, Jack, I love you, too. I love you more than I've ever loved anyone."

Jack shook his head again. "Ah, Jessica. I've been fighting my true feelings ever since the day we met. But I can't do it anymore. I have to tell you the truth."

I smiled, glad I had waited for the perfect romantic setting. No other girl in southern California could be as happy as I felt right then.

Jack gently lifted my chin, as if he were going to kiss me. Then he tore my heart in two.

"Jessica, I'm in love with your sister, Elizabeth."

My knees buckled, and Jack steadied me with a hand on my arm. I shook my head, incredulous. I must have heard him wrong! But the pity in Jack's gorgeous brown eyes was unmistakable, even in the moonlight.

"I'm sorry, Jessica," Jack whispered helplessly. "I

should have told you sooner. I didn't realize you felt so strongly. . . ."

To my horror I burst into tears. Then I shook off his hand and ran wildly down the damp, cold beach.

Jack didn't follow.

I threw open the door of my cluttered bedroom and collapsed onto the unmade bed. "I'll never get over this!" I wailed into my pillow. "Not if I live to be a hundred years old!"

I had lost Jack to Elizabeth, who barely knew he was alive. And I had humiliated myself in front of him. If there is one thing I can't bear, it's to have people feel sorry for me.

But Jack wasn't the real problem. He was only the last straw. I just couldn't stand it anymore. Elizabeth always did everything right and got everything handed to her, while I settled for second-best. I couldn't stand another day of being an inferior copy of something that was made right in the first place.

I wanted to hate Elizabeth for always coming out on top. I concentrated on summoning up some real, scream-at-the-top-of-my-lungs anger toward my sister, but I couldn't do it. I could be upset with Elizabeth, but I couldn't hate her—not after everything we'd been through together. It wasn't Elizabeth's fault that everybody loved her. Heck, *I* loved her.

"Elizabeth isn't the problem," I whispered between sobs. "*I'm* the problem. I'm the one who's not lovable."

13

Prince Albert, our family's golden retriever, ambled into the room and gazed at me with a questioning look on his face.

"Why should I expect people like Jack to love me?" I demanded of the dog. "Look at me—I'm a mess! I can't go on like this. I have to do something!"

I pounded my fist against the wall and screamed to the empty house: "I hate being a twin!"

Prince Albert raced out of the room, his tail waving behind him like a flag of surrender.

"I have to leave," I decided aloud. "I have to get away from here."

When I make up my mind about something, I act on it right away. So I ran to my closet and yanked my bulky suitcase off the top shelf. Papers, scarves, and old magazines showered down on me from the cluttered shelf, but I ignored them and threw the powder-blue suitcase onto the bed.

"I'll go somewhere where nobody knows I have a perfect twin sister," I said aloud, "where nobody can compare me to her ever again. *I hate being a twin!*"

I grabbed a wrinkled pair of faded jeans from the jumble of clothing on the floor and pushed them into the suitcase. Then I started jerking clothes almost at random off the floor and out of dresser drawers, stuffing them into the suitcase until it was full. I began fumbling with the case's zipper, ready to rush out of the house with my suitcase and never return again.

Then I remembered my secret notebooks. I couldn't leave them behind; I would be mortified if

14

anyone ever saw them. I reached under the bed for the pile of purple-covered notebooks that made up my secret diary.

Nobody knows that I keep a diary—not even Elizabeth, who knows practically everything about me. I mean, I've always given *her* a hard time for writing when it wasn't even required for school. So I was too embarrassed to tell her early this year when I started wanting to write down my own thoughts. Besides, the thoughts I record in my diary are private—too private to tell even Elizabeth.

I started to shove the purple notebooks into the overstuffed suitcase, but one just fell open in my hand. It was weird, as if it were some sort of sign. My eyes caught a glimpse of a familiar phrase—a phrase I had just screamed out to the empty house a few minutes earlier. There was no room to sit on the bed, so I slid into my desk chair, shoved aside a pile of old test papers, and began reading my secret diary.

Part 1

Dear Diary,

I hate being a twin! I really hate it. I'm serious, Diary. The worst part is that my twin happens to be Elizabeth I-Do-Everything-Right Wakefield. I wish I were somewhere else, where nobody knows I have a perfect twin sister, so nobody could compare me to her ever again. I just want to have my own identity. Is that too much to ask?

It's bad enough that Dad keeps making those corny comments about me and Liz being carbon copies. I absolutely despise that! But something worse happened the other day as I was leaving the beach party with Lila. Mr. Collins stopped me in the parking lot when I saw him there with his kid, Teddy. I wondered what in the heck he wanted with me. I mean, Mr. Collins is pretty cool for a teacher—if you have to learn about punctuation, you might as well learn it from someone who looks like Robert Redford! But I'm not the superstudent type that teachers buddy up with. In other words, I'm not like a certain other person I know—a person who looks just like me but gets better grades.

"I could have sworn you were Elizabeth," Mr. Collins said when he recognized me. I was mortified! This is a man who sees us both every day—a man who's supposed to be smart—and even he can't tell us apart. But the crowning insult was when Teddy the Brat yelled, "Which one is she, Daddy?" loud enough so that people could probably hear him clear over in Big Mesa.

I just read an article in Ingenue magazine about identity crises. I think I'm having one. I'm sick and tired of being an identical twin. Unfortunately, there isn't much I can do about it. I think I'll call Cara and Lila for an emergency ice-cream meeting. Maybe they'll have some ideas. . . .

I shifted uncomfortably on the vinyl bench of a booth at Casey's Ice Cream Parlor. I had explained my problem to Cara and Lila, but they just didn't get it.

"I always wished I had a sister," Cara said, stirring the strawberry topping into her sundae.

I sighed, disappointed. Even my very closest friends couldn't seem to understand what I was going through. What did they know about it? Cara had only a pesky little brother; her other experience with siblings was limited to her dates with *my* older brother, Steven. And Lila, an only child, thought of a sister as someone who followed you around adoringly, flattered you a lot, and tried to be like you.

Fat chance, I thought. In reality a sister is someone who shows you up by getting good grades, steals all your parents' attention, and wins over good-looking guys like blond, athletic Jeffrey French.

Until people stopped comparing me to Elizabeth, I was afraid I'd always be stuck with my sister's leftovers. I would never truly be my own person if people only thought of me as Elizabeth's dumber clone.

"Listen, guys," I said, spooning up a chunk of chocolate from my Oreo sundae. "I know exactly what's going on here. *Ingenue* magazine had a whole article on it last month."

Cara laughed. "I thought they had an article on bad posture!"

"The article was on identity crisis. Don't you realize that's exactly what's happening to me? I'm losing myself!"

"I must be dumb," Lila said, an ironic gleam in her eyes ensuring us that she knew she wasn't, "but I just don't seem to see what the crisis is, Jess. Don't you think you're making a big deal out of—"

"It *is* a big deal. Don't you think an identity crisis is a big deal?"

"Why do you have to have an identity crisis?" Cara asked in a reasonable voice. "It always seems to me that you and Liz manage to be pretty different in most respects. I wouldn't worry about people mistaking you guys, Jess. You're as different as night and day."

"You really think so?" I asked, a little less glumly.

Cara laughed. "Come on, Jess! Of course you two are different! It would be really hard to confuse the two of you."

Later Monday night

> *My mood's been up and down so many times tonight, Diary, that I feel like a yo-yo—or Lila's credit-card balance. I really did feel better for a few minutes after we left Casey's. Unfortunately, it didn't last. On the way to our cars in the parking lot of the mall, we started talking again, and it got me all depressed. But then Lila said something that actually made sense. . . .*

"I'm glad you've finally stopped worrying about this identity-crisis stuff," Cara said as we walked toward our cars. "Don't you think the whole idea was a little melodramatic?"

I whirled on her, furious that she hadn't taken anything I said seriously. "This is really beginning to get exasperating! You two are supposed to be my very best friends—and you don't even understand what's bothering me!"

"Then why don't you try to explain it to us again?" Lila suggested.

I took a deep breath and tried to put my worries into words. "It's just this—all my life I've been known for being Elizabeth's sister. When do I get a chance to be just Jessica?"

"You are just Jessica," Lila said. "Honestly, Jess, I don't see what the problem is. You're nothing like Elizabeth! Besides, you sure don't mind taking advantage of looking just like Liz when you've got something to gain from the deal."

"She's got you there, Jess," Cara agreed. "I can think of plenty of times when you've pretended to be Liz or made her pretend to be you."

"That's different!" I said, my voice rising. "Those are just pranks. This is serious. It's my *identity* we're talking about!"

Lila rolled her eyes. "I still don't understand what you're so worked up about. But I know one thing. The Jessica I know wouldn't sit around whining and feeling sorry for herself. If the situation was important to her, she'd come up with a plan for addressing the problem— even if nobody else even thought it *was* a problem."

"You're absolutely right!" I said. "I need a plan."

"What are you going to do?" Cara asked, a little warily.

I gave her a dirty look. For some reason my brilliant schemes have a reputation for getting out of hand. But that's not really fair. There's nothing wrong with my schemes. I always manage to come through them all right. "I don't know yet what I'm going to do," I said, "but I'll think of something, and soon. By the end of this week, nobody will even think about comparing me to Elizabeth!"

Tuesday afternoon

Dear Diary,

This day stunk. It blew chunks, as Bruce would say. I guess it's my own fault. I should never have been so psyched to borrow Elizabeth's new peach dress. After all, Grandma Wakefield sent it to Liz, and Grandma's old! That's OK for someone like Elizabeth, who dresses like she's sixty. But me? No way. I should have known better.

But no. I wear it to school and everyone calls me Elizabeth all day, just because they saw her in the same dress last week. Jeffrey French was so convinced I was my sister that he actually kissed me! OK, I admit that I didn't really mind that part. If you could get a look at my sister's gorgeous boyfriend, Diary, you'd understand why. He's a hunk.

But everything else was awful! Mr. Collins, Amy Sutton, our dorky principal Chrome Dome Cooper—they all thought I was Elizabeth! I've never been so humiliated in my life. Here I was, thinking I would look fantastic in that peach color that brings out my tan, and nobody even knew it was me! This is the worst day of my life. Even Lila gave me the Elizabeth treatment. . . .

I stood in front of my locker Tuesday afternoon, so frustrated I wanted to cry. I tried for a minute to add up the number of people who had mistaken me for Elizabeth, but I gave up. It was too depressing. To make matters worse, Lila had been out of school at a doctor's appointment for a lot of the day, so I didn't even have a best friend around to pour out my troubles to.

It had been a terrible day—all except that one moment in the cafeteria. As horrified as I was to have Elizabeth's own boyfriend mistake me for her, I couldn't say that I regretted that part. Jeffrey was a terrific kisser.

What am I thinking? He's Elizabeth's boyfriend, for goodness' sake!

I have to admit that I've stolen other girls' boyfriends on occasion, but Elizabeth isn't just another girl. Elizabeth is my twin sister—as everyone had been reminding me, painfully, all day. I had no business mooning over a kiss that hadn't even been meant for me, I told myself sternly. No matter how attractive Jeffrey was.

Just then Lila hurried by, a blank expression on her face. We were supposed to go to the mall together in a few minutes.

"Lila!" I called.

Lila turned and cast me one of her famous cool stares—like the ones she uses on people she isn't close to. Then she said it: *"Oh, hello, Liz."*

I could almost hear the sound barrier break as my blue depression turned to red rage. "It isn't Liz, you idiot," I seethed, trembling. "It's *me*! Can't you even tell?"

Lila's eyes narrowed. "What are you doing in that dress?" she demanded. "Isn't it Elizabeth's?"

"What difference does it make? People can only tell Liz and me apart when we wear different clothes! It's like we're the same person!"

"You don't have to shout," Lila said in a condescending voice. "Jessica, dear, don't you realize that you and Elizabeth are identical twins? Why shouldn't people get you confused every once in a while?"

I clenched my fists. I could deal with it every once in a while. It was this all-day-long stuff that was driving me bananas. I couldn't put up with it much longer.

> *If anyone else mistakes me for Elizabeth, I will start screaming and throwing things, Diary. Pointy things.*

> *Tuesday night*

Dear Diary,

> *I am brilliant—far more brilliant, even, than a certain identical twin of mine who shall remain nameless. I figured out a way to make sure no one ever mistakes me for anyone else, ever again. The idea came to me in the mall this afternoon. . . .*

"Hey, look at that," Lila said, pointing toward the cosmetics counter at Lytton & Brown department store in the Valley Mall.

The sign said FREE MAKEOVER. For a millionaire Lila was always awfully interested in anything that was free. I sighed, thinking of the suitcase full of new clothes Lila's father had just brought back for her from his recent trip to Paris. It was bad enough that Lila was an only child, who didn't have to go through life feeling like half of a pair of shoes. But the crowning injustice was that she was born a zillion times richer than I will ever be.

Of course, even if I won a million dollars, it wouldn't solve my identity problem, I reflected. People would just start referring to me as "Elizabeth's richer twin sister."

I tried to put Elizabeth out of my mind and followed Lila to the cosmetics counter. There a chic-looking cosmetician in a white smock was brushing blusher on a woman's face.

"This will give your cheeks definition," the makeup artist was saying.

She was right. The customer was kind of plain, but the dramatic sweep of color on her cheeks transformed her into somebody exotic—somebody distinctive.

Distinctive! That was it. Suddenly I had my plan.

"Uh-oh," Lila said with a groan. "You have that look on your face, Jess. That terrible I've-got-a-fantastic-idea kind of look. The kind of look that means big trouble!"

I shook my head. "No, this is perfect! Lila, I've just had a wonderful idea! What are you doing this weekend?"

"Nothing special. Daddy's going to L.A., so I'll be alone. Why?"

"How would you like a guest for the weekend?" I asked, realizing that my marvelous new plan had a fringe benefit I hadn't considered. A weekend at luxurious Fowler Crest, waited on by servants, was a definite plus in any plan.

"Jess, quit being so mysterious," Lila said, trying—unsuccessfully—to sound more bored than curious. "What's going on?"

I slipped my arm through Lila's and grinned conspiratorially. "Nothing! I just thought I'd come over this weekend and keep you company, that's all. We can have a really good time, watch movies on the VCR, play some music, have something really disgustingly sweet for dinner. . . ."

"And then what?" Lila said, pulling away and crossing her arms. She had been in on the ground floor of enough of my brainstorms to know this was the calm before the deluge. "Where's the catch, Jess? It all sounds too innocent so far."

I turned to inspect my reflection in one of the oval mirrors on the cosmetics counter, fluffing my blond hair thoughtfully as I sneaked a glance at Lila's face. She was dying from the suspense but trying to hide it. I knew just how far I could push Lila before suspense turned to irritation. It wouldn't do to irritate Lila. My wonderful scheme wouldn't work without her full cooperation.

"Lila," I announced, "with a little ingenuity, I don't see why I ever have to be mistaken for Liz again."

26

Dear Diary,

What a weekend! I've been at Lila's all afternoon, performing miracles with shampoo, mascara, and French fashions. I'm still at Lila's, but I wanted to take a minute to fill you in on the details while she's on the phone to her father. Soon I'll be heading home, to see what my family has to say about all this. They're going to go ballistic! They may not even recognize me.

If you could see, Diary, even you wouldn't recognize me. I have to admit—in total, unbiased objectivity—that I look positively gorgeous. The transformation started on Saturday morning in Lila's bedroom, when I found a photo spread of a very sophisticated model named Katrina in Vogue *magazine. . . .*

I pointed to a photograph of a slim, sultry girl with sleek black hair and dramatic makeup. "See, I think something like this would be good," I said. "I need a whole new look—something kind of slinky and mysterious."

"If you want to look like her, you're going to need more than a makeover," Lila said. She extended one graceful hand and blew on her fingernails to dry a coat of mauve nail polish. "You're going to need plastic surgery."

"Very funny." I tossed the magazine aside,

jumped to my feet, and peered at myself in the mirror over her well-stocked vanity table. "I think you're wrong."

I was wearing a nightshirt with "Sweet Valley University" blazoned across it—a gift from my brother Steven, a college freshman. But I imagined a more sophisticated, more European Jessica staring back at me from the mirror. Euro-Jessica wore a black leather jumpsuit and high boots, like the outfit Katrina modeled in the magazine.

"With a little ingenuity . . ." I began speculatively. I sucked in my cheeks and lifted my hair off my neck. "I'll need to dye my hair, of course."

"Dye your hair?" Lila shrieked. "Jess, your parents are going to murder you!"

I grinned. It took a lot to make Lila lose her composure. "You didn't believe I was serious about this, did you? Lila, let's get dressed. I want to go into town. We're going to need to raid the drugstore for some supplies."

Lila shook her head. "Jess, I think you need to take it easy. What color are you planning on dyeing it? What if it looks really weird?"

I shrugged. Lila was beginning to sound almost as cautious as stick-in-the-mud Elizabeth. My philosophy was to act first and think later. Why worry about consequences when you never really knew what would happen until you took the first step? If my hair looked bad when I dyed it, well, I'd just have to dye it back.

"It won't look weird if we do it right," I said, hoping it was true. Sure, I felt a twinge of fear, but I pushed it out of my mind. This was a time for action. I absolutely would not go through one more day of being a clone.

"Come on, Lila. I want to look like that model in *Vogue*!" I scooped up the magazine from the floor and sat down on Lila's bed. Lila was starting on a second coat of nail polish, but I knew she was hanging on every word.

"Listen to what they say about her," I urged, poking the photograph of the young, sultry model. "'Katrina is the essence of the new European beauty . . . the daughter of a ballerina and a film director. Her hobbies include Indonesian cooking, French museums, and skiing in the Alps. . . .' That's going to be me, Li. No more kid stuff." I poked at my baggy nightshirt. "No more of the old Jessica Wakefield."

Lila looked skeptical. I flopped down on my stomach on the satin-quilted bed and pored over the photograph. I wasn't sure what I could do about getting some chic European fashions. I was still paying my parents back for the last advance on my allowance. But I could certainly be like Katrina in every other way. I tried to pout seductively, but I was too excited to hold back a grin.

"The makeover's going to be just the beginning! From now on no one's going to mistake me for Elizabeth—not even for the old Jessica! It'll be just as if a new girl had moved to town!"

Lila shook her head. "I think you're going nutso,

29

Jess. I just wish you didn't have to do it while I'm stuck with you for the whole weekend."

"Don't be such a pain! You're supposed to be supportive, Li. Can't you see I'm going through an identity crisis?"

Lila groaned. "Please," she said, drawing the word out into two syllables in order to sound as exasperated as possible. "If I took every crisis you went through seriously, I'd be a nervous wreck. I think you're blowing this whole thing out of proportion."

I thought fast. Making myself over would be twice as hard without Lila's help. "Lila," I wheedled, "you know how much I need your advice. You're so good with makeup, and you know so much more than I do about fashion!"

Lila perked right up. "That's true," she agreed. "You know, some of those clothes Daddy brought back from Paris look sort of like what Katrina has on in that picture. Maybe you could borrow some of them for a while."

"Lila Fowler, you're the best friend in the entire world," I shrieked, throwing my arms around her so exuberantly that we both fell over on the bed. "Come on. Let's get dressed and go out for supplies."

Sunday evening

Dear Diary,

I'm back home now, after an amazing weekend. It's true that I was trying to flatter Lila into helping me. (Of course, I always knew she was good with clothes and makeup, but I never thought she was better than I was—just better funded.) Well, she turned out to be more of a pro than I expected!

It helps that she has a bathroom the size of the school gym. First she lathered my hair and shampooed into it this black dye called Midnight. The dye was kind of goopy, and it smelled funny going on. But, man, did it ever work! I now have raven-black—no, midnight-black hair. It's temporary, though, so I'll have to redo it every few days.

It's not just the color that's different. My hair is now straight and sleek, like Katrina's. Lila used a special gel to get rid of my bouncy waves. Bouncy hair is not Euro-so-phisticated. Katrina's hair would never bounce! Lila gets this gel stuff at the Silver Door—only the most expensive salon in town. I don't think I could afford one of their bobby pins! There are advantages to having a millionaire for a best friend.

You oughta see the clothes she let me borrow! A skintight purple jumpsuit and lots of things in black. And I just picked out the outfit to wear to school tomorrow, for the debut of the New Me.

This outfit is going to stop traffic at school tomorrow. It's a very straight olive-green skirt—leather—and it's got a slit so far

31

up the back that I've got to make sure Mom and Dad don't see me from behind in the morning, or they might not let me wear it out of the house! The blouse is totally glamorous. It's a rich, soft silk, kind of oversize. Then I'll drape this big olive-green belt kind of low on my hips—Lila showed me how. And we bought a pair of lacy black hose to wear with these to-die-for black shoes with big, square, three-inch heels—all the rage in Paris this year, according to the fashion magazines.

I haven't decided on the right jewelry for tomorrow. Normally, I don't wear much—just the gold lavaliere necklace my parents bought me for my birthday. But it's just like Elizabeth's, and the new Jessica Wakefield wouldn't be caught dead wearing anything just like Elizabeth. Besides, it's so childish. Lila lent me some chunky, dramatic European costume jewelry. I'm going to go through it tonight and make my final selection.

The only other thing is makeup, and that's been taken care of. Lila helped me work out the colors and showed me how to apply it. The effect is total drama. Black, black hair against pale, white skin. Very exotic. No more California tan for this California girl! *Vogue* says the eyes should be the focal point of the face, so I'm playing them up with heavy eyeliner and tons of mas-

cara. Katrina would be proud of me!

*Elizabeth, of course, was not. You should
have seen her face when she saw me. . . .*

My heart was pounding as I opened the door of
my house Sunday afternoon, after leaving Lila's. I
couldn't remember when I'd been so excited. And
nervous. I knew I looked terrific—the height of
glamour—but I still wasn't feeling completely com-
fortable with my new, more European image. And I
didn't know what my family would say.

Elizabeth was bounding through the doorway
from the living room as I stepped into the house. She
opened her mouth as if she were about to say something. Then her hand flew to her lips. "Jess?" she
asked uncertainly.

I tossed my straight black hair over my shoulder.
"Hi, Liz," I said, setting on the floor my bags full of
borrowed clothing. I whirled around, resplendent in
the purple jumpsuit and lizard boots. "What do you
think? Do you like the new me?"

Elizabeth's face went as pale as mine, and she
seemed to be gasping for breath. "But, Jess," she
choked out, "what have you done to yourself? What
have you done to your hair?"

I ran my hand through my gloriously straight
black locks. "Dyed it!"

"Girls!" warned Mom from the living room. She
spoke in a stage whisper, but her voice sounded annoyed. I realized my father must be taking a nap.

Elizabeth grabbed the table behind her, as if she

33

were afraid of falling. "You look completely different," she said accusingly, her voice rising again. "Jessica, why?"

"I just felt like a change. That's all," I said airily.

"Girls!" Mom said again, tiptoeing into the foyer. Then she caught sight of me, and her mouth dropped open.

"Hi, Mom!" I sang out.

"Jessica?" Alice Wakefield whispered, her eyes widening. "Jessica, what on earth—"

Elizabeth's eyes filled with tears. "You look like a stranger!" she wailed. Then she turned and ran upstairs.

I beamed, even though Katrina never would have. I looked like a stranger! That was exactly what I wanted. Never again would I be Jessica the Afterthought, born four minutes later than my perfect twin. I had shed that identity with my old clothes and my honey-gold, bouncy hair. Now I would be Jessica the Stranger—my own, unique person, apart from Elizabeth. I felt that old identity crisis melting away, like ice cream in the California sun.

I could hardly wait to get to school the next day.

Monday night

Oh, Diary, this has been an unbelievably awesome day! I blew everyone away with my new look. Even Amy Motormouth Sutton was speechless! It was better than I could have imagined. . . .

I looked sensational as I walked into homeroom, a little late (better for making a dramatic entrance). Ms. Dalton looked up with no hint of recognition on her face and actually asked if she could help me!

"It's me, Ms. Dalton," I said, enjoying her puzzled stare. "Jessica Wakefield."

After a moment of stunned silence, Cara screamed, "Jess! What have you done?"

Winston Egbert, class clown and resident nerd, jumped up and gave me a formal introduction. Then the whole class exploded. Ms. Dalton was trying to make everyone shut up and sit down, but the kids were paying attention to nobody but me. The girls were all exclaiming about my hair, and Caroline Pearce, always on the lookout for new gossip, asked where I got the clothes.

"Oh, just some little place on the Left Bank," I said airily, knowing that half the school would hear about it before lunch. It wasn't exactly a lie, you know. The outfit probably did come from the Left Bank of Paris. I just left out the part about Mr. Fowler being the one who bought it there.

Finally Ms. Dalton got us all into our seats, but everybody was still staring at me. Naturally, I loved it. Nobody paid this much attention to me when I looked like Elizabeth.

They accosted me again after homeroom. Winston, Caroline, Cara, and Regina Morrow had me surrounded as we walked to our lockers.

"Of course Elizabeth doesn't mind," I said when Regina asked about my sister's reaction. I guess I was stretching the truth a little, but I figured Elizabeth wouldn't mind, once she got used to the idea. "Elizabeth and I are very different," I continued, trying to sound ever-so-slightly British. "Why should she object, just because I've chosen to be slightly more daring than I used to be?"

"I think you look fantastic with black hair," Caroline said. "You look stunning."

"I agree," Cara said. No matter how hard a time my friends and I might give each other when we're alone, we're very loyal in public. "But aren't those heels a little high?" she ventured. "You look like you're on stilts!"

I eyed her with what I hoped was a touch of amused disdain. "Height," I said dramatically, quoting from *Vogue*, "is an important part of elegance."

"But now you're too elegant for me," said that nerd Winston. "I can't stand it! How will I ever convince you to marry me now?"

Right. As though he ever had a chance before.

A few minutes later they stared while I pulled out a copy of *Paris Match* magazine that Lila's father had brought back with him. Then I waltzed down the hallway to chemistry class.

Tuesday night

Sorry, Diary. It's been a week since I've written, but I've been caught in an absolute whirl of activity. The New moi *(that's French*

36

for "me," Diary) is still getting rave reviews. But my new image keeps me frightfully busy. I've spent eons of time hunting down foreign movie and fashion magazines, seeing sub-titled films, ordering cappuccino at out-of-the-way bistros, and buying accessories and makeup to complement Lila's French wardrobe.

This evening Lila and I went to L'Autre Chose after dinner. I ordered espresso (bitter, but fashionable). That's probably why I'm still up at this hour of the night! L'Autre Chose is such a sophisticated place. Totally cool. Even Lila, with all her money, isn't used to being so chic.

You know, I'm kind of worried about Lila. She's been acting weird. She says I'm the one who's changed. Of course I've changed. But it's a change for the better. I bet she's jealous of all the attention I'm getting. She's used to being the most sophisticated, elegant girl at school. Now she doesn't even come close. . . .

"What's the matter with you?" Lila asked at the coffee bar Wednesday night. "Robin Wilson told me you missed cheerleading practice twice."

"Cheerleading," I told her, "is so childish, Lila. I'm thinking of starting ballet lessons again instead. Ballet is so artistic and elegant, don't you think?"

It's too bad that I've wasted so much time on

juvenile activities like cheerleading. I mean, it's so . . . American. And the bouncy little pleated skirts are ridiculous, when you think about it. From now on it's sophistication all the way.

Elizabeth is the other person who just doesn't understand. She's been walking around in a funk for more than a week, as if she lost her best friend. You'd think she would be happy not to be a clone anymore. But instead of taking advantage of her new independence, she mopes around, giving me her sad puppy-dog looks.

"All you do anymore is suck your cheeks in and stare at yourself in the mirror," she whined to me the other night. Elizabeth doesn't understand anything. Sure, she's got a cute figure—for a wholesome American type—but Katrina and those other models in Vogue *are positively gaunt. Personally, I'm eating nothing but yogurt and carrots and espresso until I lose at least five pounds. Until then I need to practice sucking in my cheeks to give my cheekbones lots of definition. If Elizabeth has a problem with that, well, I guess she'll get over it.*

Luckily, I haven't seen much of Elizabeth lately, so I haven't had to put up with her acting as if I'm some sort of traitor. Now that I'm more sophisticated and independent, it would hardly do for me to spend all my time at home!

Shopping malls aren't very European, either, but until I get to Paris or Milan, I'm stuck with Valley Mall for supplementing my (Lila's) wardrobe. You'd be surprised at what you can find at the mall, if you've got taste. I found a superclassy outfit at Lisette's last night! Mother ("Mom" sounds so childish, don't you think?) is going to have a seizure when she sees that I put it on her credit card. But I swear I'll pay her back eventually. I just couldn't live without this outfit. It's all white—a slim-cut skirt, past my knee, with a sequined sweater and a beret that's just the most stylish thing you ever saw. I can't wait to wear it to school tomorrow.

Wednesday afternoon

The new outfit was a hit! I made the biggest sensation yet. The contrast of all that soft white against my stark black hair was about as dramatic as you can get. And as Vogue says, drama is everything.

My most exciting news is an idea DeeDee Gordon had at lunchtime. Normally, Lila and I don't generally hang out with artsy-fartsy types like DeeDee, but artists do understand drama—something Lila just hasn't caught on to. . . .

39

"Jess, you look fantastic!" DeeDee exclaimed, joining us at a table in the cafeteria. Lila and I used to eat outside in the school courtyard a lot, but the New Jessica doesn't go outside unless it's absolutely necessary. A suntan does horrible things to your skin. And an ivory complexion looks so sophisticated with midnight-black hair.

Lila made a face, and I knew she wanted me to find an excuse to blow DeeDee off. But here was this petite little freckle-faced artist, telling me how wonderful I looked, while Lila stared at her spaghetti and ignored me. Besides, my stomach was growling from my resolve to be as thin as a *Vogue* model. So I looked away from Lila and her spaghetti and turned to DeeDee instead. If DeeDee was willing to give me the support that my own best friend was withholding, then she was welcome to join me for lunch.

"Why aren't you eating, Jess?" Lila asked a few minutes later.

I had explained to her all about the gaunt-looking models in the fashion magazines, but Lila had been tuning me out lately. So I cast her one of those haughty looks that she taught me. "I'm watching my figure, actually."

> *Actually. Now there's a British-sounding word. I decided then and there, Diary, to use it more often.*

"Actually," I said, trying it out again, "I'd like to lose another three pounds. You can never be too thin."

40

"Or too rich," Lila said with a smirk. I glowered at her.

Meanwhile DeeDee hadn't taken her eyes off me since she sat down. "I think you look out of this world!" she said. Then came her terrific idea: "Jess, you should think about modeling. You look like you belong on the cover of a fashion magazine right now!"

Well, Diary, that got me thinking right away. We all remembered when Regina appeared on the cover of Ingenue *magazine. In fact, Lila and I had been green with envy. Especially Lila. She managed to get herself an appointment with the agent man who "discovered" Regina, but he told her she wouldn't photograph well. Lila practically had a cow. She hasn't been on the best of terms with Regina since then.*

Actually, she's the only one around who doesn't think Regina is the greatest. Even I think so, though I sure would like to have been on that Ingenue *cover instead of her. Along with being beautiful, sweet, and friendly, Regina is filthy rich—almost as rich as Lila. But it's hard to hate her for it, because of what she's had to overcome. Regina was born deaf and worked hard for years to live a regular life. Then she had some operations in Switzerland this year. Now she has almost normal hearing.*

Anyhow, if DeeDee is right, maybe Regina won't be the only cover girl at Sweet Valley High.

DeeDee's father is a Hollywood agent and knows lots of people who could help an aspiring young model. DeeDee gave me the name of one—Simon Avery, a fashion photographer. And I have an appointment to see him after school today. . . .

"It just so happens that Mr. Mahler, the art director at Lytton and Brown, just called me," Simon Avery told me in his office Thursday afternoon. "That's why I was a few minutes late. And he's looking for a young woman to model some new fashions at the store two weeks from Saturday."

Two weeks from Saturday! This was fantastic! I had never expected to be so successful so quickly. And modeling was only a first step to a career in acting. There might be talent scouts and big-city agents at the fashion show. I was sure they would take one look at me, and suddenly I'd have more movie offers than I could handle. But first I had to get through this interview. I forced myself to stay calm and listen to what Mr. Avery was saying.

"I'm sure you're aware that for most modeling, you're too short."

Too short?

The photographer barreled on. "But Mr. Mahler is looking for models for junior clothes, and junior models tend to be shorter."

Short or not, I was determined to be in that fashion

show. I smoothed my sleek black hair away from my face, hoping my fingers weren't trembling with excitement. "What do I do to apply for it?"

Mr. Avery went over the details about the photographs and other information we would need to submit.

"And you really think I might be right for the job?"

"I never like to make promises. And Mahler may have a different sort of look in mind. But you seem perfect to me. You have a really distinctive, sophisticated look—slightly European, very cool and polished. I think Mahler will like that."

My parents can be so lame. They weren't even excited about my big break. Can you believe that? They were all worried about the measly $125 it's going to cost for the photography session, even though I'm practically guaranteed to get it back in two weeks. The Lytton & Brown job pays five hundred! Think of all the sophisticated new clothes I can buy. Luckily, they finally agreed to lend me the money, but it wasn't easy. . . .

"You're going to be heavily in debt to us if the job doesn't come through," Mother warned me at the dinner table Thursday night. "A hundred twenty-five dollars is a lot of money, Jess. We don't mind lending it to you, but a loan is a loan."

43

"This wouldn't happen to Brooke Shields," I objected.

"And then there is the sixty-seven-dollar bill that just came from Lisette's."

Oops. I was hoping that wouldn't show up for another week or two. But it was infuriating that my own parents showed so little confidence in me.

"I'll pay it back," I said coldly. "Every penny. I'll even give you interest."

My parents laughed, and I realized then that they were going to lend me the money.

"That won't be necessary, Jess," my father said. "We figure you're a pretty worthwhile investment."

A few minutes later, Diary, somebody brought up the Ramsbury Fair, an annual family outing I used to enjoy when I was a child. Well, until this year. It's one of those corny events with hayrides and games and Ferris wheels.

Elizabeth brightened up for the first time in days. But I couldn't see the point. It was all too childish. "Count me out," I said. The Ramsbury Fair might be all right for Jessica Wakefield, but it was too unsophisticated for Jessa Fields.

Did I tell you about Jessa Fields, Diary? That's going to be my professional name when I'm a famous model and actress. Don't you think it sounds more elegant than plain-vanilla Jessica Wakefield?

*Well, my announcement that I was too
old for the Ramsbury Fair didn't sit well with
my former identical twin. She didn't say a
word, but I could tell. . . .*

As I jumped up from the table, I noticed
Elizabeth's eyes getting all misty. I was sure beginning to wish she would snap out of this. Her
"wounded sister" act was getting annoying. She had
no right to tell me how to dress and what makeup I
should wear.

In the last day or two Elizabeth had been even
more down in the dumps. I had no idea what else
might be bothering her. She had barely uttered a
word to *me* in days. I decided to sit her down and talk
some sense into her, sometime soon.

But not that night. I had plans to meet Lila at
L'Autre Chose.

Friday night

Diary dearest,
*I had the weirdest conversation with
Elizabeth tonight while I was getting
ready to go to the Beach Disco. She's still
freaked out because we don't look the
same. I guess I've been unsympathetic.
That was mean of me. I never meant to
hurt Elizabeth. But she can't expect me to
go back to being Twin Number Two just to
make her feel better.*
I was right that she's been even more

45

*upset in the last few days. There's something
else that's turning her into a basket case—
something incredible. . . .*

"Where are you going tonight?" Elizabeth asked,
throwing herself across my unmade bed as I finished
my makeup.

"Lila and I are going to the Beach Disco. What
about you? Aren't you going out with Jeffrey?"

Elizabeth gave this big, sad sigh and compli-
mented me on my cool black-leather jeans.

I told her Mr. Avery's assistant had suggested I
cut my hair short. It's a very contemporary look,
geometric. She just sighed again and went on to tell
me that everyone's been saying what a knockout I
am now.

Finally I couldn't stand seeing her so unhappy, so
I begged her to tell me what was wrong.

"I guess I miss the way it used to be," she said.
"When you and I looked pretty much alike. I
mean, honestly, Jess, don't you miss going places
and having people make a fuss because we look
identical?"

"Nope," I said truthfully. "Liz, can't you see how
much better it is this way—for both of us?"

I told her all about the identity-crisis article I
read, but she didn't seem impressed. She said nobody
who really knew us ever mixed us up.

I had her there. "Ha!" I said with a snort. "Then
why did Jeffrey mistake me for you the day I wore
that dress Grandma sent you?"

46

For just a moment I allowed myself to remember the touch of Jeffrey's strong hands on my shoulders in the cafeteria that day, and the soft brush of his lips on mine.

Elizabeth was looking at me strangely, and for an instant I was terrified that she could read my thoughts. But of course she had no idea that Jeffrey had kissed me. Or that I wished he would do it again.

"I hope that didn't have anything to do with this," she said bitterly.

"Well, you can see how it would be a little disturbing, can't you? I mean, I used to think the same way you do. But when my twin's own boyfriend mistakes me for her . . ."

That, dear Diary, is when Elizabeth dropped the real bombshell. . . .

"It seems pretty funny that you decided to dye your hair and everything because Jeffrey got us mixed up. He sure seems to like the results."

I dropped my lipstick. "What are you talking about?"

Elizabeth began to cry. "He's just one of your biggest fans all of a sudden."

"Jeffrey?" I asked, amazed but intrigued. "*Your* Jeffrey?"

Elizabeth nodded. "I guess once he could tell the difference between us, it was easier for him to decide who he preferred."

47

"Liz, are you sure you aren't making some kind of mistake? Jeffrey's crazy about you. Any idiot could see that!"

"Well, I hate to disagree with the idiot point of view," Elizabeth said. I hate it when she gets sarcastic. "But the fact is, I think he likes you, Jess."

"Does that mean you're not going to see him tonight?" I asked.

Elizabeth nodded. "As far as I'm concerned, we just may never speak to each other again."

Wow, Diary. Jeffrey is so gorgeous. And if Liz says she's never speaking to him again, then there isn't actually anything wrong with my being interested in him, is there? Maybe he and I should get to know each other better.

Monday afternoon

Dear Diary,

I never should have gotten out of bed today. I dressed with extra care this morning, in gray trousers, a red blouse, and a man-tailored blazer. I wanted to impress Mr. Avery in my appointment with him this afternoon—and I wanted to impress Jeffrey.

The day started going downhill at lunchtime when I began my campaign to get to know Jeffrey better. I practically threw myself at him, plus blowing my diet and gorging on french fries and ice cream. But Jeffrey is a one-woman kind of a man. And that one

48

woman is Elizabeth, no matter what she thinks about his being attracted to me. Elizabeth is blind! Jeffrey's only interest in me at lunchtime today was about whether I could give him any news of Elizabeth.

"I don't want anyone else," he told me. "That's the terrible thing, Jess. I'm nuts about your sister. I just wish I could figure out why she started acting so bizarre all of a sudden."

My only stroke of luck was that he was so hung up on Elizabeth that he didn't notice how bizarre *I* was acting all of a sudden, throwing myself at him the way I did. I came dangerously close to making a fool out of myself by flirting with a guy who doesn't know I'm alive.

I left quickly, totally depressed.

The humiliation was bad enough. But the worst part about it is that I really like Jeffrey. I mean I really, REALLY like him. Jeffrey is so sexy and fun and sweet. I've liked him since Elizabeth started seeing him. I was able to push all those feelings aside for a while, but that one kiss in the lunchroom a couple weeks ago brought them all back. Now my heart starts pounding whenever I'm near him. Is that stupid, or what?

Last night it looked as if he and Elizabeth were on the rocks. I thought I might have a chance. But he's so crazy about her that I'm sure they'll get back together. And I'll be left on the sidelines again, by myself.

Jessa Fields may be glamorous, but she's getting lonely. Every guy in school wants to talk to me in the hallway and dance with me at parties. But I haven't had a real date in ages. I guess they think I'm too sophisticated for them now. I suppose they're right. But I don't feel sophisticated around Jeffrey. I feel nervous. And happy. Help me, Diary! I have a crush on my sister's boyfriend! How pathetic.

Believe it or not, after lunch my day got worse. Massively worse. Elizabeth and I drove home from school together, but I had to stop at Mr. Avery's office to learn what Mr. Mahler had decided about a model for his fashion show. I asked Elizabeth to come inside with me for moral support.

It was horrible. While Elizabeth sat in the waiting room, I went into Mr. Avery's office, where Mr. Mahler told me I was all wrong for the fashion show. Mr. Avery tried to put in a good word for me. He's a photographer. He knows that drama sells clothes. But Mahler said he wanted a wholesome, all-American look. By the time they escorted me out to the waiting room, I was bawling like a baby. . . .

"Come on, Liz," I said between sniffles. "They don't want me. They say my image is all wrong."

Elizabeth had always said modeling was the most boring and humiliating job in the world. But she knew how important it was to me, and her eyes were full of sympathy as we prepared to leave.

But Mr. Mahler's eyes were full of Elizabeth.

"That's it!" he cried, pointing at her. "She's exactly who I'm looking for!"

I was sure I would wither up and die on the spot.

Mr. Mahler dragged us all back into the office and then started working on Elizabeth, who wasn't the least bit interested in taking the modeling job. But I still wanted it. And if wholesome and all-American was what Lytton & Brown wanted, then I could deliver it just as well as Elizabeth.

"But I really look just like her!" I insisted. "See, we're twins. But I got tired of looking exactly like Elizabeth, so I thought I'd change my image."

Mr. Mahler examined my face, but then shook his head. "I'm sorry. I just can't believe it. You two don't look anything alike. Your features are similar, but aside from that. . . ."

Elizabeth backed me up, but the art director's response was to offer her *six hundred dollars* to model in the fashion show.

Mr. Mahler made Elizabeth promise to think it over, and we got out of there. I don't think I could have stood one more minute of hearing that I'm too unconventional.

Well, Diary, I've made up my mind. I'm going to be in that fashion show, no matter what it takes.

Monday night

Dear Diary,

I feel so horribly, awfully, unspeakably bad!

After dinner tonight the doorbell rang. And there was Penny Ayala—she's the newspaper editor at school—stopping by to drop off Elizabeth's diary! I didn't know Elizabeth had lost her diary. I guess that's another reason she's been freaking out in the last few days. She left it in the newspaper office at school, and Penny picked it up accidentally, with a pile of other stuff.

I really didn't mean to read any of it, Diary. I know how awful it would be if anyone read my private thoughts. But I couldn't help myself. Most of what she'd written lately was about falling in love with Jeffrey, but one passage about me caught my eye. . . .

I'd hardly spoken with my sister in weeks, and I wanted to know what was going on in her head. I got a lot more than I bargained for:

I'm sure I'm overreacting, but looking at Jessica now is incredibly painful for me. It isn't that she doesn't look fantastic—because

52

she does! What hurts is that she doesn't look like us anymore. This whole thing has made me think very hard about what it means to be a twin. And I guess it's much more important to me than I ever realized. Being a twin isn't just looking the same, though that part (for me, at least) was always fun.

I guess for me being a twin has to do with being unusually close. It means knowing what Jessica is thinking and feeling even when no one else does. And it means she knows me better than anyone else in the whole world.

Well, that's what I'm finding hardest about Jessica's new image. Not that she looks different so much, but that she's shutting me out. If only she knew how much I cared for her and if only she understood that being identical has never kept us from having distinct identities! Maybe I could have told the old Jessica how I felt. But the new Jessica is like a stranger to me.

Oh, Diary, my eyes were so full of tears that I couldn't read another word. Yes, it's corny, but I started crying. I couldn't help it. This meant so much more to Elizabeth than I understood. I ran to Elizabeth and handed her the book, and then we hugged and hugged, both of us crying. I told her I read the passage, and she forgives me. And then we curled up on the couch and watched old *home movies—featuring two identical little blond girls in matching dresses. It was the sweetest thing.*

I understand now why Elizabeth was so sad about the glamorous new me. As soon as I put you down, Diary, I'm going to wash off my makeup and take a long, hot shower to get this black stuff out of my hair.

Elizabeth missed me. And to tell you the truth, I missed me, too.

And I know a certain modeling job that's available for a wholesome-looking blonde.

Tuesday night

Blondes really do have more fun! At least this blonde had a lot of fun today. But let me backtrack a bit, to tell you what happened after I wrote last night. . . .

"You mean Jeffrey really acted like he missed me?" Elizabeth asked incredulously when I told her all about (well, not quite *all*) my lunchtime conversation with Jeffrey.

"Missed you?" I said, wiping off my eyeliner. "Liz, the guy is nuts about you." I was resigned to the fact that Jeffrey was Elizabeth's, and I was determined that nobody—especially Elizabeth—would ever know I was attracted to him. "In fact," I told her, hiding my own chagrin, "he barely even seemed to notice who I was or to hear what I was

54

saying. He just wanted to pump me for information about you."

I was afraid Elizabeth would hyperventilate. "It's incredible," she said breathlessly. "All week I've been feeling sorry for myself because I felt I was out of a diary, a boyfriend—"

"And a twin sister," I completed for her. Then I announced that I was going to shampoo my hair, and she went ballistic.

"Jessica!" Elizabeth shrieked, bouncing off my bed. "You mean you're changing yourself back to being a plain old boring Wakefield twin?"

"When, may I ask, was being a Wakefield twin ever boring? Or *plain*?"

"Anyway, I don't have much choice," I maintained, after escaping from Elizabeth's excited embrace. "If I don't convince Mr. Mahler that I'm *you* by tomorrow afternoon, I'm going to be in debt to Mom and Dad for the rest of my life."

> *That's right, Diary. Lytton & Brown got themselves a model. So what if they think my name is Elizabeth?*

> *Saturday afternoon*
>
> Dear Diary,
> *The Wakefield twins are back! You'll never believe what happened at the fashion show today. . . .*

I was in the dressing room, as blond and bouncy

as ever. Elizabeth walked in while I was slipping into a gorgeous, glittery evening gown.

"What are you doing without the dark wig?" I demanded. "If Mr. Mahler sees you, he'll know there really are two of us. And he might figure out that I'm not you!"

Elizabeth laughed. "Your cover is blown, little sister. Mr. Mahler ran into Mom and Dad, who gushed on about how happy they were that this fashion show finally worked out for *Jessica*. Then he saw me right as Winston snatched off my wig!"

I felt my hopes for a modeling career crumbling. "Does that mean I'm fired?"

Elizabeth laughed. "Absolutely not. Mr. Mahler likes you so much he wants to get double for his money. So—"

"So we're doing the fashion show together?"

Elizabeth nodded, and I knew my own grin was as huge as the one she was wearing.

Twenty minutes later we were both dressed to the hilt in sequined evening dresses. As we stepped onto the runway, I saw that Elizabeth looked radiant. I couldn't remember ever feeling closer to her, and the best thing about it was that I knew she felt exactly the same.

You know what, Diary? I love being a twin.

Part 2

Friday afternoon

Dear Diary,

You'll never guess what I did today. I brought home a puppy! He is the sweetest, cutest, most adorable thing that ever lived. He's small and yellow and pudgy. Even Elizabeth fell in love with him at first sight. . . .

"There!" I cried triumphantly, pointing to the red Fiat convertible that Elizabeth and I shared. Despite the perfect weather, the top was up. And the world's most adorable golden retriever puppy was standing on the passenger seat, with his big, clumsy front paws resting on the partly open window. His tail was wagging as if it were battery operated, and he had this big, cute grin on his face.

I had been worried about Elizabeth's reaction to my news. Elizabeth would never bring home a

57

puppy on the spur of the moment. And she wouldn't dream of adding a dog to the Wakefield family during a weekend when our parents were on vacation.

Elizabeth tells me about a million times a day that I exaggerate all the time. But I swear I'm not exaggerating when I tell you that my sister is the world's least spontaneous person. I mean, she's the type who would decide she might like a dog and then go through a puppy-selection process about as methodical as the one she's already using to choose a college. She would get Mom and Dad's permission, check books out of the library to study the breeds that are the best pets, and then make up lists and a chart of responsibilities for who gets to walk the dog and feed the dog and clean up after the dog.

In other words, by the time Elizabeth was ready to buy a puppy, my adorable little puppy would be a grandfather. It's a good thing somebody in this family knows how to take action.

Besides, who needs research? I obviously know a perfect puppy when I see one. Luckily, Elizabeth thought so, too. As soon as she opened the car door and my puppy scrambled into her arms, I could tell my sister was hooked. Elizabeth's blue-green eyes were shining, and I couldn't tell who looked happier—her or the puppy.

I petted the dog as she held him. "This is without question the most beautiful, lovable, adorable, darling, sweet puppy in the whole world," I said.

"You're right," Elizabeth replied, her eyes still fastened on the dog.

"I know I should have asked first," I admitted. "But since Mom and Dad are away for the weekend, I figured we could keep him and hide him, then show them after we've had him for a while. Once they see he's no trouble, they'll say yes. I'm sure of it."

Well, Diary, we decided the puppy could live in my room for at least a couple of days. Nobody ever goes into my room, except me, of course, and occasionally Elizabeth. Mom and Dad say they can't stand the mess.

Personally, I don't understand why everyone has such a problem with my bedroom, Diary. I know exactly where everything is in it. And how would I ever find clothes and things if they weren't out in plain sight? I would just die if I had to live in a room as neat as Elizabeth's. BORING!

Anyhow, the state of my room is coming in handy now. Our new puppy is little. He'll be easy to hide among all the stuff I've got around. Elizabeth is convinced that Mom and Dad are going to throw a fit when they get back on Sunday. How can they throw a fit when they don't know he exists?

Of course, we can't hide a dog forever. I mean, he'll grow, eventually. We just need a little time to get used to taking care of him, to prove that we can do it. Then they'll just have to say yes.

I've already fallen in love with this little dog. I couldn't bear to give him up. No matter what anybody says, I'm keeping him, Diary. I am!

Saturday afternoon

So far, so good. All right, so our little doggy almost broke a vase. Almost. He's so wriggly that he's hard to keep hold of. And the little guy can escape from almost anywhere!

So Elizabeth said we had to buy him a collar. I hate the idea of tying him up, like an animal. But Liz said he might get away from us and run out into the street, and I almost burst into tears just thinking about our pudgy baby puppy dodging cars. So we went to the mall to buy our sweetie a collar at the Perky Pet Shop.

But a dog collar is pretty incriminating, if nobody's supposed to know you have a dog. So we went extra early, to avoid running into anyone we knew. But we almost got caught! My brilliant sister Liz saved the day. I didn't think she had it in her. . . .

We found a collar and a leash and then started cautiously out of the pet store. Our first near miss happened almost immediately. I saw Maria Santelli and Sandra Bacon walking past North's Jewelry Store, across the mall. Thank goodness they didn't turn around.

> *Gee, Diary, did I tell you about Maria? She's a cheerleader, like me. She's been sneaking around lately to date a senior named Michael Harris. Their parents don't know about it and wouldn't approve. There was a bad business deal between the families years ago, and they're still feuding. It's all terribly romantic—just like Romeo and Juliet! I heard Maria and Michael might even get engaged!*
>
> *(Wow! I wonder if she was at the jewelry store looking at diamond rings!)*
>
> *I'll have to keep my feelers out to get the real scoop on what's going on.*
>
> *But I digress, as Winston Egbert would say. I was telling you about trying not to get caught at the mall with a dog collar. . . .*

We were congratulating ourselves on avoiding Maria and Sandra when we heard someone calling our names. And there was Dana Larson, along with a brown-haired girl she introduced as her cousin Sally, who had just moved in with the Larsons.

Dana is a tall, leggy blonde. She's pretty, but she does outrageous things with her hair and clothes. I guess it's to be expected. As the lead singer of The

Droids, our school's rock-and-roll band, she's the closest we have to a punk star. That morning Dana was wearing black-and-white-checked leggings, a loose white top, and a black fringed vest.

Her cousin was just the opposite. She wore no makeup, and she had on khaki pants and an oxford shirt. In fact, Sally was dressed a lot like Elizabeth—not badly, just a little dull.

I held the pet-store bag behind my back, but it's hard to throw Dana off the scent once she knows something's up. She started pressing me about what was in the bag.

Then Elizabeth piped up, "Go ahead, Jess. It's no secret."

I thought I was going to faint. All of a sudden Elizabeth, who's never gone back on a promise in her life, was acting as if our agreement to keep quiet about the dog meant nothing at all.

"Just show them," Elizabeth urged me.

I hesitated.

"It's really a joke," Elizabeth explained. She took the bag from me and pulled out the dog collar.

Dana looked surprised—probably about as surprised as I did. "I didn't know you had a dog."

Liz laughed. "Oh, we don't! It's for a costume. Right, Jess?"

Finally I caught on. "Isn't it outrageous?" I asked. I thought I was going to explode with laughter, but I pushed it down deep, grabbed the collar, and slipped it around my neck. "It's for a punk outfit. You should wear one for a concert sometime, Dana."

Well, Diary, the dog-collar-as-fashion-statement ruse worked. What a con artist my sister is! And everyone says Elizabeth isn't as good a liar as I am. I'll have to watch her more closely from now on. Who knows what else she might be getting away with?

So you see, Diary, it won't be that hard to keep our puppy a secret. All it takes is a little ingenuity. And some creative dishonesty.

Sunday night

Dear Diary,

Mom and Dad are home. So far they don't suspect a thing. We plan to keep this up as long as we can and then to start dropping hints about wanting a dog. Then, the moment they agree to let us have one, we'll call Prince Albert out of hiding.

Isn't Prince Albert a wonderful name? It's so dignified. Elizabeth came up with it. So far Prince Albert is behaving like a prince. Well, most of the time. . . .

We were in the kitchen when we heard the folks' car pull up out front. We sort of panicked—I mean, the dog was right there, the puppy chow was out in plain sight, and our parents were about to walk in the door. Elizabeth stashed the bag of food somewhere, and I hurled the rest of Prince Albert's dinner down the garbage disposal. But when Elizabeth and I lost it, Prince Albert did too. Suddenly there was this big puddle right in the middle of the Spanish-tile floor.

I grabbed the dog and raced upstairs to throw him into my bedroom. Elizabeth got stuck wiping up the mess. She was a little annoyed, but it was probably for the best. She's much better at that kind of work than I am. I guess she told them she spilled her soda.

"Jess, this is crazy," Elizabeth whispered to me a few minutes later, after she had made a graceful exit. "It'll never work."

"Don't worry," I assured her. "I've got everything under control." And I did.

But as she trudged up the stairs, I heard her muttering under her breath, "That's exactly what I'm afraid of."

Geez, Diary. You would think that after sixteen years she would have a little more confidence in me than that! Sure, I've gotten into a few scrapes. But Liz knows I always get out of them—somehow. This time we're home free. I just know it.

Monday night

I brought Lila over to see Prince Albert after school today. (She's the only person I've told. I swear!) I'm afraid we ran into our first itty-bitty little problem. And then there was that incident at dinner. . . .

64

"He's in the basement," I told Lila, leading her down the stairs. We were keeping Prince Albert there during the day so he would have room to run around. Every day I would bring him up to my room late in the afternoon, before my parents were home. We thought it was an ideal arrangement. We thought there was nothing in the basement that a puppy could hurt.

We thought wrong.

"Did you really just get him from some stranger?" Lila asked as I greeted my adorable little puppy. "I mean, he obviously can't be a purebred dog. He didn't have any papers, did he?"

Only the papers he's peeing on, I thought. Leave it to Lila to be snobby even to a puppy.

"No, but who cares? A dog doesn't have to be expensive to be nice."

"Oh, I don't know," Lila said with her nose in the air. "I'd rather be sure of what I was getting. Bloodlines are so important."

I ignored her and played with my adorable little baby. After all, I was trying to get Prince Albert accepted into my house, not into the country club.

It took about a minute for Prince Albert to win over even Lila Snobbier-Than-Thou Fowler. In no time she was petting him and talking baby talk to him, just like me.

Then she said something that nearly gave me a heart attack: "Hey, Jessica, what's that over there? It looks like a snake."

I was petrified, but I noticed that the long black thing in the corner wasn't moving. I started toward it slowly, not wanting Lila to know I was scared. A minute later I felt silly. It was just an old piece of rubber tubing.

Prince Albert barked excitedly at the black tube, as if it were a favorite toy. Suddenly I felt sick. "Oh God!" I said to the pup. "What have you done? Where did you get this?"

Lila solved the mystery. A hose on the back of the washing machine had been chewed off.

"If I were you," she said glibly, "I'd call a repairman. Soon." She gave me one of those infuriating little smiles of hers, and then she left me to fend for myself. Some friend.

> *So, Diary, I took Lila's advice. I called the washing-machine repair place. Unfortunately, nobody can come fix the thing until Friday afternoon. I'll somehow have to keep Mom and Dad from doing any laundry until then.*
>
> *I thought my problems were over for the evening. As it turned out, they were only beginning. . . .*

I was all calmed down from the washing-machine incident, Prince Albert was safely hidden away in my bedroom, and I was beginning to think everything would be fine. Of course, it helped that Jeffrey was over for dinner. A good-looking guy always takes my mind off my problems, even a good-looking guy who's spoken for.

My father was telling us about some lawyer stuff he was working on, when suddenly I heard Prince Albert bark. Unfortunately, Dad heard it too. I stared at my chicken and potatoes and hoped the pup would shut up before Dad figured out what the noise was.

"I didn't hear anything, Ned," my mother said. "It was probably something outside."

I wanted to kiss her.

He shrugged and went on talking, but he stopped a few seconds later. "I could swear I heard some kind of howl."

I made up a story about having left my stereo on, and I raced upstairs to take care of the problem. When I opened the door of my room, there was Prince Albert, wagging his tail and all happy to see me.

"Poor doggy," I whispered, holding him. "You're all lonely up here, aren't you? But you have to be quiet now. I'll come play with you after dinner."

I wound up an old alarm clock and left it ticking near him. Somebody told me puppies like that.

"I left my stereo on," I explained to my father as I breezed into the dining room. "There was some weird song on, with a lot of screaming and stuff. That's probably what you heard, Dad."

He shook his head and laughed. "It sounded like a pair of wild dogs to me."

Elizabeth lost it. She started to giggle. Then I started to giggle, and then we both laughed hysterically. Meanwhile my parents and Jeffrey were staring at us as if we'd both started howling at the moon.

We managed to calm down, and by the time we finished eating, I thought our problems were over for the night. Then my mother announced that she was going to do a load of laundry.

"No!" I yelled. She looked at me as if I were crazy. So I jumped up and told her she'd been working too hard, and I offered to do the laundry for her. Then I dashed out of the room to bundle up the clothes. I guess I went too far. Everybody had to realize something was up. I mean, my family knows that if it was up to me, I'd throw away dirty clothes and buy new, clean ones, rather than do laundry. But what can I say? I panicked.

My parents must have thought it was even weirder when Elizabeth offered to help me and even dragged Jeffrey along—as if it would take three people to throw a load of clothes into the washer.

I know, Diary. It was a little crazy to take the bag of dirty clothes and climb out the little basement window with them. But that's exactly what I was doing when Elizabeth and Jeffrey got to the washing machine.

"Jessica!" Elizabeth cried. "What's going on? Where are you going?"

68

Jeffrey gave me one of those what-has-Jess-gotten-herself-into looks that my family and friends do so well.

"*He* ate the washing machine!" I whispered frantically. I explained that I was taking the laundry next door to the Beckwiths' house.

Jeffrey's expression turned into that Jess-has-finally-flipped-out look that I also know rather well.

Elizabeth wanted to tell Mom and Dad about the dog.

"No!" I shrieked. "If we tell them now, they'll never let us keep him!"

Meanwhile poor Jeffrey was still trying to figure out who ate the washing machine. I finished crawling out the window and ran next door, leaving Elizabeth to explain the situation to him.

> *But everything's fine now, Diary. Really. I told Mr. Beckwith our washing machine broke. Mom's clothes got cleaned, and I brought them back through the basement window. She never knew the difference. So there's no problem—as long as she and Dad don't try to do any more laundry before Friday.*
>
> *Tuesday night*
>
> *Prince Albert is still the world's most adorable dog, and he's getting more adorable every day. It's funny—he looks so pudgy and clumsy, but when he wants to, he can race*

around the house like you wouldn't believe. Lila says he's not a purebred. Maybe he's part greyhound. Luckily, he's tons cuter than an ugly old greyhound. I love him, Diary. I really do.

Elizabeth said Dana Larson's cousin, Sally, came into the *Oracle* office this afternoon and talked as if she might like to write for the school paper. I can't see the attraction. (No offense, Diary. Writing to you is nothing like writing for other people, where you have to worry about spelling and punctuation. As I always say, a truly creative person can find more than one way to spell a word!)

Anyhow, I was kind of surprised to hear that Sally might be a writer. I barely know her, but I heard she's getting involved with The Droids. It's hard to imagine someone being both a writer and a punk rocker. Also, she's dressing a lot wilder for school than she did this weekend, with a new hairdo and makeup job, too. I wonder just what Sally's story is.

Friday night

The washing machine is fixed, thank goodness. But it cost me every cent I had saved—fifty dollars! I'll have to borrow some from Elizabeth just to keep me in milk

shakes and movies until I get my allowance.
But it was worth it, if it helps us keep
Prince Albert.

Speaking of Prince Albert, we began to
work on Mom and Dad tonight at the dinner
table. . . .

"Wouldn't it be fun to get a pet, like a dog?" I
asked, as if I had just thought of it. "A cute, fuzzy little puppy?"

They were skeptical, to say the least. For some
reason I have a reputation for being irresponsible—
just because I don't *flaunt* my dependability, the way
Elizabeth does.

Elizabeth tried to help. "It wouldn't have to be an
expensive dog," she said. "I mean, we could get one
free."

"There's no such thing as a free puppy, sweetheart," Mom said. "There are vet's bills and li-
censes—not to mention dog food."

And washing-machine repair bills, I added silently.

I wasn't ready to give up. "But what if I can prove
I can take care of a puppy and keep it out of trouble
and everything?"

"I don't know," my father said. "I don't see how
you could prove that without actually getting a
dog, and if it didn't work out, you'd have to take it
back."

No! I'm absolutely not going to take him
back. Mom and Dad didn't exactly say no in

71

the end, but they didn't say yes, either. It was one of those infuriating "we'll see" decisions that parents make when they want to drive their kids crazy.

I can't stand the suspense. They have to let me keep him! They have to!

Sunday night

He's lost! Our helpless baby puppy is lost. I don't know what to do. . . .

Elizabeth and I were walking Prince Albert. He was being as cute and pudgy as ever, wagging his tail and giving us those big puppy-dog grins as he waddled along. But he suddenly decided he didn't want to go any farther. He sat down in the middle of the sidewalk and wouldn't budge, no matter how much we pulled on his leash.

Then the collar slipped right over his head. As soon as he realized he was free, Prince Albert sprang to his fuzzy paws and trotted across the street. We ran after him as fast as we could, but he's awfully fast for a little baby. And he's so small that it's easy for him to hide. Within a few minutes he was out of sight. We searched for hours, but we couldn't find him.

I looked at Elizabeth, and I knew she was thinking the same thing I was thinking. We were both imagining a tiny golden puppy, wandering lost and frightened through unfamiliar streets as darkness fell.

I sat on the sidewalk and burst into tears.

Diary, I am so miserable I want to curl up and die. Our poor little pup is gone! I'll never be happy again.

Monday evening

Dear Diary,
  There's lots of news to report tonight. Guess what? Elizabeth and I were helping with dinner, feeling depressed about poor Prince Albert. Then Dad showed up with the surprise of the century. . . .

I was scraping carrots for dinner. But I guess my mind was on our cute little lost puppy, because I scraped enough carrots to make salad for an army of rabbits. I was afraid I would burst into tears in front of my mother, so I headed upstairs as soon as I finished the carrots. But I saw Dad standing in the doorway, and I stopped, not believing my eyes.

In his arms was a squirming, happy golden-retriever puppy with big, clumsy, furry paws. Prince Albert!

"Dad!" Elizabeth screamed, running in from the kitchen. "Where did you get him?"

Dad laughed. "Your mom and I decided it would be all right to get a dog," he explained. "So I stopped by the animal shelter on the way home, for a surprise!"

I couldn't say a word. And I couldn't take my eyes off Prince Albert. I took him in my arms, and I was so happy I could hardly stand it.

"You know, I've got a great name for him," I said finally, with a wink for Elizabeth. "Prince Albert!"

Prince Albert gave an excited yip and began to nuzzle my chin.

"Jessica!" Mom exclaimed. "I swear he knew you were talking about him. And he just seems to adore you already."

If she only knew.

Dad began quizzing me about taking responsibility for the dog, and I nodded. "He won't be any trouble at all," I said. "You won't even know he's in the house!"

Elizabeth couldn't help laughing then. "Oh, Jessica," she said. "You're too much!"

> *I really am, Diary. Aren't I?*
> *I can't believe that out of all the dogs in the pound, Dad picked our very own Prince Albert! It's truly amazing. So now we have our wonderful puppy back home with us, and we don't have to hide him anymore.*
> *Well, Diary, that wasn't the only happy ending today. Elizabeth got a call from John Pfeifer this evening, and he told her the most incredible story about Dana Larson's cousin Sally. . . .*

Sally had been having trouble fitting in at Sweet Valley High—and at the Larson home. Dana tried to make her feel welcome, but Dana and her brother Jeremy both found it difficult to adjust to having another person in the family. Sally had lived in foster homes for most of her life. Now that she had a real family, she desperately wanted to stay with them.

Sally liked conservative clothes and wanted to write for the school paper. But she wanted Dana to like her, so she faked enthusiasm when Dana outfitted her in punk clothes and invited her to join The Droids.

That afternoon Sally was riding home from school with Dana and Jeremy. Mrs. Larson had announced a family meeting after school that day. Sally was sure she was going to be sent away to another foster home. So she was feeling pretty hopeless on the way home that afternoon.

Then Jeremy picked up two hitchhikers.

The hitchhikers began harassing Dana. Then they hijacked the car and made Jeremy take them to Kelly's, a seedy bar in a rough part of town.

"There's a couple things we need first—like your wallet," said the first hitchhiker when they had reached the bar. "Or my friend here will think of something to take from your sister here."

Jeremy handed over the wallet. Then the hitchhikers announced that they were taking both girls into the bar.

Dana was rigid with fear. Sally was afraid, too. But protecting her cousins was her first priority. She told the guys that Dana was a bore, and that she, Sally, knew how to have a good time. She insisted that living with the Larsons had been a total drag, and she told her cousins to leave her there.

Jeremy and Dana rolled away, but they raced back to Kelly's a few minutes later—with three other boys from school. Against six angry teenagers, the hitchhikers backed off. The cousins had a tearful reunion, and Dana and Jeremy apologized for the way they'd treated Sally.

Then they all returned home to find that the Larsons hadn't wanted to send Sally away, after all. They'd wanted to adopt her!

> *What a story! I had no idea Sally was so brave.*
> *Well, as if that wasn't enough excitement for one day, we also heard something wild about Maria and Michael this evening. As I mentioned last week, Maria and Michael have been dating each other in secret, because their parents have this silly feud. Well, right after we got Prince Albert back this evening, Cara Walker came to the door with awesome news. . . .*

Cara's dark eyes were huge with excitement. "I just saw Maria Santelli," she said. "She and Michael just got engaged!"

"What?" screamed Elizabeth, stunned.

"You're kidding!" I cried. "Did she tell you that?"

Cara nodded. "But it's a huge secret, because they don't want their parents to know."

For all her love of Shakespeare, Elizabeth can't seem to appreciate a Romeo-and-Juliet romance when it happens right under her nose. "But if they can't tell their parents," she asked, "doesn't that mean they probably shouldn't get married? Besides, they're still in high school."

Personally, Diary, I think Liz can be a real spoilsport. Maria and Michael are engaged to be married! I think it's terribly romantic! I can't wait to talk to Maria at school tomorrow.

Part 3

Friday afternoon

Dear Diary,

Maria and Michael's engagement is the most romantic thing I've ever heard! Everyone at school is buzzing about it. In fact, my sister seems to be the only spoilsport in the crowd. You should have heard her this afternoon, as we sat on the lawn at Sweet Valley High after school let out. . . .

"It's so wonderful!" I exclaimed, hugging my knees with excitement. "I can't believe someone in our very own class is getting married! I wonder if I'll get to be a bridesmaid. I can wear flowers in my hair and everything—and maybe I'll catch the bouquet!"

Elizabeth wrecked the mood right away. "Jess," she said in that I'm-the-older-sister voice that irks me so much. "I don't think you realize how serious this whole thing is. There's more to marriage than just a ring and a wedding. Maria's only sixteen, and Michael can't be much more than seventeen!"

"Who cares?" I asked, as amazed as ever at Elizabeth's unworldliness when it comes to love. Then I got her good. I quoted her favorite teacher back at her. "Mr. Collins says Juliet was only fourteen when she met Romeo. Age has nothing to do with anything."

It was easy to get swept up in the drama of Maria and Michael's love affair. I imagined myself as Juliet, intent on marrying my true love despite our parents' bitter feud.

> *Fat chance, Diary. I don't even have a steady boyfriend!*
>
> *The closest I'm likely to get to marriage anytime soon is a social-studies project we're doing next week on family life. To learn about day-to-day issues adults face, Mr. Jaworski is pairing up some juniors and seniors into "husband and wife" teams on Monday. I'm not sure if it'll be a ton of fun or a total drag—I guess it depends on who I get stuck being "married" to!*
>
> *Of course, most of the time I don't really want a steady relationship. I like playing the field. Why tie yourself down to one guy when it's so much more exciting to date somebody new every week? I hate being bored.*
>
> *But I have to tell you something private,*

Diary. Sometimes, when I look at my sister's relationship with Jeffrey, I feel a pang of envy. Jeffrey is tall, blond, and athletic—the ideal romantic hero! As much as I love my sister, I sometimes think he's wasted on someone as practical and levelheaded as Elizabeth.

"Liz, don't you wish Jeffrey's parents were feuding with Mom and Dad?" I asked. "Don't you think it would make everything more *interesting* between you two?"

Elizabeth gave me a look as if I had suggested that she and Jeffrey eat live goldfish.

I don't get it, Diary. Here she is, my own flesh and blood, and Elizabeth doesn't have a single romantic bone in her whole body! It's a good thing I've got enough romance for both of us.

After my talk with Elizabeth I decided to put all these romantic bones to good use and get the whole scoop from Maria about her star-crossed love affair. (I'm not sure what that means, exactly, but everybody always says that about Romeo and Juliet, and it certainly sounds romantic.)

Luckily, Maria was finally ready to talk at cheerleading practice. . . .

"Maria, it's gorgeous!" said Robin Wilson, my cheerleading cocaptain, as she leaned over to admire

Maria's engagement ring. "I can't believe he really gave you a diamond."

"Well, we *are* engaged," Maria said. The ring was exquisite—a simple gold band with a small, perfectly round, sparkling diamond. Maria's smile was just as radiant.

"You mean it's all out in the open now?" Amy asked.

Maria blushed. "Well, not really. I mean, we're telling our friends. But we're not letting our parents know—not for now, anyway. So keep it quiet."

Then Maria told us about the feud between the Santellis and the Harrises.

Maria's father and Michael's father were college roommates and then business partners. When Maria and Michael were small, their fathers even joked about their growing up and marrying each other.

Little did they know!

When Maria was about twelve years old, there was a huge fight between the two couples about a business deal that fell through. The partnership and the friendship collapsed, and Maria's parents told her they would never see the Harrises again.

"A few months ago Michael and I ended up working on a project for the film society together," Maria explained. "We hadn't spoken in years. We were really weird around each other at first, and then we found out we still liked each other. A lot. Only, by then we weren't kids anymore."

"But what about your parents?" I asked.

"They found out about it and told us to stop see-

82

ing each other. I thought we should bring it out in the open, but Michael didn't want to upset his dad. So we just continued to meet anyway, without their knowing. They think we broke up."

Monday night

Dear Diary,

We started the marriage project in Mr. Jaworski's class today. Amazing coincidence, huh? And guess what? I'm married to Winston Egbert—Mr. Dork-Brain himself. One thing's for certain. I'm keeping my own name! I would hate to have to go through life as an Egbert. But at least he makes me laugh. . . .

In class each girl drew a boy's name from a box. I went first, and everybody applauded when I read Winston's name out loud. Elizabeth was second, and she got Bruce Patman. Lucky her! Bruce, the richest, handsomest guy in the senior class, had always been a pain in the neck. But he'd mellowed since he'd started dating Regina Morrow and was actually fun to be around in those days.

I noticed Elizabeth draw a sigh of relief when Olivia Davidson got Jeffrey's name. Olivia works on *The Oracle* with Elizabeth, and I know my sister trusts her. It would have killed Liz to have Jeffrey end up with somebody like Lila or Amy. Lila, by the way, got Bill Chase, the surfer. He's cute, but kind of dull.

Maria was one of the last few girls to choose a name, and every person in the class watched her face as she reached into the box. Everyone applauded when she read aloud, "Michael Harris."

"Let's get started," Mr. Jaworski said after everyone had chosen a name. "Now, each 'wife' has been given a folder with a fact sheet inside it. Boys, why don't you join your classroom 'spouses' and find out where you live, what you do, and anything else that's in your folder."

Winston and I opened the folder, and I was absolutely mortified. I was married to a bus driver!

"What's wrong with that?" Winston asked. "Consider it a golden chariot, my dear." Winston was running for student representative to the PTA and was already promising people whatever they wanted to hear. Then he looked down at the fact sheet with an evil grin. "Besides, we'll have plenty of room for our seven children."

Actually, Diary, it was a real hoot! But I wish I hadn't gotten saddled with seven brats and a part-time job in a beauty parlor—especially after my recent experience with makeovers. The very best part of the day was when Lila cried, "At least your husband has a job. It looks like I'm doomed to the breadline. Bill's unemployed!"

So there you have it, Diary. Lila Fowler, daughter of a millionaire, is the wife of a surfer. She's a short-order cook, and he's out of work! Bruce and Liz did OK. She's a doctor, he teaches fourth-graders, and they have two children. Olivia and Jeffrey own a small business. Amy ended up married to Roger Patman, Bruce's cousin. Amy's a lawyer and Roger's a banker, so she was lording it over everyone, bragging about the fantastic vacations they're going to budget for. But of course it was Maria and Michael that everyone was the most interested in. . . .

"Michael's a veterinarian, and I'm a housewife," she said. "Can you believe it? I must be the only 'wife' who didn't get a job."

"Being a housewife is a job," Michael said.

Maria rolled her eyes. "I mean a *real* job."

Then Mr. Jaworski told us all to turn to the page about budgets. We each had a number at the top of our page, which was our yearly joint income, after taxes.

"This is impossible," Lila said with a moan. "Bill, that must be the wrong page number. No one can live on that little money!"

Lila's real monthly credit-card bill is as much as she and Bill make in a year! It'll be fun to watch her trying to live on Bill's unemployment checks.

We have until Wednesday to budget our money. Then we'll start reporting to the class on how we've decided to spend it.

Luckily for Lila, a more pleasant topic came along later in the afternoon, courtesy of

yours truly. It certainly gave her something
else to think about. I caught up with Lila and
Cara near their lockers. That's when I pro-
posed my brilliant idea. . . .

"Seeing Michael and Maria together today gave me a great idea!" I said as we stood in the crowded hallway. "Don't you think we should have a party for them?"

Lila raised her eyebrows. "Like a bridal shower?"

"No. I mean an engagement party," I said. "Something for both of them. I mean, it seems so unfair that they can't even tell their parents. They're probably dying to celebrate."

Lila nodded, and I could see her brain kick into party-planning gear. "Something formal, I think. Something really big and exciting."

Within minutes we had decided on a surprise party at Fowler Crest, to be held the following Saturday night. We'd have a wedding cake, lots of silver bells and white decorations, and food for at least thirty guests. Well, maybe fifty.

"I don't know, you guys," Cara said. "Didn't Maria say she and Michael wanted to keep this really quiet? Maybe having a big party isn't such a good idea."

I swear, Diary, Cara's spending too much
time at our house since she started dating my
brother. She's beginning to sound just like
stick-in-the-mud Elizabeth. Who could object
to a party?

In the end we won Cara over. So we're doing it. We're throwing a surprise engagement party for Maria and Michael at Lila's house Saturday night. I'm psyched!

Tuesday afternoon

Lila came over today to start planning the party. Elizabeth told us it was "inappropriate." I hate that word. She says the Harrises and the Santellis might find out, blah blah blah. Who in their right mind would tell them? As long as the people we invite don't spill the beans to their parents, Maria's and Michael's families don't have to know anything about it.

But before Lila arrived, Liz and I were out by the pool. We had a conversation that I can't seem to get out of my head. . . .

"Do you think you and Jeffrey will end up getting married?" I asked her.

Elizabeth looked up from her math book with a surprised stare on her face. "Jeffrey and I don't even know what movie we're going to see this weekend, let alone what we'll be doing months from now. How could we possibly guess the future?"

I didn't understand how the girlfriend of someone as gorgeous as Jeffrey could keep from speculating about marrying him. "What I mean is, do you think he's the sort of guy you could imagine being married to?"

Elizabeth chewed the end of her pencil, which she always does when she's thinking hard about something. "Isn't it strange?" she said, still not answering my question. "I don't think you and I have ever talked about the sort of man we'd imagine as a husband."

"Well, I sure hope I don't end up marrying Winston Egbert in real life," I said, suddenly depressed. "Not to mention having to fight over clothing budgets. Winston and I figured out that I only get fifty dollars a year to cover my entire wardrobe!"

Elizabeth laughed. "At the rate you're going, I bet you'll never settle down and get married. You can't even go out with the same guy two weekends in a row."

I pretended that my pout was a joke, but I was kind of hurt. Elizabeth had a perfect boyfriend who was madly in love with her. It didn't seem fair for her to make fun of me.

"You think I'm going to be a spinster, don't you?"

"Oh, I don't know," Elizabeth said playfully. "Maybe someday you'll find someone crazy enough to put up with you."

I threw a towel at her.

"I know you think Maria and Michael's engagement is the world's most romantic event," Elizabeth said, more seriously. "But I guess I think of marriage as something bigger than romance. I mean, think about it, Jess. Imagine spending the rest of your life with someone!"

Again I felt depressed—and scared. "I can't," I

admitted. But the alternative didn't seem any better. "You don't think I'll end up an old maid, do you? So far I haven't been very good at long-term relationships. You're the one who's good at that."

Wouldn't you know it, Diary? I really could have used some of that big-sisterly advice Liz always wants to hand out when I don't need it. But just then Lila arrived, and the conversation turned to Michael and Maria. As I said, Elizabeth thinks their engagement is a mistake.

I think Elizabeth should get a life.

Thursday night

Dear Diary,

Winston and I made our marriage presentation today. It was a blast! But Maria and Michael didn't seem to be having nearly as much fun. It must be a lot different when you're doing it for real.

In addition to our budgets, each couple was given some sort of crisis to handle. The rest of the class took the discussions as kind of a joke, but Maria and Michael were dead serious. I was sitting near enough to hear the whole thing. . . .

"I still don't think we've got this budget right," Maria objected. "But I guess we can't do any better than this, since we've only got your salary to work with. If I had a job, we'd be able to afford summer camp for the kids."

"Who needs summer camp?" Michael scoffed. "Anyway, I'm glad you don't have a job. Otherwise, who'd be around to take care of the kids?"

I'm not a die-hard feminist, like Liz, but I know my mouth dropped open at how sexist he sounded. I closed it quickly so they wouldn't know I was listening. I didn't want them to lower their voices.

"Michael, you can't be serious!" Maria said. "Nobody talks that way anymore."

"Nobody—except Michael Harris!" he said, as if it were something to be proud of. I was beginning to dislike Maria's fiancé intensely. "I don't want my wife to work!" he continued. "I want her to be able to stay at home and take care of my kids. Like in the good old days."

Right, I thought. *The dark ages.*

They let the argument drop and went on to their family crisis. Their twelve-year-old son had been caught shoplifting and could be sent to reform school. A psychologist had suggested family therapy, and Maria was inclined to agree. Michael was not.

"We just tell the kid to get in line, or else," he said. "And I'll see to it he doesn't do it again, whatever it takes."

Maria's eyes widened. "You don't mean you'd hit him, do you?"

"Why not? It sounds like he needs it."

"You're not going to hit our son, Michael," Maria insisted. "He obviously needs a psychologist. Your attitude is probably the reason he's doing this in the first place!"

The apartment building Winston and I lived in burned down. But compared to Maria and Michael's argument, our crisis seemed minor.

Michael was stubborn and Maria was angry, and their voices were loud enough so that other people started to notice. Luckily, Mr. Jaworski called for us to start our reports. Winston and I were asked to talk about our budget.

"I earn seventeen thousand dollars a year," Winston began. "And Jessica—my dear wife—earns six thousand dollars."

We explained that we lived in an apartment because we couldn't afford a house. "However," I said, "I've convinced my husband to let me have half my yearly salary for clothing and entertainment."

The class cracked up. I guess they knew me too well. Maria seemed to be the only person in the classroom who looked serious. In fact, she looked downright dismal.

A few minutes later Mr. Jaworski asked Maria and Michael to give their report on their family crisis. Michael did all the talking, and Maria didn't contradict him when he said they had decided that "firmer discipline" rather than therapy would keep their son in line.

I'm sure Maria and Michael will work it all out. I mean, that's what this exercise is for—practice. They'll use this to work the kinks out, so they'll be OK by the time they get married.

I heard something else about Maria and Michael today. She was Winston's campaign manager for his PTA election, but she dropped out. Caroline Pearce says it's because Michael was jealous of the time she's been spending with Winston. Jealous of a nerd like Winston? Michael's gone overboard. But I know it's only because he loves Maria so much. How romantic, to have somebody love you so much that he'd be jealous of every second spent with another boy.

As for me, I'm finding that marriage is a snap. Even marriage to a dork like Winston.

Friday afternoon

We had a party-planning session at lunch today. Lila thought of a cover for inviting Maria and Michael to her house tomorrow night. She told them she's throwing a party because her cousin is visiting and especially wants to see them both.

Actually, she nearly blew it—subtlety isn't Lila's strong point. Maria and Michael looked mystified about the whole thing. They had hardly spoken to her cousin the last time he was in town, so they couldn't figure out why he wanted them there. And Lila practically beat them over the head, telling them they had to arrive at exactly eight o'clock, on the dot.

Cara and I laughed until we were in tears. Michael and Maria must think Lila's a lunatic, but I don't think they caught on that it's a surprise party for them. I guess they're too wrapped up in each other to notice anything else.

I can't wait for tomorrow night! Unfortunately, I couldn't afford to buy a new dress—not after that fiasco with Prince Albert and the washing-machine repair bill. I fell in love with a silver party dress at Lisette's the other day. But I can't afford it. So I'm stuck with my ancient aquamarine halter. It will just have to do.

Why can't I be rich, like Lila? After this party is over, I'm going to look into some ways of increasing my net worth. Mr. Jaworski taught us that phrase in our budgeting project. Net worth. Don't you think it sounds mature and sophisticated?

Anyhow, I'm excited about the party. Michael and Maria are going to be blown away!

Saturday night, really late

I was right. Michael and Maria were blown away. They were also blown apart. Meaning they aren't even engaged anymore. What a drag.

Lila outdid herself with the party preparations. Silver bells and white balloons festooned the walls of the Fowlers' formal drawing room. An enormous banner screamed HAPPY ENGAGEMENT, MARIA AND MICHAEL! A table was heaped with scrumptious-looking desserts—especially a two-tiered wedding cake with butter-cream frosting and a little bride and groom on top.

When Maria and Michael walked in, Dana and The Droids struck up "The Wedding March," and everyone rushed forward to congratulate the guests of honor.

They looked surprised, but they also looked tense, as if maybe they'd had an argument on the way over. I figured it would blow over. Two people who were that much in love wouldn't hold a grudge. And there's nothing like a party to get your mind off a disagreement, I figured.

I figured wrong, it turned out.

Lila and I stood near the refreshments table— Lila having the nerve to wear the same silver dress *I* couldn't afford to buy at Lisette's. I tried not to think about it as we watched Maria across the room.

"She looks great in white," I said, admiring the way Maria's simple white dress set off her dark hair. "I can just see her in her wedding gown."

Then Dana grabbed the microphone and announced a new Droids song called "Hold on Tight," written especially for Maria and Michael.

I thought I was going to faint away right then, it was all so romantic. Maria's eyes shone with tears of happiness as she and Michael whirled around the floor.

After that I danced with Michael, and Maria danced with Winston. I noticed Michael watching them dance. He had a thoughtful look on his face, but he didn't seem jealous or angry. I decided Caroline's gossip about Michael being jealous of Winston was just that—gossip.

A few minutes later I realized how wrong I was.

Michael took the microphone to thank everyone for the party. "I also want to thank Maria," he added. "Sometimes it's hard to tell someone how special she really is—even when she's closer to you than anyone else in the world. The wonderful thing about Maria is that she understands. It's what I love most about her."

Maria's eyes filled with tears again, and I have to admit that my own did as well.

"I have one more thing I want to announce," Michael continued. "This is kind of late in the race, but I've decided to run for the student representative to the PTA. And with Maria's help I'm sure I stand a very good chance."

He acted as if she'd agreed to help him. But Maria's eyes opened wide, and I knew she hadn't even heard that he was running. Besides, it didn't make sense for a senior to campaign for a position that would last into the following school year.

Winston looked as if he'd been slapped in the face. "There's nothing to explain," I heard him tell Maria in a flat voice. Apparently, she had given him a flimsy excuse for dropping out as his campaign manager, and now he thought she'd planned to help his competition the whole time. "I guess even someone as thick as I am can take a hint." He spun on his heel and ran out the door.

Maria hurried after him. "Wait!" she cried.

But Michael stopped her. "Let him go," he said roughly, grabbing her arm. "Let him go. You hear me?"

"Let go of me!" Maria insisted, her voice rising. The room went silent as everyone stopped to listen. "You think you own me just because you gave me this ring. Well, you don't! I'm my own person. And you have no right to treat me the way you just did. I made a promise to Winston, and you've made me look like a real jerk!"

"You care so much about what you've promised him," Michael said. "Well, what about what you've promised me?"

"What have I promised you that I haven't done?" Maria demanded. "You're the one who won't keep a promise. What about telling our parents? What happened to that?"

The color drained out of Michael's face, and his lips set in a thin line. "If you go chasing after Winston, Maria, it's going to be all over between us."

Maria stared at him, oblivious to the people around them. Then she looked at the ring on her finger. "Michael, I don't think this is right. We've stopped having fun together. We fight all the time." Tears began coursing down her cheeks, but Maria's voice was calm. "We'll talk later. Now I've got to go apologize to Winston."

Maria's fingers trembled as she dropped the engagement ring into Michael's hand. Then she rushed out of the room while Michael stared after her.

I thought things couldn't get any crazier, Diary. But they did. Suddenly, who should show up on the scene but Maria's and Michael's parents. I found out later that Caroline Pearce told her mother about the party, and Mrs. Pearce blabbed it to the Santellis.

Like mother, like daughter, Diary. Don't you think?

The parents were practically breathing fire. But once they found out Maria and Michael had called off the engagement on their own, they calmed down and started talking about it like civilized people. The upshot is that the families made up, and Maria and Michael are going to be allowed to be friends again, which seems to be all that either of them wants at the moment.

It certainly was the world's weirdest engagement party.

The funniest part of the evening was watching Lila try to preserve the mood, even after the engagement was off. "No one can leave!" she kept yelling. "Have fun, everybody! I spent a lot of time and money on this party!"

As Elizabeth said at the time, Lila's such a sentimentalist.

Monday afternoon

We gave our final presentations in Jaworski's class today. Michael and Maria

97

went last. They seemed nervous, but I guess
they had a long talk after the party and got
things settled between them, because I could
tell that they're friends again. Their presenta-
tion was kind of touching. (Sorry. I hate that
word; it's so sappy.) But it really was. . . .

"I think we learned how important compromise is," Maria said, after reviewing the problems that had come up in the course of their project. "And also how difficult it is to agree when two people have opposing ideas about something.

"We also learned how important it is to communicate our differences. In the seminar I finally went along with Michael's decision to use discipline instead of therapy in the case of our problem son. If that had really happened, I would have been resentful because I was totally opposed to his decision. But I was unable to communicate how strongly opposed I was."

Michael cleared his throat. "Maria and I both agreed that we learned as much from what this project left out as what it put in. Mr. Jaworski, your folders gave us all the information we needed to be a real married couple. We knew our occupations, our family size, our ages—all sorts of things. But your folder didn't say anything about how we felt about each other. You didn't tell us where we met." He smiled at Maria. "Or what made me first fall in love with her. Or what I think about when I can't be with her."

The class was utterly silent as Michael spoke.

"We appreciate the project very much because we

think most kids our age probably don't give the serious, adult side of marriage much thought. But we also want to put in a word for just plain love. The problems we had to deal with were all hard. Without love they would probably be impossible. Our final conclusion is that a marriage without genuine love and trust just isn't going to make it, however carefully worked out all the other things are."

Everyone clapped as Maria and Michael sat down.

I hate what I'm about to write. Don't ever breathe a word of this, Diary. But Elizabeth was right. Maria and Michael weren't ready for marriage. None of us are. It sure seemed romantic, though.

The only new development now is that I'm getting the feeling that something is brewing between Maria and Winston! It was all perfectly innocent when Michael was being jealous. Win's too much of a chicken to go after another guy's girlfriend. But now that Michael is out of the picture, it looks like old Win is stepping in to fill the void. From Romeo to Egbert. What a letdown.

Well, Maria is welcome to my ex-husband. The family-life project is over. And I'm happy to say I'm a single woman again.

Look out, world!

Part 4

Monday afternoon

Dear Diary,

   I'm going to be a millionaire. Stop laughing. I am. I'm becoming a Tofu-Glo girl. You say you haven't heard of Tofu-Glo? It's the latest and greatest thing for your skin. It's all natural and made from soybeans. And I just happen to be the best salesperson of all time. I can convince anyone of practically anything. Consider the way I talked Elizabeth out of fifty dollars to get this thing off the ground. . . .

"For starters I'll have a Tofu-Glo party," I told Elizabeth in my bedroom that afternoon. "You know, invite everybody over and tell them all about it. It'll be so much fun! I thought I could invite all the girls from Pi Beta Alpha over a week from Wednesday. I'll have the party then."

Like me, Elizabeth was also a member of the most exclusive sorority at school, but she always said she joined just to humor me, and she never took it seriously. But for once she actually seemed interested in an activity involving the sorority.

"Good idea," she said, an enthusiastic smile on her face. "But why wait until then? Can't you start sooner?"

Elizabeth's early support of my Tofu-Glo career was encouraging. She didn't know it yet, but I was preparing to make a different kind of sales pitch altogether—with Elizabeth as the target.

"I need to get my sales pitch ready," I told her in a serious, practical tone that I knew would win her respect. "I don't want to start selling until I've got it perfect. Besides, by then I'll have my samples. And," I added, thinking fast, "I'll invite some girls who aren't in PBA, too. I want to have everybody I know come."

Just in time I had remembered that Elizabeth's biggest problem with Pi Beta Alpha activities was their exclusive nature. Personally, I don't understand why anyone would want to join a sorority that *wasn't* exclusive, but I was buttering Elizabeth up for the Big Favor, so it was important to phrase everything in exactly the right way. So far I had her right where I wanted her.

"Will you go door to door, too?" she asked. "You'll have to rehearse your sales pitch, so you sound professional."

"Oh, right. You can help me with that, Liz." I

watched her eagerly and bit my lower lip as if I were worried about my sales ability. "I really want to be good."

That part wasn't completely a scam. Elizabeth is a great partner for rehearsing things like that. I really did need her help.

"You will be, Jess," she said earnestly. "I know you will."

Now it was time to move in for the kill.

"There's only one problem," I said, nervously pleating the material of my bedspread. I looked up quickly. "I need a hundred fifty dollars to buy the starter kit, and I've only got a hundred. So can I borrow fifty dollars?"

There. I had popped the big question. I watched her face as she debated with herself. This was going to be close. It wasn't the first time I had asked Liz for money. In fact, it wasn't the second, third, or tenth time, either. And I have to admit, I don't always manage to pay her back. But this was different. This was a sure thing.

I was lucky I needed only fifty dollars. I had finally paid my parents everything I owed them, so that I had some allowance to speak of again. Extra baby-sitting jobs had helped replenish my savings, and a timely gift from Aunt Nancy had made up the rest of the first hundred. Elizabeth was my best bet for the rest. I crossed my fingers behind my back and tried to look as though I didn't want her to feel guilty if she refused. Still, she hesitated.

"OK," I said with a big, sad sigh. "It doesn't matter." I turned away with just the right touch of melo-drama. "I'll have to ask Lila, I guess."

I suppose I overdid it with that suggestion. Elizabeth knew perfectly well that I would never admit to Lila that I needed her help, even though fifty dollars was nothing to my best friend.

"But, Jess," Elizabeth began, getting all reasonable on me, "why do you have to start out by handing over a hundred fifty dollars? It doesn't make much sense to me."

I sighed. Elizabeth was so naive about the business world. Everybody knew you had to spend money to make money. "But I'll make it all back selling just a third of the stuff I get. Really!" I grabbed her hand. "Please, Lizzie? I'll pay you right back, I swear!"

Elizabeth laughed, and I knew she was beaten. "OK, OK! I give up! I can't have you begging in the streets, can I?"

"Oh, I knew you would!" I cried, giving her a hug. "That means I can get started right away. I'll call them right now and tell them I'm signing up."

> So, Diary, what do you think? Am I the world's greatest salesperson, or what? I can't wait to kick off my new career with my Tofu-Glo party next Wednesday. I don't even think I'll tell Lila about it until I've got the cosmetics here and I'm ready to start. Until then it'll be my little secret.
>
> Oops. I almost forgot the parental units, as Winston would say. I suppose I'll have to

*tell them about it right away. I can't wait to
get started selling Tofu-Glo products. I was
born to be rich.*

Monday night

*I sprang my plan on Mom and Dad as we
were getting Mexican food ready for dinner
tonight. As I predicted, they didn't see the
brilliance of it at first. Jeffrey was over for
dinner, and he wasn't very supportive, either.
Not everyone has my eye for business oppor-
tunities. At least Mom and Dad didn't tell me
I couldn't do it. . . .*

First I explained that Tofu-Glo has a network of
salesgirls throughout the country. The sales reps pay
for the initial package of shampoo, skin cream, and
other products, and then sell them to friends and
neighbors.

"Since everything is made from soybeans, it's all
totally natural and healthy!" I said.

"Soybeans?" Jeffrey asked. He tried to hide a gri-
mace by staring intently at the cheese he was shred-
ding. I ignored his skeptical look.

"I can't lose," I insisted. "Everyone will want to
buy Tofu-Glo from me, and I'll make a fortune!"

Jeffrey leaned over and whispered into
Elizabeth's ear, but I heard every word: "Sounds
pretty gross to me."

One more crack like that, I decided, and Jeffrey

might lose his status as the World's Most Perfect Boyfriend.

"Just how thoroughly have you researched this company, Jessica?" my father asked, sounding a lot like Elizabeth. "There are a lot of dishonest firms out there."

I swear, sometimes my parents have no confidence at all in my judgment. I wish they wouldn't treat me as if I'm six instead of sixteen.

"Oh, Dad! Do you think I'd get involved in something that wasn't completely legit?"

"I think I'll pass on that one."

My frustration turned to rage. If they refused to give me permission to sell Tofu-Glo, I'd be in big trouble. I had already sent in the $150 for the introductory package.

"I'm only kidding, honey," my father said quickly, realizing he'd made me angry. "All I'm saying is that you might find yourself caught up in something with unpleasant surprises. That's all."

"Dad, you don't—"

"Oh, I don't know, Ned," my mother cut in, smiling. "I sold cleaning products once door to door, when I was in college. Remember? And to tell you the truth, I thought it was a lot of fun. I think it would be a good experience for Jessica."

Diary, when I make my first million, I'm buying that woman a mink coat! Right after I buy one for me.

106

"Yeah, Dad," Elizabeth added. "Steven sold magazine subscriptions when he was in the Boy Scouts, remember? You didn't mind his doing it."

I'd buy Liz a mink coat with my millions, as well—but she's into saving the rain forests and the whales and pretty much everything else, so I doubt she'd wear it.

Even Dad couldn't hold out against all three of us—especially after the Reasonable Twin spoke up in my favor. (Doesn't that just bite? He won't agree to something when it's just me, but as soon as it has the Liz Seal of Approval, he gives in!) But at least he did give in.

The only real question left is what I'm going to buy when I sell my first shipment of Tofu-Glo and start becoming disgustingly rich—a Chanel bag, or a new pair of Doc Martens.

OK, Diary, you've convinced me. I'll get both.

Tuesday afternoon

The latest gossip at school is that Aaron Dallas ticked off everyone at soccer practice yesterday.

Isn't it crummy, Diary? My own sister was right there, waiting for Jeffrey, but I had to hear the news at school today from

Caroline. Doesn't Elizabeth realize how bad it makes me look when I don't know an important piece of gossip involving my very own sister's boyfriend's best friend? Liz ought to be more considerate and fill me in on these things herself. . . .

Sweet Valley High's soccer team was one of the best in the district, and Aaron was our top scorer. Aaron had always been popular—handsome, friendly, and fun to be with. In fact, I had gone out with him occasionally myself. But lately he had been getting on people's nerves.

Monday afternoon during a practice game, Aaron had control of the ball—until Tony Esteban slipped in ahead of him and stole it away. There was a scramble, and the ball went out of bounds.

"It's out on Dallas!" Tony called.

"Are you blind?" Aaron demanded. "It went out on you!"

Tony shrugged. "No way, Dallas."

Tony began to walk away, but Aaron grabbed him by the shoulder and jerked him around. "What do you think you're doing, calling a foul on me?"

Jeffrey took Aaron by the arm and tried to calm him down, but Aaron kept cursing and gesturing angrily at Tony.

"OK!" Coach Horner yelled, cutting the conflict short. "Time to pack it in! Hit the showers!" But he stopped Jeffrey and Aaron for a terse conversation before he let them go to the locker room.

I don't know what the coach said to Aaron, but I bet Elizabeth does, since Jeffrey was there. So far she's not talking. Caroline claims the coach told Aaron he would be off the soccer team if he couldn't learn to hold his temper. I can't believe that, Diary. No coach in his right mind would kick his star player off the team so close to the championship. I'll have to work on Elizabeth to get the real story.

You know, Diary—now that I think about it, this isn't the first weird thing I've heard about Aaron. Robin Wilson was having a cow on Friday because he accused her of cheating off his math test. She says she only leaned over to pick up her pencil. Robin's a pain in the neck, but she's good at math—better than Aaron. She wouldn't need to cheat off him.

And Lila mentioned something that happened at the Engagement Party of the Century a couple weeks ago. She said Aaron threatened to beat up Roger Patman on the dance floor, just because Roger accidentally stepped on his foot.

Caroline says Aaron's parents are getting a divorce and that's why he's being such a dork-brain. That's too bad. I'm glad my parents would never do anything that awful. I would just die. Still, that's no excuse for treating his friends like dirt.

I don't know how someone as sweet and

friendly as Jeffrey is putting up with Aaron's short fuse. And I don't understand how Aaron's girlfriend, Heather Sanford, can stand him. I hardly know Heather; she's only a sophomore. But she's got a wardrobe to rival Lila's. Anyone with clothes that awesome has to have some sense.

Monday afternoon

All right, all right. I haven't written in almost a week. So, I'm a delinquent. Sue me.

My first shipment arrived! I'm so excited I can hardly stand it. Twenty-four boxes of Tofu-Glo! I have to admit, it looks like a lot more than I expected. . . .

"There's a whole bunch of boxes for you," said the young delivery man who stood at the door. He was cute—a little skinny, but tall and sandy-haired, with nice eyes. Besides, I love getting presents. So I gave him one of my most radiant smiles.

"From the Tofu-Glo company," he continued.

I almost hugged him. "You're kidding! I can't believe it's here. Let me help you. Oh, this is great!"

A few minutes later he set the first box down on the curb. I ripped into it and pulled out a glass bottle with "Tofu-Shampu" written in gold script on a green label.

Green like money.

"I'll just take these on up to your porch," the man said, balancing a stack of four other boxes in his arms.

One by one, I pulled the beautiful, wonderful bottles of shampoo out of the first box and laid them on the sidewalk. "This is going to be so fantastic," I said aloud, wondering how long it would take me to sell $150 worth of the stuff.

The delivery man returned from setting the boxes on the front porch. I was about to thank him, but he swung another tower of boxes out of the back of the van and carried them up to the house. I gulped. This was a lot of tofu.

"All of that?" I asked when he returned.

"Not quite," he said, heaving three more boxes out of the truck. "There. That's it. Biggest single delivery this week."

What have I gotten myself into? said a little voice inside my head. *Can I really sell all this stuff?*

"I—I didn't know there would be so much."

"Don't worry," he said with a grin and a shrug. "I hear the stuff is really hot."

That cheered me up right away. "Hey, don't be surprised if you have another load to deliver pretty soon. I'm going to sell this stuff in no time."

Liz got home just after I finished carting the last box of Tofu-Glo up the stairs to my room. "So this is your ticket to fiscal happiness, huh?" she said.

Yes, those were her exact words as she stood in the doorway of my room, with her

111

arms folded and that Jessica's-at-it-again look on her face.

She can be such a drag, Diary. She doesn't take me seriously. Nobody does. I hate it when she gives me that amused, superior look—as if she wants to laugh, but she won't because she's being polite. She treats me like a child. But I'll show her. I'll show everybody.

Maybe I'll have a career as a salesperson. I could start with Tofu-Glo and then work my way up. Eventually, I'll sell something important, like stocks and bonds. Or something glamorous, like expensive perfume. Or something big, like real estate. I'll have scads of money, and a parking space that says, "Jessica Wakefield, Salesperson of the Year," and I'll go on business trips to classy places like Paris and exotic places like Hong Kong and important places like Washington, D.C., and the New York Stock Exchange.

And Elizabeth will stop treating me like her baby sister. And nobody will ever give me those amused-but-too-polite-to-laugh looks again.

But I digress, Diary. For now I decided to ignore Liz's Superior Twin act. I need her support if I'm going to become Tofu-Glo's number-one salesperson.

To tell you the truth, it only took me a minute to stop being annoyed with

Elizabeth. I mean, she suddenly turned supportive—and even interested in my Tofu-Glo. So I reached for the nearest box and pulled out a jar of Soya-Soft moisturizing cream. . . .

"Soya-Soft cream is a revolution in skin care," I read from the label, trying to sound professional. "Its totally natural ingredients work in harmony to hydrate, tone, and rejuvenate the skin."

"Will it make me look years younger?" Elizabeth asked, eyes twinkling.

"Are you kidding? You'll be fifteen again! Let me just read you what's inside." I cleared my throat. "'Active ingredients: deionized mineral springwater, soy, aloe vera.' Sounds good so far."

"Oh, tell me more, Tofu-Glo girl!"

I grinned. "'PABA, keratin, peach-kernel oil, essence of beeswax, petroleum, okra extract, fish-bone meal, sebum, hydrolyzed albumen.'"

Elizabeth's mouth dropped open. And with each ingredient I read aloud, even *I* was feeling more and more skeptical. Of course, a good salesperson would never let her prospect know that.

"See?" I concluded. "It's all totally natural and wonderful."

"Jess, that sounds kind of—"

"Oh, don't be so squeamish," I said. "It's good for you. Well, anyway, we've got to start calling people. My Tofu-Glo party is the day after tomorrow, you know."

We made up a list of most of the girls we know from school. I even told Elizabeth she could invite boring old Enid. Why not? I figured. The bigger my list of clientele, the bigger my profits. Right? Then I started making calls and inviting people to my party.

Unfortunately, the first person I called was Lila. She's such a wet blanket. Like the thunderstorm on a parade, the anchovies on a pizza, or the chaperons at a school dance. Well, you get the idea. She wouldn't recognize a good idea if it smacked her in the head.

Smacking her in the head, now there's an idea. . . .

Lila's voice through the phone line was dripping with scorn. "You mean you're going to be a *salesperson*?"

You would think I'd told her I wanted to join the Chess Club or date Chrome Dome Cooper, the principal. "Yeah! What's wrong with that?"

"Oh, it's just—well, all I can say is, I'd never do anything so—so déclassé."

It's bad enough that I have to put up with my sister acting superior. But where did Lila get off, using words like "déclassé" with me? I glared at the telephone receiver.

"I'm sure you never would, Lila," I said sweetly. "I can see how living off your father's money might make it hard for you to take any kind of initiative."

I looked up to see Elizabeth still standing in my doorway, a shocked look on her face. I winked at her, but I wondered privately if I'd pushed Lila too far.

Despite her cash flow, I've always felt a little sorry for Lila. All the silver party dresses in the world can't make up for the fact that she doesn't have a mother. And her father never has much time for her. Then again, Lila has no right to be snotty to me. It isn't my fault her father's more interested in business than in his own kid.

I vowed to be nice to my own kids someday, after I'm a world-famous salesperson and even richer than Lila.

In the end Lila said she'd come to the party. I hung up the phone with a sigh of relief. Despite all our arguments, I really like Lila a lot. I don't want her to be mad at me. Besides, she could afford more Tofu-Glo than any girl at school. I bet she's feeling a little threatened because eventually I'm going to be even richer than she is.

She'll get over it.

Wednesday night

My party was a total success. It was awesome! Everyone I invited came. I offered healthy snacks like soy chips, granola, sunflower seeds, and mineral water. The Tofu-Glo sales brochure suggested those things, to fit the all-natural theme of the cosmetics.

But, man, was I tense at the beginning! I don't think I've ever been so excited and nervous in my whole entire life as when I stood there in the middle of my living room, ready to start my Tofu-Glo sales pitch, with a dozen girls staring at me.

Nobody knows this, Diary, but I get a horrible, sick feeling every time I have to talk in front of people. My palms sweat, and my heart pounds, and I find myself holding my breath. Then I'm afraid I'm going to faint, like one of those simpering, old-fashioned romance-novel women with the vapors. I'm all right once I start talking, but the beginning is hard. It's so hard that I always want to turn around and run.

But I'm Jessica. I'm supposed to be bubbly and outrageous and bask in the attention. So, as always, I plastered a big smile on my face, I took a deep breath, and I jumped right in. . . .

"Well, I guess you all want to know what this is all about," I began. I swallowed hard, as if I could gulp down my stage fright. I forced myself to breathe. What if nobody bought anything? I wanted so badly for this to work. It had to work.

I remembered the advice from the Tofu-Glo sales brochure: "Relax. Enjoy yourself. Knowing that these products are 100 percent pure should set you and your client completely at ease. Remember, Tofu-Glo is good for you."

That helped. Suddenly I found that I was breathing like a normal person. I bought myself a little more time by pointing out the snacks and encouraging people to help themselves. By the time they were crunching on granola bars, I felt better.

"I know it's a little unusual," I said, "but I'd like to talk to you about a company I recently found out about. They make beauty and health-care products that are completely natural."

I paused for dramatic effect and noticed Elizabeth, standing in the back and nodding at me, with a big, proud smile on her face.

"The company is called Tofu-Glo," I said, back to my usual self. "And I'm a Tofu-Glo girl."

After they digested that, I went on to describe the whole line of Tofu-Glo products.

"I'd like you all to try Tofu-Shampu, Tofu-Clean, Soya-Soft, and Soya-Life dietary supplement," I said, placing a container of each on the coffee table. "These products are guaranteed to make your skin, your hair, your whole body, look and feel great."

As I described each product in detail, I saw that every girl in the room was listening to me intently.

I'm really good at this, I realized with a warm glow. I felt as if I could fly. "As I said, the main active ingredient in each of these things is soybeans, the same stuff those chips are made of."

Cara examined the soy chip she had been nibbling. "Does it taste the same?" she asked.

"Actually, Cara, I haven't eaten the shampoo. But go ahead and taste it if you want."

Everyone laughed, and I suddenly knew, beyond any doubt, that I would sell a ton of Tofu-Glo that day.

"How about this Tofu-Shampu, Jess?" Maria asked. "I have to wash my hair after cheerleading practice, besides washing it every morning. Is it safe to use that often?"

"Sure! No problem!"

"Sounds good!" Maria decided. "I guess I'll give it a try."

I wanted to dance across the room. Instead I smiled at her. "My first customer!" I said. "So for you the shampoo is free!" I turned to the rest of the group. "Now, who's next?"

Everybody started placing orders faster than I could take them. As soon as I saw they were buying, I concentrated on ways to get them to buy as much as possible.

"Hey, Julie," I said to Julie Porter. "Why don't you get some for your sister, too? I'm sorry I couldn't invite her. I don't know where she hangs out these days."

Julie's face reddened, and I felt guilty for bringing up Johanna, who had dropped out of school the year before. But it worked. Julie took another bottle of shampoo.

It was so incredible. Almost every person who came bought something! It's not official Tofu-Glo policy, but I decided to offer a money-back guarantee. And it worked like a charm.

*Heather Sanford picked out a whole arm-
ful of stuff. And even Enid took a bottle of the
shampoo. I figure Elizabeth put her up to it,
but I accepted her cash just the same. A sale
is a sale, right?*

*Speaking of Elizabeth, she floored us all
at the end of the party. After Heather left, my
sister began making some very un-Elizabeth-
like remarks. . . .*

I was on the other side of the room, taking Cara's
order, while Elizabeth sat on the couch with a few of
her friends. But I kept one ear cocked to hear what
she was saying. I had known that Elizabeth and
Jeffrey had been spending a lot of time with Aaron
and Heather in the last few weeks. But I hadn't realized just how much Elizabeth disliked Heather.

"What really drives me out of my mind more than
anything," Elizabeth continued, "is that she *baby
talks*! And I really mean baby talk! We went out a
week ago Friday, and Aaron was mad about something, as usual. And Heather tried to get him to cheer
up." Her voice rose several octaves. "'Oh, Aaron—
peez don't be angway!'"

Everybody laughed appreciatively, though Jessica
noticed a look of surprise on Enid's face. For once
Jessica sympathized with Enid. She didn't particularly
care whether Elizabeth liked Heather, but it seemed
strange to hear sensitive Elizabeth maliciously making fun of someone.

"I've heard her, too," DeeDee said. "It's really

amazing. I think she believes it's perfectly normal for a high-school student to sound like a three-year-old."

Elizabeth grinned. "What was it she said he was? Oh, right: 'Gwumpy'!"

A few minutes later the girls were rocking with laughter as they mimicked Heather's baby-talk voice, in a conversation about how good Tofu-Glo would make them look. Then I noticed Elizabeth blush, apparently ashamed of herself. She jumped up quickly to carry some empty bowls into the kitchen. Her friends were laughing so hard, they didn't seem to notice how abruptly she left the room.

I don't know what to make of that. I'll have to have a talk with Elizabeth and see what's really going on with Heather. And Aaron.

But maybe not just now. If Tofu-Glo sells as well door to door as it does in parties like that one, I'll be very busy in the next few days. And very rich sometime soon!

I've never felt so much affection for soybeans.

Uh-oh, Diary. Something smells funny. I really mean it. There's a strange, yucky smell in my bedroom. I hope Prince Albert didn't leave me any surprises. I'd better check around.

Thursday night

Wow. Aaron got into more trouble at soccer practice today. And only a week before

120

the big championship game with Big Mesa.
It's hard to believe that Aaron has turned
into such a bully. He was always so nice and
easygoing. But Amy was there and saw the
whole thing. . . .

Aaron was expertly guiding the ball downfield, to get into position for a score. Then Brad Tomasi cut in from the left and kicked the ball away. Aaron tripped and fell, but he was up instantly, chasing Brad.

Everyone figured Aaron was after him because he wanted to steal the ball back. Instead Aaron tackled Brad and began pounding him in the face. "You jerk!" he screamed. "You nearly broke my leg back there!"

Brad, caught by surprise and pinned underneath Aaron's weight, could hardly move to defend himself.

Then the coach's whistle screeched, and the other players surged forward to break up the fight.

Aaron struggled against Jeffrey's hold as Coach Horner examined Brad's injuries. After the coach sent Brad to the nurse's office with two boys to help him, he turned on Aaron. "I ought to punch you out for that one, Dallas, but I'd be arrested."

"He's a clumsy idiot!" Aaron shouted. "He deliberately tripped me! Everyone saw him do it."

"And everyone saw you attack him," the coach retorted, his voice full of warning. "There is absolutely no excuse for what you just pulled, Dallas. I'm putting you on notice: one more fight, one more shout out of you—anywhere in this town—and you're off the team. Do I make myself perfectly clear?"

121

Aaron looked as if he would have liked to tackle the coach. "But you can't do that!"

The coach's voice became low and intense. "I will do exactly what I choose. And I do not choose to tolerate that kind of infantile, prima donna behavior on my team. So you are hereby suspended until Tuesday."

There was an audible gasp from Aaron's teammates.

"And," the coach continued, "if you want to play in Thursday's game, you will *enjoy* being suspended."

He blew the whistle again and yelled at the team to hit the showers.

This stuff with Aaron is making Elizabeth freak out. She doesn't want to talk about it. But, frankly, I haven't had time to pay much attention—learning everything there is to know about Tofu-Glo is taking up every spare minute. Tomorrow afternoon I plan to start selling door to door!

Anyhow, my guess is that Elizabeth, who hates violence more than anyone, thinks Aaron is being a jerk. But Jeffrey is Aaron's best friend, so I doubt he was happy to hear that.

Now she's convinced Jeffrey is never going to talk to her again after The Oracle *comes out on Monday.*

You see, Elizabeth went to soccer practice today, to write about the team's preparation for the championship game with Big Mesa.

122

For somebody who's supposed to be so smart, my sister ought to have her head examined. She could have supported her team and kept her boyfriend. Instead she decided to write about what really happened at practice and may alienate Jeffrey in the process. She says it's a matter of "journalistic integrity." I think it's a matter of journalistic insanity. Why risk losing a hunk like Jeffrey?

Sometimes—like practically every minute of every day—it's hard to believe Elizabeth and I are related.

Friday afternoon

You can't win 'em all. But you can win most of 'em! At least you can if you're as wonderful a salesperson as I am. I took Tofu-Glo door to door today and had four great successes and one dud. . . .

"Hi!" I said brightly as soon as the door opened to my first customer's house, on Moonglow Terrace. "My name is Jessica Wakefield, and I'm your Tofu-Glo girl." I held up my canvas sample bag. "Can I show you some of our health and beauty products today?"

"Well . . ." began the middle-aged woman in the doorway.

"It'll only take a few moments, ma'am," I said politely, smiling so hard my teeth hurt. "I'm sure you'll be very interested."

123

Finally the woman nodded and smiled back. "All right, dear. Come on in."

"This is a lovely house," I said as soon as I stepped inside. Then I got a good look at the decorating job and realized that my flattery was sincere. The house was exquisite. "My mom couldn't have done a better job," I said. "And she's an interior designer."

The woman gave me a surprised smile. "Did you say your name is Wakefield?"

"Yes."

"What a coincidence!" she replied with a laugh. "Your mother did do my house! She's Alice Wakefield, right?"

I wanted to give her a high-five sign right there, Diary, but I restrained myself. The sale was in the bag! But you would be proud of me, Diary. I acted like a complete professional. As I said, I'm really good at this.

I described the Tofu-Glo product line to the woman, Mrs. Bowen.

"Why don't I just take one of each, Jessica?" she said as soon as I finished. "How would that be?"

How would that be? How would that be? That would be totally rad. It would be too awesome for words. She even told me I could tell her neighbors she was a customer of mine. I did, and it worked at the next three houses. I made those three sales in no time. Then I hit house number five, and I got totally stumped.

"May I try some first?" the woman asked. She had

a face like a hatchet. *Try some?* I couldn't think of any good reason to refuse, so I let her.

It took her a long time to open the jar of Soya-Soft, and I was getting kind of embarrassed. I mean, I didn't want customers to think Tofu-Glo uses inferior jars and lids. But I was even more embarrassed when she opened it. She wrinkled her nose, and I guess I did, too.

"Is that smell from the cream?" the woman demanded.

"Oh, well, you see—" I groped for an explanation. Then inspiration hit. "They don't put in artificial fragrances, you see. The smell goes away after you use it."

The woman eyed the open jar with a skeptical look on her face.

"Go on," I urged. "Try some. Please?"

She dabbed some of the cream onto her hands and began massaging it in. She must have heard my heart pounding in the silence of the house, as she rubbed and rubbed and rubbed, waiting for the cream to soak into her skin. The cream just lay there like a coating of smelly grease.

I was floored. *There must be something wrong with this woman's hands.* Who ever heard of skin that wouldn't absorb moisturizing cream?

"Don't you like it?" I asked.

"I think I'll go wash this off," the woman said, her hatchet face all puckered up as if she had eaten a lime. "You can show yourself out, I'm sure."

And that was the end of my winning streak. I was too tired to face any other house

125

*but my own, so I jumped in the Fiat and
came back here.*

*Now I'm lying on my bed, still trying to
figure out where in my room Prince Albert
left me his smelly surprise. I know what
you're going to say, Diary. If my room was
neat, like Elizabeth's, I would be able to see
exactly where the problem was. But with all
the junk all over the floor in here, the whole
dog—let alone one little pile of, well, you
know—could be hidden under my laundry or
under a stack of papers.*

Whose idea was it to get a dog, anyway?

*Well, I hear someone downstairs. I guess
Mom just got home. 'Bye.*

Friday night

*My life is over. I'm going into one of those
witness-relocation programs. I'm going to
join a convent. No, I'm going to become a
worm farmer in Utah.*

*I am not joking. This is the worst night
of my life. . . .*

The phone rang as I was talking to my mother before dinner. Cara was on the line.

"You know how I bought some shampoo from you
on Wednesday?" Cara asked.

"Yeah," I said hesitantly.

"Well, I tried it this afternoon," Cara said, her voice

full of dismay. "And it won't rinse out of my hair!"

I suddenly had the sensation that I was slowly sinking into a big, messy, greasy swamp of Tofu-Glo.

"Jess?" Cara asked.

"I'm here," I said, trying to make my voice sound normal. "What do you mean, it won't rinse out?"

I caught my mother's eye from across the room and made a sour face at her.

"I mean, it won't rinse out!" Cara said sharply. "I tried for half an hour. And it won't come out! My hair is totally disgusting!"

"But, Cara—"

"And I'm supposed to go out with Steven tonight, but obviously I can't now! So what about the money-back guarantee, Jess?"

I gulped. "What?"

"The money-back guarantee! You said if I'm not satisfied with—"

"I know what I said," I snapped. "Oh, all right. I'll give you your money back. And I'll explain to Steven, too," I added, knowing my brother was expected home from college for the weekend and would be arriving any minute.

"Oh, honey," my mother said after I hung up the phone. "That's too bad. Did you have the same problem when you used the shampoo?"

"Well, actually, Mom, I haven't tried it."

Mom was surprised that I had sold the stuff to other people without trying it out on myself first. So I decided to go upstairs to try the whole product line. I crossed my fingers, desperately hoping that Cara and the hatchet woman had mutant skin and hair, and that everybody else loved their Tofu-Glo.

"And, Jess," Mom called after me as I trudged upstairs, "I think Prince Albert might have dragged something under your bed. A piece of food or something. There's some kind of a smell."

I grabbed a bottle of Tofu-Shampu and a jar of Soya-Clean and climbed into the shower to try them out.

I opened the shampoo bottle and was hit with a wave of smell. It had the same foul stink as the Soya-Soft moisturizing cream. But I held my breath and began washing my hair with it.

So far, so good, I thought. *It's nice and sudsy. So what's the problem? I can live with a little odor.*

I stepped under the steaming rush of water to rinse out the shampoo. I kept rinsing and rinsing. But my hair still felt soapy. Cara was right. The shampoo would not come out.

I jumped out of the shower and tried to dry my hair with a towel. My beautiful, silky hair was sticking together in funny clumps. I sighed.

"So something's wrong with the shampoo," I said aloud. "I can live with that."

I screwed open the jar of Soya-Clean and found that it smelled as awful as the rest of the stuff. So I gritted my teeth, screwed up my nerves, and dabbed some on my face. I was worried that it wouldn't wash out either, but a few splashes of water did the trick.

"No problem," I said happily, watching my dripping face in the mirror. But as the water evaporated, my skin began to get kind of tight and shiny. It stung like crazy and turned a yucky, shiny red. I leaned over the sink in a panic, splashing cold water on my face. The stinging went away, but my face was bright pink.

"Oh, no!" I said with a groan. "I look terrible!" *So much for my date with Neil Freemount tonight.*

Then Elizabeth poked her head into the bathroom. "What's the smell?" Then her eyes widened. "Jess, what happened to your face?

I practically threw the jar of Soya-Clean at her. "This! This is what happened. I can't believe it!"

"And your hair? Did the Tofu-Glo do that, too?"

I nodded, feeling as if I were drowning in that Tofu-Glo swamp.

"Oh, wow!" Elizabeth said, totally sympathetic. "That's awful, Jess. I'm really sorry." But her pity was the last thing I wanted.

"*You're* sorry? You don't look like this!" I wailed, holding out a lock of stringy, sticky hair. "It won't come out. My face looks like a tomato. And I have a date tonight!"

A few minutes later Mrs. Bowen called to say she wanted to return all her Tofu-Glo products. Before dinner even started, I got calls from five more dissatisfied customers. And during dinner Steven kept asking me how I managed to poison Cara.

"And what's this smell?" my father asked, wrinkling his nose.

The phone rang again, and I sank lower into my chair. "I can't talk to anyone else today! Please!"

"I told you to do some in-depth research," Dad reminded me.

"Ned, please!" Mom chided, patting my hand. "I don't think that's very helpful right now."

"Why would you want to sell Cara tofu to put on her hair?" Steven asked, annoyed about his canceled date. "I don't get it."

The crowning insult was when Prince Albert appeared in the doorway, holding a container of Soya-Life in his mouth. He dropped it onto the floor and began barking at it.

I burst into tears and ran from the room.

Now everyone wants her money back. And worst of all, I've ruined my own looks. I'm finished. See you in Utah.

Monday afternoon

My face turned back to its normal color over the weekend. That's the only good thing that's happened.

Mom made me move the whole nauseating pile of tofu-goo out to the garage. Now it's attracted every dog in the neighborhood. I can't even think straight because they're all howling and sniffing around out there.

But wait, Diary. It gets worse. . . .

"What do you mean, you have to keep it refrigerated?" I screamed into the phone.

The Tofu-Glo representative's voice sounded mechanical. "The label on the bottom of each jar clearly states—"

"On the bottom of the jar? I never saw—"

"The label clearly states that Tofu-Glo products must be kept refrigerated," the woman finished.

"But how am I supposed to keep twelve cases—"

"Tofu-Glo is made with all-natural, organic ingredients, miss," the woman responded. "We use no preservatives."

"So you mean it's *rotting*?"

The woman started to explain about the breakdown of organic ingredients, but I was too stunned to understand what she was saying.

"Well, then," I interrupted, "I'd like to return everything I haven't sold—"

"We don't accept returns in cases like this, miss. You failed to follow the storage instructions, so Tofu-Glo will be unable to cover your costs."

"OK," I said in a small voice. "I understand."

I hung up the phone and bit my lip, trying not to cry. Only then did I notice Elizabeth standing in the doorway. "Oh, Lizzie!" I wailed. "What am I going to do? I didn't know you had to keep the stuff cold! Whoever heard of putting shampoo in the refrigerator? It isn't fair!"

"But they'll take it back, won't they?" she asked in a reasonable voice.

I shook my head forlornly.

"And you gave a money-back guarantee," she said, looking almost as sorry as I felt.

"I know!" I said, bursting into tears. "I have to buy every single bottle of rotting tofu back myself! Oh, Lizzie, what am I going to do?"

So there you have it, Diary. The stupid junk rotted! The label on the bottom of the jars is so small, you need a microscope to read it. But the stuff is supposed to be refrigerated. How was I supposed to know that? What do I look like, a scientist?

Monday night

Jeffrey's mad at Elizabeth for the article she wrote about Aaron losing his temper. I don't blame him. She should have known better.

For some reason Heather isn't mad at Elizabeth, even though she's Aaron's girlfriend. Elizabeth says she misjudged Heather completely—that Heather talks baby talk to Aaron because it's the only thing that calms him down when he's in one of his rages. And Heather even designs and sews all those gorgeous clothes she wears. Anyway, Elizabeth says Heather hopes the newspaper article will help Aaron see what a creep he's been.

Jeffrey doesn't agree. He's still defending Aaron.

What if Jeffrey and Liz break up over this? What if they aren't a couple anymore, and then he notices me? I wouldn't want to hurt Elizabeth's feelings. But maybe Jeffrey and I were meant to be. I can see it now. He stops me at lunchtime one day, in the school courtyard, and pulls me behind a tree.

"Jessica," he says, "I don't know how I could be so blind. You are the one I love. The one I've always loved." Then he takes me in those strong arms and kisses me—just like that time he mistook me for Elizabeth in the cafeteria. Only this time his kiss is meant only for me. It's warm and tender and passionate. And I stare into those dark-green eyes and I know that he's the one boy for me.

Sigh. I'm sorry, Diary. I didn't mean to get weird on you. I'm just so depressed about this tofu-goo that I want to drown myself in fantasies. But dreaming about Jeffrey is even more depressing. He'll never leave Elizabeth. I don't stand a chance.

I think I'll go downstairs and overdose on large quantities of chocolate.

Tuesday night

I'm too depressed about my Tofu-Glo disaster to really care about soccer. But everybody else is in a snit about Aaron and whether he'll get kicked off the team. His temporary suspension ended today, but if Coach Horner hears about Aaron losing his temper—even once—before the big game

Thursday, Aaron is out. And Sweet Valley High loses the championship.

Elizabeth and Jeffrey made up, even though they still disagree about Aaron.

And the Tofu-Glo in the garage is stinking up the whole neighborhood now. My parents say it's up to me to get rid of it.

If I had any money left, I'd buy that plane ticket to Utah. Worm farming is looking better and better.

Thursday lunchtime

Hi, Diary. I'm sitting under a tree in the courtyard, trying to pretend I don't exist. The girls who bought Tofu-Glo from me have been giving me dirty looks all week. At least the big stink about Aaron Dallas has become a bigger topic of gossip than the big tofu stink in my garage. Apparently Aaron said some mean things to Elizabeth today about her article.

Cara caught up with me a few minutes ago and gave me all the details. . . .

"Jessica!" I heard Cara's breathless voice behind me. "Did you hear what happened?"

The only news I wanted to hear was that my entire garage had been swallowed up by an earthquake.

"Cara, believe me," I said, trying to remember the gist of what I'd heard. "Jeffrey would never hit anyone."

"No! It was the other way around. They were in

a fight about Liz! And Aaron hit Jeffrey!"

I knew neither boy had actually been hurt, so I barely listened as Cara rambled on.

"Liz's article said Aaron would get kicked off the team if he got into another fight, right?" she said. "So he can't play this afternoon!"

"Who cares?"

Cara gave me an annoyed look. "Boy, what concern! What's the matter? Still stuck with that disgusting tofu?"

I cast her a menacing glare I learned from Lila. "Give me a break, will you? Don't rub it in."

"I thought that was the problem," Cara teased. "That you can't rub it in. Or rinse it out."

I whirled on her. "For your information, Cara, I've lost every single penny I made, plus I owe Liz a ton of money, plus I have a whole garage full of rotting tofu, plus my mom is ready to kill me if I don't get rid of it. Plus," I added, seething now, "every single dog in Sweet Valley is snooping around the house, trying to figure out what the smell is. There, satisfied?"

Cara tried to suppress a giggle.

"Don't laugh," I warned her, making my eyes steely. "It's the most horrible and humiliating thing that's ever happened to me in my whole life."

Thursday night

Life is unfair. I actually had to pay to get rid of that rot!

I guess I should back up, Diary. I had just

135

*come home from the soccer game. (By the
way, we won the championship. Aaron admitted to Coach Horner that he hit Jeffrey.
He must have shown that he really was sorry,
so Horner let him play. So that's over.)*

*So is my life among the soybeans. But the
whole experience has cost me a fortune. . . .*

I called Dirty Don's Disposal company this morning, to arrange to have the tofu-glop carted away.

"Fifty dollars to take it away?" I cried into the
phone. "Don't you pick it up for free?"

"Lady, what do you think we are? A philanthropic
organization or something? Fifty bucks. That's as low
as I go."

"OK," I agreed limply. "But can you come today?"

"Sure—for another ten bucks. But not before
five o'clock."

I rushed home from the game instead of going
out to Guido's Pizza Palace with the soccer players
and the other cheerleaders. Then I stood in the living
room and watched through the curtains while Dirty
Don tossed the twelve cases of Tofu-Glo into the
back of a fluorescent-orange truck. The window was
open, and the diesel fumes mingled disgustingly with
the scent of rotting Tofu-Glo and the stink of Don's
cigar.

In the driveway the neighborhood dogs circled,
snarling and baying.

My mother had signed a blank check for me that
morning. I was tempted to use it to move to Utah.

Instead I sighed and pulled it out when Dirty Don came to the door after loading his truck.

"I'm done," he said abruptly. "That's sixty-five bucks."

"You said sixty on the phone."

"You didn't mention on the phone that the stuff stinks. Sixty-five bucks."

I was too depressed to argue. "OK, OK. How do I make out the check?"

"No checks."

I couldn't help myself. I dissolved into tears. "But I don't have any money!" I cried between sobs.

"OK, OK. Quit bawling. Just write 'Dirty Don' and let me get that junk out of here, all right?"

My fingers were shaking as I wrote the check. But a few minutes later the horrible man was gone. And so was that horrible Tofu-Glo. I would be in debt for the rest of my life, but my career in soybeans was over. I leaned against the front door, trying to compose myself. Then the door opened outward, and I fell back—right into Jeffrey's arms.

"Whoa!" he said. His sexy laughter—and the feel of his arms around me—cheered me up a little. "I've heard of dropping in to see someone," he said, "but dropping out?"

Behind him Elizabeth, Aaron, and Heather paraded into the room, looking all happy and excited about the game. I could tell that the four of them were friends again. But I didn't really care. I was too upset.

I will never be able to pay back Elizabeth or my parents. I will never be able to afford

*to buy anything, or to do anything fun, ever
again. I'm going into seclusion for the rest of
my life.*

I hate soybeans.

Friday night

*This is so intense. You are not going to be-
lieve it. My father called right after Elizabeth
came in this afternoon. He told me the best
news I've heard in ages. Cancel my room at
the convent. . . .*

"Hi, Jess," Dad said on the phone. "Liz just told
me you had the Tofu-Glo carted away. How much did
it cost?"

"Oh, Dad! Did you have to call just to remind me
to pay you back? I will, I swear!"

"No, honey. That's not it."

"Then why did you?"

He cleared his throat. "Well, you know I wasn't
very satisfied with this Tofu-Glo company, even before all this happened. So I did some checking."

Great, I thought. *He called to say "I told me so."
That's exactly the kind of fatherly support I need
right now.*

"It seems somebody had brought a suit against
Tofu-Glo, someone who had a similar experience.
Anyway, to make a long story short, the company lost
the suit, and all Tofu-Glo girls are to be reimbursed
for the money they sent to the company."

My heart leaped into my throat.

"And damages," he added.

"Dad!" I screamed. "You're kidding!"

He chuckled. "Now, it's only three hundred dollars in your case—"

"So I can pay back Liz? And you and Mom?"

"And you might even have a little left over."

I was speechless.

"Jess?"

"I'm here, Dad. I just can't believe it!"

"Well, OK, honey. But listen—" His voice became serious. "Just because you came out on your feet doesn't mean disasters always end up so well."

"I know, Dad," I said, feeling contrite. "I know."

So that's that, Diary. I made money on Tofu-Glo after all! How lucky can I be?

But from now on I promise to stay away from get-rich-quick schemes. You know, Diary, there are more important things in life than money.

Part 5

Wednesday afternoon

Dear Diary,

 I found the most gorgeous dress at Bibi's the other day, for the PTA dance. It's all bare and filmy. Really sexy. There are only two problems.

 First, it's a size four. I'm going on a diet tomorrow. I figure I can lose three or four pounds between now and then, and then if I don't eat anything the day of the dance, I should be able to squeeze into it.

 Second, I don't have a date. I'm so bored with all the guys at Sweet Valley High. Maybe I'll ask Rob Atkins, the guy from Bridgewater High I met at the big soccer game last week.

 It's not just the guys that are boring. Everything at school has become so routine.

141

It's the same old stuff, over and over again. The same people, the same couples, the same classes, day in and day out. Even the same uneaten leftovers served day after day in the cafeteria, I suspect. I wish I could think of something to do to liven up everyone's lives.

I know what you're thinking, Diary. You're thinking that I'm contradicting myself. You say I've been envying Liz like crazy for the last month because she's in a stable relationship. I guess I have been. But no more. Jeffrey is her boyfriend, not mine. I have to get used to it and stop mooning over him. But it still isn't fair! If I can't have a special boyfriend, why should everyone else be able to?

But basically, I'm sick of stable, boring couples! It's not just Elizabeth and Jeffrey. I'm sick of Cara and Steven, too. And Winston and Maria. And Regina and Bruce. And Susan Stewart and Gordon Stoddard. Even Amy Sutton, Miss Boy-Crazy herself, won't shut up about Peter DeHaven, who's cute enough, but too brainy and too conceited.

My friends and family obviously need more variety in their lives. Can you imagine anything more predictable than a date with the same old person every Friday night? I'm so glad I'm a free agent. I didn't realize how much of a rut everyone's in until a bunch of

*the boring old married folks started talking
at lunchtime today. . . .*

"I'm glad Steven's going to be in town," Cara said
after I mentioned my lack of interest in going to the
dance with any of the guys from school. "I don't know
what I'd do if I couldn't go with him," she continued.
"I can't think of a single guy at Sweet Valley High I'd
feel like going with, either."

She doesn't know what she'd do without him?
Cara was turning into a wimp. She needed to be
more independent, I decided. She barely had any social life at all these days, except for when Steven was
in town. And she hardly talked about anything but
him. When Elizabeth joined us a moment later, I was
glad for the distraction. But then she started in on
the same topic.

"I'm so excited about Steven's coming home,"
Elizabeth declared.

Cara's face lit up, and the two of them began cata-
loging Steven's good points. I glanced over to Winston
and Maria. No help there. They were wrapped up in
each other, as usual. So I shook my head and concentrated on eating half of Elizabeth's sandwich.

Amy pulled a chair up to the table. "Hi, guys!" she
greeted us. "I bet you're all wondering whether or
not I'm still going to have a predance party at my
house next week, aren't you?"

Finally, Winston tore his eyes off Maria.
"Anticipation," he announced, "has us all breathless."

Maria giggled as if that were the funniest state-

143

ment anyone had ever made in the history of the world. Another lost cause.

"Of course," Amy began, "this party is going to be a really big deal for Peter and me. I mean, it's the first party we'll be—you know—giving together."

Elizabeth looked confused. "Peter?"

"Peter DeHaven," I supplied. Honestly, for someone who was writing the gossip column in the school newspaper, my sister was hopelessly behind on the news. "He and Amy have been going out."

Elizabeth looked incredulous, and I knew exactly what she was thinking. *Someone as smart as Peter DeHaven is going out with Amy?* She had a point. Peter's going to MIT next year, and every time he turns around, somebody hands him a science or math award.

"Peter's *mad* about me," Amy confided, unwrapping a brownie. "In fact, I'm getting a little nervous. I mean, he *is* older and everything. And you know how serious he is."

"I never really thought Peter was your type, Amy," Cara said, with a wink for me and Elizabeth. "Isn't he kind of—I don't know—kind of a workaholic?"

Amy looked indignant. "Not at all! Peter's just good at everything he does. He can't help being a superstar, can he?"

"No, he can't," Cara said diplomatically. "I just meant, are you really all that compatible? I didn't think you were interested in science."

"Science," Amy repeated, as if it were a Klingon word. "Oh, well, I'm not. I think it's about the most boring thing in the world. But Peter's adorable.

144

And he never talks about any of that stuff when we're together. I wouldn't let him, even if he tried. We talk about fun things—like the party next week."

Amy would have gone on endlessly about Peter. Luckily, Julie Porter came by just then. I don't know Julie very well, though I know she's a great pianist. It figures, since she's the kid of two professional musicians. Despite that, I feel sorry for Julie. Her mother, a famous opera singer, was killed in an accident six months ago. How horrible! I can't even imagine anything awful happening to Mom.

As hard as her mother's death hit Julie, she seems to be adjusting all right, mostly by throwing herself into her music. Her older sister, Johanna, is having more trouble. Johanna is gorgeous, with long, thick auburn hair and deep-green eyes. In fact, she doesn't look anything like Julie, who's little, with red hair. Johanna got the beauty in the family, but Julie got the brains. Johanna was always a rotten student—even worse than Amy, whose grades are atrocious. But after her mother died, Johanna gave up altogether and dropped out of school. She's been waitressing ever since.

But I'd heard rumors that Johanna was planning to return to Sweet Valley High.

Sure enough, Julie brought it up as soon as she sat down. . . .

"I guess you've all heard the news," Julie said.

"What news?" Winston asked.

"It's Johanna," Julie said. "She's decided to come back to school to give it another chance. Today's her first day. She's in the office right now, filling out all the forms." She paused. "She's going to be a junior again, so she'll be in some of your classes."

"Wow!" Amy said, licking chocolate off her finger. "I think I'd just die of mortification if my sister—"

"Amy!" Elizabeth hissed, cutting her off. "I think it's great! Johanna must have a lot of courage. I bet it isn't easy starting over again."

"I don't think it is," Julie said quietly. "And I think we're all going to have to do what we can to help her. Otherwise . . ."

Julie didn't finish what she was saying, Diary, but I think I can fill in the rest. Otherwise, Johanna will never make it. She might not make it anyhow, to be honest.

Wednesday night

Liz and Cara and I went to the beach after school today, and I began working on Cara. . . .

"'Is Your Relationship All It Could Be?'" Cara read from a copy of *Ingenue* magazine as we lay on the beach.

146

"I hate that word," I said vehemently.

"What word?" Elizabeth asked, turning on her side on her beach towel.

"'Relationship'!" I nearly spat it out. "It's so *boring*." I gave Cara a meaningful look. "Especially for people our age."

"Something tells me I'm about to get the famous Jessica Wakefield you're-too-young-to-get-tied-down-to-someone lecture. Honestly, Jess, you're as bad as my mother sometimes!"

I glanced at Elizabeth. "It's bad enough doing everything with the same guy when he's close by, like you and Jeffrey," I said, though I knew that if hunky Jeffrey were *my* boyfriend, I'd want to spend every minute with him. "But, Cara, think about it! What's the point in sticking with Steven when he isn't even around half the time?"

Cara grinned. "I knew it. Come on, Jess, let's hear it. I know you're going to be miserable until you've persuaded me, so go ahead and try."

I sniffed. "I don't like your attitude, Cara. Isn't it true I'm one of your very best friends? Don't I selflessly put my feelings for you in front of my feelings for my own brother?"

Cara laughed and opened a bottle of suntan lotion. "I'm not persuaded yet," she said. "Maybe you should try that line about how my image will be destroyed if I don't go with someone new every week."

"That's right!" I said. "People are going to think you're just waiting around for Steve because you can't

147

do any better. I bet Steve thinks that himself."

A slight frown crossed Cara's face, and I knew I had scored. "Steve would never think that."

"Of course he wouldn't," Elizabeth assured her, giving me a dirty look.

"Don't bet on it," I warned. "If I know Steve, it probably wouldn't hurt one little bit to make him realize there are other guys interested in you, too. For example, when was the last time he sent you a dozen roses?"

Cara blinked. "Uh—well, I guess never," she admitted. "Is that a bad sign?"

I had her eating out of my hand. I clapped it to my forehead. "Is that a bad sign? Cara, are you kidding? He obviously doesn't even *respect* you. I bet if you agreed to go to the PTA dance with Ken Matthews, Steve would start sending you roses faster than you could say—"

"Jessica!" Elizabeth warned, raising her sunglasses so that I could see the look in her eyes.

"Right! Faster than you could say 'Jessica,'" I said with a laugh.

Cara's brown eyes looked troubled, and I knew I had planted the seeds of doubt in her mind. I felt guilty for a second, but I shook it off. The seeds would never take hold if the ground wasn't fertile.

I know, Diary. I was the one who pushed Cara and Steven together in the first place. I used to think a romance between them was a great idea. But now I'm not so sure. I never thought they'd get so—serious. They're both too young to tie themselves down. And I'm just the right person to help them out of their rut.

Friday night

My brother got home this afternoon. I can't exactly come right out and tell him to cool things off with Cara. I have to be more subtle. You know, drop a few hints and lead him to making the logical conclusion. . . .

Elizabeth and I were helping Steven unpack his yellow Volkswagen. "What have you got in here?" I demanded, struggling to lift one of his bags. "Rocks?"

"Just clothes and shoes and things," Steven said with a shrug. "And a few presents for Cara. We have an anniversary coming up, you know."

Those two are too sappy for words.

"Well, that's hardly a surprise," I said, "considering you guys celebrate practically every *week* since you met."

Elizabeth ignored me and gave Steven a big smile. "I think that's really sweet, Steve. I'm sure Cara will be so happy."

She swung a laundry bag onto her shoulder and began walking up the driveway.

"It's funny," I said to Steven as soon as she was out of earshot. "I don't seem to remember Cara mentioning anything about an anniversary. I guess she's just been so busy lately she kind of forgot about it."

Steven glanced at me, a spark of fear in his brown eyes. "Busy? What do you mean?"

"Oh, nothing," I said as we began walking toward the door. "I mean, nothing *important*. You know how it is. You go to a party here, another party there. Before you know it, you've barely even got time to think! Let alone time to remember something like an *anniversary*."

Steven cleared his throat. "I didn't know Cara was going out so much."

"Really? You're kidding," I said, filling my voice with surprise. "I'm sure it doesn't mean anything— her keeping it quiet, I mean."

I attacked again as Steven and I brought the bags into his bedroom.

"I bet it'll be nice for you two to be together again," I said, staring thoughtfully at a photograph of Cara that was sitting on my brother's desk. "I mean, it must be so hard having to deal with all these separations. And then the stress of dating other people—"

Steven looked up. "Who dates other people? I don't. And as far as I know, Cara doesn't, either."

I laughed.

"Jessica, is there something going on that I should know about, or are you just losing your mind?"

I raised my eyebrows. "I'm sure Cara wouldn't even *consider* them dates," I assured him. "It's just that I know she's got some good friends who happen to be guys—that's all. It's not a big deal. For heaven's sake, Steve, you can't expect the poor girl to sit around *knitting* or something while you're off at college having a great time."

"I never expected that!" Steven snapped. "As far as I'm concerned, she's perfectly free to do whatever she wants to do. I guess I just hoped she wouldn't *want* to go out with other guys. That's all."

I patted him on the shoulder. "That's OK, Steven," I said. "It's hard not to be possessive. You can't help it."

The score for the first inning: Jessica, two points; relationship, zip!

Oh, Diary. I am wicked, aren't I? But it's for their own good. They'll see that someday, and they'll thank me.

Sunday afternoon

Cara and I met at the Box Tree Cafe this afternoon before we went to play tennis at Bruce's. It looks as if she and Steven are fighting. See? I knew I was right. How good can their relationship be if it falls apart after just a few teeny tiny hints?

151

Cara sipped her iced tea, a dejected look on her face. "I just don't understand how we ended up getting into another stupid argument. It just all came out of nowhere, and we'd just finished making up!"

I looked down at my glass so that Cara wouldn't see the tiny grin I couldn't quite hide. Operation Breakup was proceeding on schedule.

"He kept asking if I felt tied down, and I kept saying I didn't," Cara continued. "And then I started getting suspicious, wondering whether he didn't just want me to say I felt tied down because *he* feels tied down. And the next thing I knew, we were furious with each other again!"

"I told you that long-distance love leads to nothing but problems," I said. "I wouldn't worry about it. I'm sure Steve will come crawling back in no time."

"So you don't think I should call and apologize? I really think I was the one who was being totally irrational."

I gasped. "Never! Cara, do you want him to start taking you for granted? Just assuming he can treat you like dirt and walk all over you and you'll still come back to him?"

Cara shook her head. "He didn't—"

"And besides, I happen to think Steve needs to realize that you're willing to stand up to him. Maybe once he sees that, he'll stop seeing all those women up at school."

Cara's face turned as white as her tennis dress. "What women?" she croaked out.

152

"Oh, no one special," I said with a nonchalant wave of my hand. "You know how it is. A little dance here, a movie there—"

Cara looked as if she was practically in tears. "He never told me he was going out with anyone!"

I shook my head. "Cara, of course he didn't." Actually, he hadn't told *me* he was going out with anyone at school, either. But I was sure that he must be. Even if he wasn't, I reasoned, it couldn't hurt for Cara to think that he might be. "He wants to keep you dangling on a string," I said. "That way, whenever he drops into town, you'll be ready and waiting for him."

I sighed, as if I were totally disgusted by Cara's innocence. "Wise up. If you keep this up, Cara, he'll just completely lose respect for you. It's much better to get out while you've still got some tiny little bit of self-respect left."

"That rotten creep," Cara muttered. "If I'd had any idea he was seeing girls up at school . . . and the whole time I've been turning down dates right and left!"

"I told you," I said with some satisfaction. "What could possibly be more stupid than turning down a date?"

I just had a thought, Diary. I wonder if Operation Breakup would work on Elizabeth and Jeffrey. . . . No, I guess not. Besides, I'd be afraid to try it. What if it did work? If Jeffrey was suddenly free, I would be tempted

*to go out with him. And if I went out with
him, my sister would probably never speak to
me again. But, darn it, he's so good-looking!*

*I guess I'll stick with Cara and Steven.
It's a lot less complicated.*

*Speaking of Elizabeth, she told me some-
thing surprising about Johanna Porter today.
Liz has been tutoring Johanna in English,
and they've become friendly.*

*It turns out that Johanna the dummy is
some kind of math genius. At least my sister
thinks so. While the two of them were struggling through a short story, Steven came in,
all in a snit about some math problems he
was stumped on. Johanna took one look and
solved them in her head! College math problems! Maybe she's not as dumb as we
thought.*

Sunday night

*Amy will be livid! She will have a hyper-
conniption fit. A super hyperconniption fit!*

*Elizabeth told me what Peter is doing
while Amy is out of town with her parents
this weekend. Of course, Lizzie said not to
tell anyone. But you're not just anyone,
Diary. . . .*

Elizabeth ran into my room this evening as I
was starting my new exercise routine to fit into the

size-four party dress. She started pumping me for information about Amy and Peter, mostly about whether Amy was really serious about him. I said that she was.

I was going to start in on how dull steady couples can be, but Elizabeth interrupted me. "So he really matters to Amy," she said in a thoughtful voice, as if she were talking to herself.

"Why the sudden interest in Amy Sutton? I thought you'd decided she was too flaky for you these days."

Suddenly Elizabeth looked troubled. "If I tell you why, do you swear not to tell a single soul?"

This was beginning to sound interesting.

"Of course!"

Elizabeth's eyes narrowed. "No. I mean it, Jess. If you tell Amy—or Lila—or Cara—or *anyone* that I told you, I'll never speak to you again as long as I live!"

And everyone says *I'm* the melodramatic twin.

"I promise! Come on, what's up?"

Elizabeth sat on the bed. "Well, apparently Peter asked Johanna Porter out Friday night. I'm really worried about it, too. Johanna seems so vulnerable right now. She says she's always had kind of a crush on him, and it sounds like he might be taking advantage of that."

Wow. This was serious stuff. "You mean he asked Johanna out while Amy was away this weekend?

What a creep! Amy would absolutely *die* if she ever found out."

> I guess I sound like a hypocrite, Diary. One minute I say teenagers shouldn't date just one person. And then I call Peter a creep for dating more than one person. But this is different! Really! As long as two people have an agreement to go steady, they should stick to it. But having an agreement in the first place is a pretty stupid idea, if you ask me.
>
> Can Johanna really be fooling around with Peter? It's hard to picture. He's such a brain, and she's kind of dumb—unless Liz is right about her being a math whiz.
>
> But in all honesty, Amy is no rocket scientist, either.
>
> I'm worried about Amy's reaction. And Elizabeth is worried about Johanna. She says Johanna is vulnerable right now, that she might fall apart if Peter rejects her. I wonder if that would make her drop out of school again.
>
> I'm not a horrible person (I hope). I don't want anyone to get hurt. But I have to admit that this turn of events is more entertaining than all these boring old couples who are surgically attached to each other.
>
> Variety is the spice of life.

Guess what? I asked Rob to the PTA dance, and he was totally psyched. And I bought the sexy size-four party dress from Bibi's. But the real news is Cara's date. . . .

Cara and Lila and I were eating lunch on the school's patio. Cara was in a crummy mood, because of Steven.

"I can't understand it!" she said. "All of a sudden we seem to be having communication problems. We keep getting into these ridiculous fights. He's convinced I've been seeing other guys, which is crazy. I think *he's* the one who's been cheating, to tell you the truth. Anyway, last night I was so miserable I just didn't care anymore. I figured I'd just go ahead and invite him to the dance on Friday."

I held my breath. She couldn't be so stupid, I told myself. Not after all my hard work.

But Cara continued, her eyes filling with tears. "And he got really angry! He started saying I should go with one of the guys I've been seeing. I don't even know what he's talking about. What guys? You two know I haven't gone out with anybody but Steven!"

I moved in for the score. "Maybe that's part of the problem," I said. "Don't you think so, Lila?"

Lila was gaping at a photo spread called "Enhance Your Cheekbones" in a recent issue of *Ingenue*. "It could be," she said vaguely, fingering

157

her own cheekbones. Obviously, she wouldn't be much help.

"Trust me," I insisted to Cara. By this time any nerd could see that Cara and Steven weren't right for each other.

"Well, I *do* want to go to the dance," Cara admitted. She gazed across the courtyard at tall, blond Ken Matthews, captain of the football team. "I guess I might have kind of a good time with Ken."

"Of course you will!" I assured her. "Now, go over and ask him right now, before someone else nabs him."

And she did! That was just so healthy of her. Don't you think so, Diary?

I like watching the effect that a few carefully chosen words can have on another person. Elizabeth says things like that about writing. But writing is different. When Elizabeth writes an article, it takes a whole week before it appears in the school paper. And she's not there to see people's reactions as they read it.

Operation Breakup has instant gratification. I can drop a hint and then watch Cara's face as she picks up on it. Or Steven's. Then I use that reaction to decide what to say next. By the next day there's tangible evidence—usually another fight—that proves that my words made a difference. It gives me a real rush—you know, like power!

I've always been good at matchmaking.
But maybe my true calling is matchbreaking!

Wednesday night

Elizabeth is ticked off at me. Count on
her to overreact. You see, Amy was annoying
me in the locker room today after cheerlead-
ing practice, so I sort of mentioned to her
that thing about Peter and Johanna. . . .

Amy was surprised when I told her Cara was
going to the dance with Ken instead of Steve.

"It's just that they were really in a rut," I explained. "You know how it is. You start seeing someone, and then things get more and more obsessive,
and sooner or later, well, the spark is gone."

Amy's gray eyes were huge. "Who felt that way?"
she asked. "Cara or Steve?"

I laughed. "To tell you the truth, neither of
them. I have to admit, I kind of pulled a few
strings, dropping a little hint here, another little
hint there."

Amy looked downright shocked. "You mean you
deliberately tried to split them up?"

I shrugged. Amy had no right to be all high-and-
mighty with me. I had seen her try to steal Lila's cute
cousin Christopher right out from under Enid's nose
just a few weeks before. At least *my* motives for
breaking up Steve and Cara were purely altruistic. I
didn't have anything to gain from it.

159

"I *was* the one who got them together in the first place," I reminded her. "I couldn't split them up if their relationship was really stable, could I? Anyway, you can never tell while you're right in the middle of something that things have gotten stale. That's what friends are for."

Amy shook her head. "It's one thing getting two people together. But deliberately breaking up Steve and Cara, just because *you* think they're stale. . . ."

Her sanctimonious act was getting irritating. As a matter of fact, I didn't like her attitude at all.

"I wouldn't concern myself with it," I said. "Besides, I think you have your own share of problems, with Peter running around behind your back like he's been doing lately."

Amy reeled as if she'd been slapped. *There,* I thought. *That'll teach her to judge me.*

> *OK, I admit it. It was probably a rotten way to tell her. Peter was Amy's first steady boyfriend at Sweet Valley High, and I knew how totally in love with him she was. I also knew she was insanely jealous of other girls. Even more important, I had sworn to Elizabeth that I wouldn't tell a soul. But nobody talks that way to Jessica Wakefield and gets away with it!*

Amy gripped the edge of the sink. "What do you mean? Who's Peter seeing?"

Oh well, I figured. *If Elizabeth's going to kill me*

160

for blabbing anyhow, I might as well blab the whole story.

"Johanna Porter," I said. "It's all over the whole school, Amy. I can't believe you haven't heard by now."

Amy turned white. I can't blame her. It's bad enough being cheated on. But being cheated on with someone dumb enough to actually flunk out of school is really embarrassing. "I'm going to kill him!"

She grabbed her quilted makeup bag and raced out of the room.

Anyway, I'm not sorry I told her the truth. Amy is still my friend. And I know I would want to hear the truth if I had a boyfriend who was running around behind my back with someone who's practically illiterate (even if she is good at geometry problems).

Elizabeth didn't see it that way. She came chasing after me in the parking lot a while later and jumped down my throat. I don't see why it was supposed to be such a big secret. Luckily, Liz is rotten at holding a grudge.

Friday night

There was only one good thing about tonight: my date. Rob was good-looking, fun, and a great dancer. It's excellent that he lives in Bridgewater. Lila says the Bridgewater

161

Ball is coming up soon; if I play my cards right, maybe he'll ask me!

Actually, there was one other good thing about tonight: my size-four dress—even if it was only the second-most-fabulous outfit in the room. (Susan Stewart, as usual, had on a strapless cornflower-blue number that was to die for. She's always as well dressed as Lila My-Daddy's-a-Millionaire Fowler.)

Besides my date and my dress, the party and dance were pretty much a bust. . . .

As Amy's predance party began, everyone seemed mad at somebody else. Amy and I were still mad at each other. She was mad at Peter, and he was mad at her for being mad. Elizabeth was mad at me for telling Amy about Johanna. Johanna had stayed home, but she was mad, too—because she thought Elizabeth had spilled the beans about her and Peter. Cara and Steven were mad at each other. They stood at the party with their separate dates but glared jealously across the room at each other.

At the dance in the school gym, Cara and Steven somehow ended up dancing together. Standing with Lila, I watched their faces from across the room.

First, they were kind of sad and uncertain. Then they started talking. Suddenly Cara's eyes got as big as softballs. My heart thudded down around my ankles as I read her lips. She said just one word: *Jessica.*

162

Then their conversation got fast and excited, with lots of meaningful glares in my direction. Operation Breakup was unmasked.

Cara and Steven were holding hands when they came stalking across the dance floor to me. They were not smiling.

"Time for me to get lost," Lila said cheerfully before slipping away. *Some friend.*

"Jessica, we want an explanation," Cara began.

Steven was less diplomatic. "More than an explanation!" he demanded with a growl. "We want revenge!"

I gulped. "I was only testing you two," I improvised. "I figured if you really loved each other, you'd never fall for any of that stuff I said."

Sometimes I'm at my most brilliant when I don't mean to be. Steven started getting on my case again, but Cara looked thoughtful.

"She's right, Steve," Cara said in a soft voice. "We're really the ones at fault. We should have trusted each other."

Steven sighed. "Maybe you're right," he said, holding her close.

I breathed a sigh of relief. I was off the hook—temporarily, at least. As soon as Steven was at home, without Cara around to put that starry-eyed look on his face, I was sure he'd remember to be mad at me.

Cara and Steven were lovey-dovey for the rest of the night. Gag me with a spoon. I guess my plan to break them up backfired. Those two are hopeless.

Monday lunchtime

Everyone is gossiping about Peter and Johanna at school today. Amy is fit to be tied.

First of all, Johanna got the only A on Mr. Russo's tough chemistry test last week! And we've all been ragging on her for being stupid.

Elizabeth thinks Johanna's too good for Peter. I never thought I'd hear myself saying this, but maybe she's right. Peter has been going out with Johanna at night and then ignoring her in school so that Amy doesn't catch on. In other words, he's treating them both rotten. Apparently, Peter is too stuck on himself to care about anyone else.

Monday night

Oh God, Diary. Johanna dropped out of school today—for good! She's going back to being a waitress.

I just had a horrifying thought. Could I have done this? Did Johanna quit school because she was upset that Amy learned about Peter and her? I never meant to ruin

164

Johanna's life. I was only trying to take Amy down a notch.

Dear Diary,

Liz gave me the lowdown on the Johanna Porter situation.

First of all, it wasn't my fault Johanna left school! I'm so relieved. Elizabeth said Johanna overheard some girls saying mean things about her in the locker room Monday, and just lost it. I can imagine. I've heard people criticizing her terribly. It was the last straw. Poor Johanna ran out of the building and went straight to the Whistle Stop Diner, back to her old job as a waitress.

But everything's OK now. Johanna changed her mind and came back to school. She and Liz are friends again, but she decided to cool it with Peter, after the way he treated her. Speaking of Peter, I don't think there's much of a future for him and Amy, either. Amy is furious with him.

I have to admit that Johanna is pretty cool. I'm ashamed at myself for being mean to her earlier. Don't tell anyone I said that.

But the Sweet Valley High grapevine always finds new subjects. Lila was dishing out gossip today about the Susan Stewart wardrobe-money mystery. We were in the *cafeteria at lunchtime and noticed tall, red-haired Susan come in with her rich boy-friend, Gordon. . . .*

"I couldn't help overhearing Susan talking to Regina Morrow today in the bathroom," Lila said, eyes fastened on Susan and Gordon as they came out of the lunch line and scanned the room for an empty table. "You should have heard the way Susan was going on about Helen!"

"Who's Helen?"

"The woman she lives with, the one who raised her," Lila replied, as though I should have known. "Anyway, Susan was going on and on about how Helen won't tell her who her real parents are. Do you think her mother really is someone famous, like everyone says?"

I shrugged. "I think she must be. You can tell things like this just by the way a girl looks and carries herself. Susan Stewart is obviously incredibly high-born. Just look at her posture! Look at the way she dresses! She's got 'class' written all over her!"

Gordon had "class" written all over him, too, I thought, watching the way he pulled out Susan's chair for her. That sure was unusual behavior for the school cafeteria. Of course, Gordon was used to country clubs and elegant restaurants. His parents weren't as filthy rich as the Patmans or the Fowlers, but they were executive types. I mean, they weren't exactly eating TV dinners and shopping at the Salvation Army.

"The whole thing sounds like Cinderella, doesn't it?" I concluded, thinking of Susan's absent but generous mother, who obviously sent her tons of cash to buy clothes fit for a princess.

"It does," Lila agreed. "The only question is how much longer is Susan going to have to put up with living in the cinders over on Trowbridge Street!"

I had to laugh at that. Trowbridge Street isn't Country Club Drive. In fact, the houses aren't even as big as on my own street, Calico Drive. But it's a perfectly nice suburban neighborhood with ranch-style homes and an occasional orange tree. You know, normal California.

Maybe Susan's real mother is royalty, or a famous ballerina, or a theatrical star. Maybe there's a tragic reason why she couldn't raise her daughter herself.

What do you think, Diary? Who is Susan's mother? Everyone says Susan's guardian has promised to tell her when Susan turns eighteen. But I doubt she can wait that long. I sure couldn't, if it were me.

Part 6

Monday afternoon

Dear Diary,

Everybody is talking about the Bridge-water Ball, which is the ritziest, glitziest party of the year. Unfortunately, you can't go to the Bridgewater Ball unless you live in classy old Bridgewater or are rich and well connected, like Lila. I thought I had it made when I went to the PTA dance with Rob Atkins. But that romance fizzled out quickly.

Of course, Lila is having her own problems getting an invitation. That is so great! We talked about the ball in health class this morning, before the bell rang. . . .

"So are you going to the Bridgewater Ball?" I asked, knowing very well she still didn't have a date.

Lila—always the coolest, most unflusterable person around—actually *blushed*. "Of course."

"Well, who are you going with?" I pushed.

"Well, no one's exactly asked me yet. But I *am* going. The Fowlers always go."

I suppressed the urge to make a sarcastic remark. After all, Lila is my best friend, and I realized she was feeling major trauma about not having a date. But I was enjoying the conversation, all the same.

"Well, do you know who else is going?" I asked instead.

"Girls from Whitehead, mostly," Lila said, referring to a private girls' school in Bridgewater. "Hardly anyone from Sweet Valley High, of course."

"I bet Susan Stewart is going," I speculated, "with Gordon Stoddard, of course."

We watched Susan take a seat near the front of the room. Lila and I usually made a point of sitting near the back—far enough back so that teachers don't notice you, but not so far back that they think you're trying to hide and call on you anyway. Also, if you sit far enough back, you have the best view of what everyone else is doing.

"Listen, Jess," Lila said in her I'm-OK-you're-a-peasant voice. "*Nobodies* don't go to the Bridgewater Ball."

That surprised me, even coming from Lila. "*Nobodies?* Come on! Susan probably is a somebody, and you know it." I pointed out that Susan's real mother was obviously sending her enough money to buy most of Valley Mall, if the girl's incredible clothes were any indication.

"They're OK," Lila muttered. "If you like that style."

It was true that Susan dressed differently from Lila—simpler and more understated—but she was every bit as elegant.

"I really doubt she'll be going, Jessica," Lila said, a hint of acid in her voice. "It's quite exclusive."

"Well, why don't I just ask her?" I suggested.

OK, I admit it. I knew that would piss off my best friend. I guess my longing to see Lila squirm overpowered my desire to keep her happy.

"We were just talking about the Bridgewater Ball," I called up the aisle to Susan. "And I wondered whether you're going."

Susan smiled. "Yes. I'm going with Gordon and his parents."

I shot Lila a triumphant look. Maria Santelli, who was sitting nearby, gasped. "You're kidding!" she exclaimed to Susan. "That's supposed to be the ritziest social event of the whole year. I can't believe you're actually going."

Susan shrugged. "I don't really know that much about it. All I know is that it's at the country club over in Bridgewater and it has the theme of Old Vienna."

Maria's brown eyes were wide with admiration. "Only the most important people in Sweet Valley go, you know."

Susan turned around in her chair. "You'll be going, won't you, Lila?"

I braced myself for possible fireworks. Either Lila would be gratified that Susan naturally thought of her as one of "the most important people in Sweet Valley," or she would be mortified that she had to admit in front of the whole class that she didn't have a date.

Winston saved her from having to say anything at all, but embarrassed her even more in the process.

"Lila, I'll be glad to take you!" he offered.

"Give me a break, Winston," she said, rolling her eyes. "That's the stupidest thing I ever heard."

He jumped up and walked over to her desk. "I've been saving up to buy a car, and I could use the money for tickets instead. No problem."

"Winston, cut it out." Lila's voice was venomous. I'd seen Lila angry plenty of times, but I'd never seen her this—intensely quiet. I actually began to wish that Ms. Rice wasn't late for class. I was afraid Lila would murder somebody before the teacher arrived. Or hire someone to do it for her, knowing Lila.

Winston was making himself an excellent candidate for murder victim. He kneeled, moaning. "Lila, please!" he cried in a voice that carried all over the room. "Please say you'll go with me to the Bridgewater Ball! I'll do anything! *Anything!*"

"Winston!" Maria gasped at her boyfriend in mock despair. "What about me?"

"Sorry, Maria," Winston said, brushing her aside with a grand gesture. "Lila Fowler can get me into a higher social position. That's the breaks. So, what do you say, Lila? Is it a date?"

He clasped his hands together and gazed up at her with desperate, pleading eyes. "If that isn't enough, I could take all the money my parents have saved to send me to college! Please! I'll spend any amount to take you to the Bridgewater Ball! How much are tickets? Two thousand? Three thousand? Even a million dollars would be a bargain!"

Dana Larson made a ridiculous comment about classy events like the ball being elitist. And Winston immediately thought up a fake Poor People's Cotillion and began waltzing around the classroom with Ken Matthews.

Luckily, Winston's craziness took the focus off Lila, who was positively livid with anger.

I have to admit that I enjoyed seeing Lila mortified. But I was worried, too. I knew Lila well enough to know she would find a way to vent that anger. And I sure didn't want to be in her path when the time came.

Then Ms. Rice walked in to start health class. She started discussing human fertility problems and how old you could be and still have a baby. She said even someone in her forties can have a baby. Jeepers! That's as old as my mom. I think that's tacky. Can you imagine?

But I was zoning out, anyhow, thinking instead about Susan's mysterious mother and about Lila and the Bridgewater Ball. I sure wish now that I had been listening; Ms. Rice is giving a quiz tomorrow. A quiz in health class! How bogus.

Tuesday night

Oh, man, Diary. I have big, big news. Humongous news. MY MOM IS PREGNANT! She hasn't actually said so, but I'm almost sure. I was in the living room studying my health textbook for the quiz tomorrow on reproductive science and overheard my parents talking. They must've thought I was too engrossed in my book to be listening. . . .

"Did you go to see Dr. Quentin this afternoon?" Dad asked Mom in a low voice.

Out of the corner of my eye, I saw Mom nod and place her finger to her lips. I went back to my health book.

As the hormone levels change, I read silently, *feelings of irritability are common. Some women claim to have cravings for unusual foods.*

Suddenly Mom looked up from the television set and turned to Dad. "Ned, do we have any ice cream?"

"I don't think so."

"I want some ice cream. I'd really love some ice cream right now. Pistachio."

"Pistachio?" he asked, his forehead wrinkling up. "You want pistachio ice cream?"

Mom crossed her arms and got this stubborn look on her face. "Yes. What's wrong with wanting pistachio ice cream?"

Dad shrugged. "Well, I've just never in my whole life seen you eat pistachio ice cream, that's all."

Suddenly an outrageous thought dawned in my head. I reread the paragraph about irritability and unusual cravings. *No,* I thought. *It couldn't be.*

Then I remembered the remark about a doctor's visit. And I recalled something weird Mom had said Monday morning—about Andrew and Andrea being nice names!

"Honey," my father said, "I'm too tired to go out and get ice cream tonight. Can't you eat something we've already got in the house?"

"Oh, Ned!" my mother cried angrily. She jumped up and stalked out of the room. "I'm going out for pistachio ice cream!"

The kitchen door slammed.

"Dad," I began tentatively, "is—"

He cut me off. "I think I'll go look over my case notes for tomorrow," he said, rising abruptly. "I'll be in my study."

As soon as Elizabeth got home from her date, I dragged her into my bedroom and reviewed the evidence for her.

"Are you trying to say Mom is pregnant?"

"Yes!"

"But, Jessica, that's ridiculous!"

"And why is it so ridiculous?"

Elizabeth opened her mouth and then closed it,

speechless. "Because it is, that's why," she finally managed.

"Well, what about all this? Can you think of a reason for all these things? Anything that would tie them all together?"

"Well, no, but—"

I grabbed her hand. "Listen, has she said or done anything else lately that you didn't think about at the time but that would make sense if she's having a baby? Anything?"

I watched her face as she paused. "Actually," she said reluctantly, "a couple days ago I was toasting some English muffins. . . ."

"Yeah?"

"Oh, Jess! It's too dumb. It didn't mean anything."

I faced her squarely. "Elizabeth, this is very important. What about the English muffins?"

Elizabeth sighed. "Well, Mom just said something like, it was such a pain having everything come in packages of six when there are five of us in the family, because there's always one left over. She said families with four kids were better off because they didn't have to fight over who got the last muffin."

"See? You see? Four kids! She wants to have another kid!"

Elizabeth picked up a silk scarf from the floor and fingered it absentmindedly. Finally she looked up. "Why don't we just ask her, Jess?"

"Ask her? Ask her? Are you crazy?"

"Why not?"

I whirled around. "Don't you see how secretive

176

she's being about it? I mean, if she wanted us to know, wouldn't she tell us? Come on, Liz, wouldn't she?"

Elizabeth nodded slowly. "I guess you're right. But how can we know for sure?"

I couldn't keep from flashing a grin. "Well, I think in a case like this we have every right to spy on her."

"Jessica!"

"Well, we do! I mean, it's not as if she were just planning to buy a new refrigerator or something. We're talking about our little brother or sister!"

The disapproval on Elizabeth's face melted into a look of wonder. "A little baby," she cooed. "Gosh, can you imagine?"

"Wow," I said, stunned. Believe it or not, I had been thinking so hard about the pregnancy that I hadn't stopped to envision the baby.

Then Elizabeth broke out into the world's most radiant smile. Or should I say one of the *two* most radiant smiles? The one on my own face completed the matched set.

Did I say it was tacky for a woman my mother's age to have a baby? I was wrong, Diary. I was dead wrong.

"I can't believe it!" I said. "I can't believe it!"

"We don't know for sure," Elizabeth reminded me a minute later, getting serious again. "So we've got to *make* sure."

"What should we do?"

177

Elizabeth grinned again. "Just what you said," she replied. "We've got to spy on her. But carefully!"

We've decided that I should finally return all of the zillions of clothes I've borrowed from Mom in the last two months or so and forgotten to give back. And if I should just happen to see something while I'm in her room putting things away, well, it's not my fault, Diary.

Elizabeth says I'm about as subtle as a hand grenade, but I'll be great. When it comes to spying, I can be totally smooth—as smooth as a baby's bottom.

A little baby! Can you believe it?

Wednesday afternoon

I'm more sure than ever. Guess what I found in my parents' room?

Mom and Dad were still at work when I tiptoed into their bedroom after school today, lugging a bundle of borrowed clothes. Prince Albert caught me at the door, smiling one of his big, goofy doggy grins. I knew he wouldn't tell on me, so I let him help.

I tossed the clothes onto the bed and gazed around the room. The first thing I noticed was the group of framed photos on my mother's dresser. There was a much younger Dad, holding up a chubby baby Steven. There were blond-haired three-year-old twins, celebrating their birthday in pink-checkered pinafores. I was the one reaching for the stack of presents.

Looking at the photos gave me this huge rush. Mom would be adding a few more frames soon.

Prince Albert ambled over to the walk-in closet and sniffed at the door handle. It seemed like a reasonable place to start searching, so I opened the door and stepped inside. I poked around for a few minutes—and Prince Albert sniffed around. And in a few minutes we found the evidence.

The pink-and-blue paper bag was marked "Great Expectations," the name of a downtown maternity and baby shop. And inside was a tiny yellow crocheted sweater and cap.

Wednesday night

In a minute, Diary, I'll get to the latest on my mother's upcoming tax deduction. But first let me update you on Lila.

To tell you the truth, I've been so busy thinking about the baby that I haven't paid much attention to anything else. And no, I haven't told anyone at school about Mom. Elizabeth thinks we should wait until we hear it officially. I guess she's right, but it's so hard not to say anything!

Anyhow, Lila is still dateless for the Bridgewater Ball. And every time Susan is around, I can almost see poison darts flying

at her from Lila's brown eyes. Lila is mad at
Susan for being a "nobody" with a date to the
biggest social event of the season, when Lila,
who thinks of herself as a somebody, doesn't
have one. Besides, she was humiliated in
health class the other day, and somebody has
to pay. It looks as if Susan's elected. I don't
know what Lila will do to get back at her, but
I'm sure she's planning to teach Susan a les-
son. I'm just glad I'm not in the line of fire.

Now back to the really important update.
Before dinner I told Elizabeth about the baby
sweater and bonnet. We were going to con-
front Mom right then, but we overheard her
and Dad talking in his den.

"I don't know, Ned," came my mother's voice
from behind the closed door. "I'd rather not tell
them until we're sure. I don't know how they'll
take it."

"Come on, sweetheart. They're old enough to
handle the responsibility."

"I know, I know. But I just don't know how to
break it to them, that's all. Let's just wait until it's definite, OK?"

Elizabeth and I decided right then and
there to start dropping hints. We have to let
our parents know that we love the idea of
having a new baby in the house. If they
know we'd be thrilled, they would both feel a

*lot better about it. And they'd be less afraid
of telling us the news.*

*Unfortunately, the brilliant plan for get-
ting Mom to confess her news totally fizzled.
I feel so stupid.*

We began trying just before dinner. "What's this
powwow about?" Mom asked, walking in on me and
Elizabeth in the kitchen.

"Oh, we were just talking, Mom," I said. "We
were talking about, you know, kids."

"Oh."

"Yeah," I continued. "Having kids. Liz said she
wants to have lots of kids."

Elizabeth jumped, but then she recovered and
played along. "That's right," she declared. "I love big
families. Lots of kids."

"Well, that's nice, Liz. Is dinner ready yet?"

A little while later we were all sitting at the dinner
table with Jeffrey, when Elizabeth took a deep breath
and started in again. "I always wished we had more
brothers and sisters."

"Me, too," I chimed in. "I always used to pretend
my dolls were my baby brothers and sisters and I had
to take care of them. But I was glad to do it."

Jeffrey was staring at me strangely, but I ignored
him. I was even willing to let the World's Most Attractive
Boy think I was totally nuts, in order to make my mother
feel better about adding another kid to the family.

Mom looked a little surprised, too. "I never knew
that, Jess."

"Oh, sure. All I ever wanted was to have a baby to take care of," I insisted.

"Yeah," Elizabeth agreed. "And I always thought it would be fun to have someone younger to give advice to and help with homework and stuff."

Right, I thought. *As if she never tries to force her advice on me, as it is.*

My parents exchanged a look of surprise. Mom seemed worried.

"I just love babies," Elizabeth continued.

Dad gave Jeffrey a wry smile. "Listen, Jeff," he warned. "I think it's time you reconsidered your association with this family. Obviously Liz is cracking up."

"Liz isn't crazy, Dad," I said. "It's just that, well, the mother of a friend of ours at school had a baby, and we thought that must be fantastic for her. You know, to have a baby in the house."

"Girls," Mom said after an awkward silence, "I'd like to talk to you both after dinner, all right?"

I grinned at Elizabeth across the table. *Jackpot!*

> *Well, Diary, our jackpot turned out to be lemons. I don't think I've ever been so embarrassed in my life as when Mom sat me and Liz down at the kitchen table and asked, "Which one of you is in trouble?"*
>
> *OK, so maybe we overdid it. But I'm not about to stop—not when we are so close to our goal. I just know she's almost ready to tell us. I just know it!*
>
> *You know, Diary, poor Steven is com-*

*pletely out of the loop, off at college. He has
no idea what's going on. I think I'll call him
and tell him to get here as fast as he can.*

Thursday morning

*I heard such cool news this morning that
I actually stopped thinking about the baby
for five minutes. . . .*

Mom was glancing over the front page of the
Sweet Valley News at the breakfast table this morning. "It says here that Jackson Croft, that famous
movie director, is coming to Sweet Valley to make a
film. And, girls!" Mom said. "Listen to this: 'Next
Saturday he will be holding an open casting call for
extras at the Hampton Place shopping center parking
lot.' That sounds like a lot of fun, doesn't it?"

*Fun? It sounds HEAVENLY! I could see
myself showing up at the casting call. Jackson
Croft takes one look at me and says my talent
and beauty would be wasted if I were only an
extra. He learns about my experience. After
all, I had the lead in the school production of*
Splendor in the Grass, *I was in that fashion
show at the department store in the mall, and
I once appeared on a national talk show as a
typical high-school student.*
*Croft casts me in a small but key role in
his film, perhaps a light romantic comedy.*

After my Oscar nomination for best support-
ing actress, I'm chosen to star in his next ro-
mance. From there I move to heavy, powerful
dramas. I give the acceptance speech for my
first Oscar while wearing a long white—no,
black sequined gown. Strapless, backless, and
very sexy, with a slit to midthigh. And—
    Elizabeth was looking at me with that
amused, condescending gleam in her eye.
One drawback of being twins, Diary, is that
a twin can read what you're thinking like no-
body else can.

"Think you'll go to this casting call?" Elizabeth
asked, trying to hide her grin.

   Is Chrome Dome Cooper bald?

I stuck out my tongue. "Maybe. Well, sure.
Why not?"
My mother was grinning too. It was obviously a
conspiracy. "Oh, Jess," Mom said, "you're so transpar-
ent. You think you'll be in Hollywood by the end of
the month, don't you?"

   Did I say only twins can read each other
   like a book? Mothers share that same annoy-
   ing trait.

"All she has to do is hear 'movie director,' and she
starts plotting," Elizabeth said as if I weren't in the

room—the same way you'd talk about a five-year-old.

Just see if I thank them in my Oscar acceptance speech!

"I am not plotting!" I said. "I just happen to think it would be very interesting to go to a casting call, that's all."

"Oh, right," Elizabeth said with a nod. But her eyes were still twinkling.

"And besides, Jackson Croft is a very famous and respected film director. I'd be honored just to see him."

My own family doesn't take me seriously as an actress, but they're wrong. I can feel it in my bones, Diary. This will be my big break! I can't wait until Saturday!

Thursday afternoon

Lila told me the most awful thing about Susan today. It must be all around school by now.

People are saying that Susan Stewart's real mother is in a hospital for the criminally insane! Nobody knows exactly what she did to be put there. Cara thinks she may have killed some people. Wouldn't it be horrible to have a mother like that?

Everyone's afraid to talk to Susan now. We're not sure what to say or how to act. Even her boyfriend Gordon seems to be

185

*avoiding her. I feel bad about it. Susan
looked so lonely in the cafeteria today.*

*On the other hand, Susan's been lying to
us all. Well, I guess she never actually said
she was somebody important. But she sure
acted like it. What a phony.*

*I barely know Susan, really. But even
Gordon and her other friends are acting as if
she's got the plague. I guess they would
know. So the rumors about her mother must
be true. It gives me the creeps every time I
look at Susan. Does insanity run in families?*

*Speaking of mothers—or insanity, I guess—
things are pretty crazy at my house. Steven got
my message that we had a family emergency,
and he came home today. He was blown away,
Diary. You should have seen his face. . . .*

I was totally psyched when I got home from
school and saw Steven's Volkswagen in the driveway. I
raced inside and found him in the kitchen, talking
with Elizabeth. But I realized in an instant that he
hadn't heard the news yet.

"Didn't you tell him, Liz?"

Steve rose to his feet. "Tell me what?"

I took a deep breath. "That Mom's pregnant."

Steve's mouth dropped open. Then he sank back
into his chair. "Would you say that again?"

Elizabeth laughed. "Oh, Steve! You look so funny!"

I told him about the clues we pieced together. And
I explained our plan to let Mom and Dad know that

186

we loved babies and would be happy to hear the news.

My brother just stared at me in reply.

"Well?" I asked. "Come on, Steve. Say something."

Then a huge grin spread across his face. He slapped his thigh and started laughing. "OK, OK, Jess! You really had me going there. That's a good one, though. Mom's pregnant! Right!"

Elizabeth and I were not laughing.

"But, Steve," Elizabeth tried, "it's no joke. Honest."

His face froze. "No joke?"

The news finally sank in, and Steven decided the best course of action was to keep up the "We love babies" campaign. Then Mom staggered in with two bags of groceries.

"Steve!" she began, surprised but pleased to see him. "I saw your car outside and—"

"Mom!" Steve screamed. He sprang to his feet with a look of horror. "Give me those bags! Here. Sit down. Don't tire yourself out like that."

Very subtle, big brother, I thought. *And people say I'm the dramatic one.*

My mother's mouth was hanging open, a lot like Steve's had been a little earlier. "Hello, Steve," she said uncertainly. "What are you doing home from college?"

"I just wanted to see you, Mom. How are you feeling? Can I get you anything?"

My mother's blue eyes were practically popping out of their sockets. "How am I *feeling?*"

"Let me take your jacket," Steven continued. "Do you want Liz to make you some tea or something?"

As Steven draped her jacket over a chair, Mom

187

turned to Elizabeth. "What's with him?" she mouthed.

"Uh, Steve just wanted to come home and spend some time with the family," Elizabeth explained weakly. "He loves family life."

"Yeah," Steven said quickly. "That's right. There's nothing like being with your own family."

Our mother eyed him suspiciously before turning to glance at Elizabeth and me. I shrugged and gave her my most innocent look.

"I'm going upstairs to change my clothes," Mom announced. "When I come down again, I hope my real children will have returned."

Thursday night

I just got off the phone with Lila. More amazing news . . .

"I never realized before what a total jerk Gordon Stoddard is," Lila's voice came over the phone. "I mean, how could he do it?"

"What did he do?" I asked, thumbing through a copy of *Glamour.*

"Well, I was at the club with Daddy having dinner—we do that when he's in town, you know."

"What did Gordon do?"

"The Stoddards were there—not Gordon, though, the jerk—and they said they'd never been so shocked in their whole lives as when they heard about Susan Stewart."

I dropped my magazine. "And?"

188

"And they said wasn't she awful to try to trap Gordon into a relationship, and that they had told him to stop seeing her, and that he broke their date for the Bridgewater Ball!"

"No! You're kidding!" I read between the lines of Lila's story. "Maybe he'll ask you, then."

"Oh, I'd never go anywhere with someone who was so shallow," Lila said quickly, in a tone that told me she darn well would go if Gordon asked. "I mean, just because there's a *rumor* that Susan's, well . . ."

"Yeah, yeah," I said, a plan beginning to form in my mind. Before I could act, I needed to make sure Lila's intentions were perfectly clear. "But seriously, Lila. Are you saying you wouldn't go to the Bridgewater Ball with Gordon if he asked you to?"

"I wouldn't go to the end of the street with him if it was up to me," Lila said. "But you know what social obligations are. I might have to go for my father's sake, even though, to tell you the truth, I think the whole idea is sickening. But the Fowlers and the Stoddards have always been friends."

As usual Lila was laying it on a little thick. She managed to make it sound as if the Fowlers had been millionaire socialites for years instead of the "new money" that they really are.

Not that I wouldn't mind a little money of my own—new, old, or anywhere in between.

"So you would go if Gordon asked you, in other words," I said slowly.

"Well, you know how it is—"

"Yeah, no one else might ask."

189

"That's not true!"

I smiled. "Oh, of course not. Sorry, Lila."

"All I'm saying is, I'm not going out of my way to get him to ask me, but—"

That was everything I needed to know. "Yeah, I know," I replied airily. "Social obligations and everything."

After I hung up the phone, I put the pieces of my plan into place. I know exactly who rich, handsome Gordon should take to the Bridgewater Ball, dear Diary. And it sure isn't Lila.

I suppose it's too bad Susan's feelings have to be hurt. I mean, it's not her fault her mother's a lunatic. But I can't blame Gordon for not wanting to take Susan to the ball. What would people think?

Elizabeth says that drip, Allen Walters, likes Susan. A week ago I would have said she was way out of his league. But now she's not an aristocrat anymore. What a letdown—to go from someone as classy as Gordon to a bookworm like Allen! He's not even good-looking! But maybe Susan doesn't deserve any better, after deceiving us about being the kid of someone important.

Friday afternoon

My idea bombed. I borrowed Elizabeth's gorgeous new blue dress—the one Heather made for her. I figured an aristocratic type like Gordon would go for the conservative look. But he barely got a chance to see it. Lila managed to snatch him out from under my nose at lunchtime today. Now she has a date to the ball, and I don't.

Even Susan Stewart is going out that night, though not to the ball. I heard Allen Walters asked her out for that same night, and she accepted.

I think I'll just resign myself to baby-sitting for the rest of my life.

By the way, it may be more baby-sitting than I bargained for! Elizabeth borrowed my health book and read in a later chapter that women who have twins once have a good chance of having them again. What an outrageous thought.

Saturday afternoon

You'll never believe what happened at the casting call today. No, I didn't get a part, but it was almost as awesome. . . .

Jackson Croft was there, all right, a tall, sandy-haired man standing on a makeshift platform. Elizabeth, Enid, and I were there together. Dozens of other people crowded around, trying to get a good look as he explained that his assistant would be casting high-school boys first.

Elizabeth didn't care about being in the movie, but she was hoping to interview Jackson Croft for the newspaper. She had found out that his teenage son was killed by a drunk driver, and that Croft was donating his proceeds from this movie to Students Against Drunk Driving. She kept saying what a great story that was. And she thought she could set up an appointment while everyone else was busy casting the high-school football team.

I wasn't interested in Elizabeth's newspaper story, but I went along just the same. If she really did get to talk to the director, I knew he would take one look at me and realize I was perfect for a role in his movie.

"We'll be seeing girls in a few minutes," the director said when we pushed our way through to where he was sitting behind the stage.

"Oh, I know," Elizabeth said in her journalist voice, "but that's not why I came. I write for our school newspaper, and I was wondering if I could interview you about—"

"About my movies?"

"No, not exactly. I—I read that you're donating your profits to Students Against Drunk Driving."

"I see. I'd be glad to talk to you," Croft said. "What school do you go to?"

"Sweet Valley High. I'm Elizabeth Wakefield, and this is my sister, Jessica, and my friend, Enid Rollins. We're all big fans of yours."

I decided it was time to take the bull by the horns. "That's right," I said, shaking the director's hand. "And I think I'd be terrific in your movie."

"Jessica!" Elizabeth cried.

"That's all right, Elizabeth," said Croft. "I can see your sister has the makings of a real celebrity."

For once in my life I was speechless. I wanted to grab him and give him the world's hugest hug. Instead I stood there like an idiot, blushing to the roots of my hair and trying to think of something halfway intelligent to say.

"So you go to Sweet Valley High?" Mr. Croft asked. "Is that a good school?"

"Sure," said Enid. "It's a very good school."

The world's greatest director (he's got to be the greatest, to have picked up on my impending stardom so quickly) pulled out a few chairs for us so that Elizabeth could interview him right then and there.

A minute later I thought I would faint from shock.

Croft jumped up, a wide grin on his face. "Susan!" he cried, holding out his arms.

Susan Stewart was standing behind us, looking nervously at the director. Not only did he know her, but he seemed thrilled to see her. Even Elizabeth seemed as if she were about to lose it.

"I had to talk to you," Susan told him. "I had to tell you that I can't—"

"You talked to your mother."

Susan nodded. "I'd love to come to stay with you, visit you in L.A. for a while, but I can't leave her now."

They spoke for a couple minutes longer, until Croft's assistant called him away. Then we pounced on Susan, begging to know what was going on and how she knew Jackson Croft.

"It's like a dream," Susan said softly. "He's my father, you know."

Well, there you have it, Diary. Susan Stewart is somebody important, after all. Her father is Jackson Croft, the famous film director. And she didn't even know it until yesterday.

Also, Susan's mother has been right there all the time! Helen Reister, the woman who's been raising her, is actually her mother! Jackson Croft broke up with her years ago, not knowing she was pregnant. Helen didn't want her daughter to live with the stigma of being born to an unmarried mother. So she had pretended all these years to Susan that her real mother was out there somewhere.

As for the lunatic story, that really was just a nasty rumor. I'd bet a million bucks that Lila was the one who started it.

Gotta go! Elizabeth, Steven, and I are meeting at the beach for a strategy meeting about Baby Wakefield.

Later

Oops. I blew it, Diary. I mean, I REALLY blew it, big time. . . .

Steven, Elizabeth, and I decided at the beach today that it was time to confront our parents and get them to tell us the truth about Mom's pregnancy. So we stalked into the living room and stood in a line in front of them, like a firing squad.

Steven took control. "Mom, Dad, we've got to talk."

My parents looked surprised. "Mmmm. Sounds serious," Dad said. "What is it?"

"We know everything."

Mom nodded slowly. "You do, huh?"

Elizabeth took a deep breath. "We want you to know that we're really happy about it. So you don't have to hide it anymore."

Our parents stared at each other, puzzled. "Something tells me I'm going to regret this," Mom started, "but just what are we hiding that you're so happy about?"

"The *baby*, Mom," Steve said in an exasperated voice. "We know."

Mom's mouth hung open. "The what?"

Dad laughed. "I'm sure he said 'baby.' But just why he said it, I haven't the vaguest idea."

I began to feel a sick sensation in my stomach. "Mom, we *know* you're pregnant!" I insisted.

Mom gasped. "What on earth ever gave you that idea?"

Steven blushed bright red. "Are you saying you're not?"

"No, I'm not!"

"But Mom," Elizabeth said, "you've been talking about—about names, and getting cravings for pistachio ice cream—"

Dad began to hoot with laughter. "And that made you think your mother was pregnant?"

I began gliding toward the door.

"Yes!" Elizabeth said, turning as red as Steven. "But it wasn't my idea to begin with." She cast me a menacing glare.

A jolt of panic raced through me. "Wait a minute!" I protested. "I found baby clothes in your closet! How do you explain that?"

Mom looked surprised. "I'm going to a baby shower next week. And how do you explain digging around in my closet, young lady?"

"And we heard you and Daddy talking about not telling us something until it was definite. What was that all about?"

My parents exchanged another surprised look. "Something tells me we've been under surveillance," Dad said dryly. "We were discussing the possibility of taking a month-long vacation and leaving you girls here by yourselves. That's all."

Suddenly Mom began to laugh. "Now it all makes sense," she said between gasps. "All this bizarre talk about babies—I thought all three of you were going insane!"

Elizabeth and Steven turned to glare at me. Then they both wheeled around and stalked out of the room.

I gave my parents a sheepish grin.

"Ooops."

Late Saturday night

We went to the Beach Disco tonight. I wanted to be somewhere loud to drown out the sounds of my brother and sister laughing at me. Now that they're not angry anymore, they think it's hysterical.

I'm glad I'm not getting another sibling.

Once my sister finished trashing me in front of everyone, we were all sitting around listening to the music. And I was trying to drown out the sound of Elizabeth pressing Regina Morrow to tell her more about Switzerland, where Regina went for the treatments that gave her normal hearing. Now that she can hear, though, she's got to listen like the rest of us while Elizabeth constantly begs for boring stories about Switzerland.

But then Susan Stewart showed up at our table, and things got real interesting, real fast. In fact, I have some major gossip. . . .

"Whew!" said Susan, squeezing in at our table at the disco. "I haven't danced so much in ages. It's incredible how nice everyone's being to me tonight."

Of course they're being nice, I thought, *now that your father is a famous movie director. It's only natural.*

"Elizabeth, you'll never believe what happened just now," Susan said, an excited smile lighting her face. "I was dancing with Gordon, and he said he realized what a terrible mistake he'd made, and could I still go to the Bridgewater Ball with him. Isn't that great?"

Lila choked on her diet soda. *"What?"*

"Yes!" Susan continued, oblivious to Lila's dismay. "I can't believe it!"

Lila's voice quavered with anger, and I knew Gordon was in for it. "Neither can I."

Elizabeth was looking shocked and disappointed, as if Susan should have turned down a chance to go to the classiest event of the year with a rich, handsome guy. "Susan," Elizabeth began, trying to sound diplomatic, "it's none of my business, but I thought Allen—"

"Oh!" Susan said in a tiny little voice. "Maybe—I think he just asked me out of pity, don't you? He knew I was feeling so alone. . . ."

She opened her mouth to speak again, but suddenly Allen was there, smiling. "Hi," he said, taking the seat next to her. "Susan, congratulations about everything."

"Allen! Thanks, I—about our date—"

"That's what I wanted to talk to you about." He launched into a description of a corny Japanese restaurant. Then he stopped, noticing her expression. "Oh, I guess you'll probably be too busy now, going to Hollywood parties and meeting interesting people. I can understand how you wouldn't want to bother with a guy like me."

Susan's expression changed, and she actually laughed. "Allen! Would you shut up? The most important and interesting thing on my schedule is to go out with you." She glanced at Elizabeth. "I know who my real friends are now, Allen. And you're the best of them all."

198

Gag me with a spoon.

Allen and Susan headed toward the dance floor, but we all heard what happened when Gordon caught up with them.

"Gordon," Susan said. "I completely forgot, I'm busy the night of the ball, and I'll be busy every night from now on. So you can take your snobbery and your stupid Bridgewater Ball and go jump in Secca Lake! Good-bye!"

Allen's mouth was gaping open, but Susan steered him onto the dance floor, leaving Gordon staring after her. Then he saw us all watching.

"Lila!" he cried feebly. "I've been meaning to talk to you."

"So have I, Gordon," Lila said, a smile frozen on her face. "And this is what I wanted to say." She stood up—the picture of dignity—and dumped her diet soda over his aristocratic head.

And that, dear Diary, is about the classiest thing I've ever seen Lila do.

Part 7

Dear Diary,

Awesome boy-watching at the beach this afternoon. Unfortunately, Elizabeth was in one of her duller than dull moods and kept reading brochures about that boarding school in Switzerland. Honestly, my sister is such a dork sometimes.

Sure, traveling to new and exotic places sounds fantastic. But I'm talking vacation. I'm talking great-looking, well-dressed European men, incredible food, and hotels with room service. I'm talking sight-seeing and skiing and buying French clothes and Italian shoes. But studying, going to classes, and writing papers? Not!

The only good things about school are hanging out with friends and scoping guys *and getting invited to parties. But we can do all that right here in Sweet Valley. So why go halfway across the world for school? As I said, my sister can be a real dork.*

Her priorities are definitely screwed up. Randy Lloyd lent me a pair of binoculars, which added a whole new dimension to boy-watching on the beach today. I could see every muscle in their arms and every sinew on their legs. But Elizabeth couldn't care less. While I was comparing gorgeous surfer bods, only Enid (still the World's Most Boring Teenager) was paying attention. Elizabeth was reading about that nerdy school in Switzerland where people study writing. I don't understand the attraction. . . .

"Do you think Randy knew you were going to put his present to this kind of use?" Enid asked me as she fished in her jute beach bag for a comb.

"Of course not," I said. Naturally, I had let Randy think I was interested only in him—not in surfers' biceps. Otherwise, he never would have let me use his binoculars. But try to explain something as obvious as that to someone as clueless as Enid. "I don't care what Randy thinks," I continued. "He's too boring."

Not surprisingly, boring must be what Enid looks for in a guy, because she came right back with, "I think Randy is cute. He's nice, Jessica. And he really cares about you."

I could tell from the look on her face that she was criticizing me. Enid likes me about as much as I like her, but we both play nice when Elizabeth is around. So I ignored the reproach in her voice. "He is nice," I agreed with a shrug. "And he owns expensive binoculars. If he keeps lending me things, who knows how long I'll stay interested?"

"You're awful," Elizabeth scolded. But she was adopting the big-sister act more out of habit than anything else. She was barely following our conversation. Even as she spoke, Elizabeth was drooling over pictures of Alps and descriptions of writing assignments.

I had better things to drool over.

"Wow!" I said, scanning the horizon. "This is really terrific. I mean, look at this place! A beach, palm trees, gorgeous guys. The mountains just a couple hours away. Who could ask for anything more than Sweet Valley?"

"How about your twin, for starters?" Enid asked in that voice she uses when she thinks I'm not being thoughtful of my sister. "Or haven't you noticed that Liz is halfway to Switzerland even as we speak?"

"Liz, put that brochure away," I ordered. "I thought we were through with this Switzerland business!"

"Come on, Jess," Elizabeth protested. "Switzerland happens to be a fascinating country. Regina Morrow says it's incredibly beautiful. Up in the Alps, she says—"

"Stop!" I commanded. "How many times do we have to hear about what Regina Morrow has to say about Switzerland?"

203

Actually, Diary, Regina is one of the nic-
est people we know. And smart. And stun-
ningly beautiful. And filthy rich. But the
thing is, you can't hate Regina for any of it,
because she's so brave and so sweet and has
been through so much. But since she had her
hearing restored at some fancy-schmancy
Swiss clinic, I am sick to death of hearing her
blab on and on about how Switzerland is the
most glorious place on earth.

Gag me with a ski pole.

"Come on, you two," Elizabeth urged, ignoring my objections. "Just look at this."

She spread the brochure out in front of us on the beach towel. I had to agree that the scene was pretty. The school building looked like a life-size version of one of those old-fashioned Swiss cuckoo clocks, set smack in the middle of snow-covered mountains that were mirrored in a glassy blue lake with lots of evergreen trees around it.

But I still couldn't believe she would seriously consider going to school a zillion miles away. And without her better half (me)!

For once in her life Enid actually agreed with me. "You're really serious about this place, aren't you?" she asked, sounding worried.

Elizabeth nodded. "Now it's just a question of waiting to hear from Mr. Hummel, the headmaster."

I felt my stomach thudding down around my ankles.

"It's probably out of the question," Elizabeth conceded, making me feel a little less hopeless. "I bet I'm too late to apply for a scholarship next year. See, they have a special creative-writing program that starts in the summer and lasts for all of the senior year. Can you imagine taking creative-writing classes while looking out at the Alps for inspiration?"

Personally, I thought California surfers in tiny bathing suits were all the inspiration anyone could need.

Elizabeth just sighed and stared out over the Pacific Ocean, but I had a feeling she was seeing a snow-dusted mountain meadow, maybe with a little girl in pigtails, herding goats. "I think it would be the most wonderful thing in the whole world."

"I don't want to sound selfish, but I hope this Mr. Himmel says it's too late," Enid piped up, expressing my views exactly. "I couldn't stand the thought of you going so far away for so long!"

"It's Mr. Hummel, not Mr. Himmel," Elizabeth said—as if we really cared. "And it wouldn't be that long, Enid. Not when you consider that it's an opportunity to really live and write in Europe! I keep telling myself not to get excited when the whole thing seems so unlikely. But I can't help it!"

I lowered the binoculars. Even surfers didn't seem important when compared to the prospect of losing my sister. "I thought twins were supposed to be close. Haven't you always said how important it is for us to spend time together, Liz? I'd like to know how much time we're going to get to spend together when you're off somewhere wearing lederhosen and yodeling and chasing goats."

Elizabeth had the nerve to laugh. "You make it sound ridiculous, Jess!" She started to rave about what a great school this Interlochen place was, but I cut her off.

"I know, I know. The Interlochen School happens to be heaven on earth. But it also happens to be heaven on the other side of the earth! Couldn't you find someplace a little less remote if you're so bent on spending a year in boarding school?"

Tahoe, I thought. Elizabeth can go to school in Lake Tahoe. She'd have her mountains, and I could still see her. Besides, Lake Tahoe was full of great-looking skiers.

"You don't understand," Elizabeth said, abruptly ending my dreams of spending every weekend on the ski slopes. "It isn't the boarding-school part that matters. It's Switzerland. I can't really explain why I feel the way I do, but I just know I have to go there."

I silently cursed Mr. Collins for assigning my sister F. Scott Fitzgerald's *Tender Is the Night* as an extra-credit project. Ever since she'd read the dumb book, Elizabeth had been all starry-eyed about going to Geneva. I thought it was just a phase she was going through, but it hadn't worn off.

Elizabeth gave a big, dreamy sigh. "I know the Interlochen School would be the most marvelous place in the world to study creative writing!"

I looked at Enid, and Enid looked at me. Neither of us liked the sound of this—not one bit. Elizabeth had gone way overboard. I was afraid my sister would do something I would regret.

206

Sunday night

I wish Elizabeth would quit blabbing about Switzerland. How could she even think of leaving Sweet Valley? Even more important, how could she even think of leaving me?

She was still at it at dinner tonight. Mom and Dad and Liz and I met Steven at Pedro's, a Mexican restaurant near Steve's college. Again Elizabeth couldn't stop talking about the Interlochen School. . . .

"You won't be able to eat Mexican food in Switzerland," I reminded Elizabeth just before I popped a nacho into my mouth.

Steven raised his eyebrows. "Still Switzerland?" he asked her. "I was sure you'd have given up by now, Liz, and decided that the good old U.S.A. isn't that bad after all."

"Don't tease your sister, you two," Mom said.

Honestly, I thought. *Can't my parents see that this is a life-or-death situation? Why aren't they doing anything about it?*

"Europe has really had it, anyway," I said, trying a new tactic. "It's completely decaying over there, Liz. Why would you want to go sit around in some chalet when you could be right here on the beach, keeping up your tan?"

"Don't you remember how wonderful it was when we went to France during spring vacation?" Elizabeth asked me. "You loved it! Besides, generation after generation of artists and writers have gone to Europe to soak up culture so they could perfect their visions. And if Mr. Hummel lets me apply for that scholarship, I could go, too!"

That was different. One little spring vacation wasn't a whole year. And Elizabeth and I had been together.

"I think your vision isn't the only thing that needs perfecting," Steven grumbled. "It sounds to me as if your whole thought processes need a little reorganization."

I almost applauded.

"You aren't being fair," Elizabeth said, a pout on her face. "If I get in—"

Dad held up his hand. "I think that all of this is contingent upon too many 'ifs' right now. Why don't we wait until we have a little more information before we get so excited about the whole thing?"

But it's already too late. I feel as if I'm losing my sister. Elizabeth is so excited that I barely recognize her as my look-before-you-leap twin. This is getting serious, Diary. I'm scared.

Monday night

The most unbelievable thing happened tonight.

Winston had a party for the big lottery drawing on television this evening. We only

*went over to his house for the heck of it. I
mean, nobody thought Winston would actually win the lottery. . . .*

We all crowded around the television as Ollie
Perold, a disc jockey from Los Angeles, prepared to
announce the winning lottery number. Elizabeth and
I were there, along with Jeffrey, Lila, Maria, Bruce,
Regina, and several other kids.

"Ladies and gentlemen, it's the moment you've all
been waiting for!" the disc jockey began. "Now, as
you all know, the jackpot has been growing. Today's
winner will receive—yes, folks, it's true—twenty-five
thousand dollars!"

We all applauded, though nobody really thought
Winston would win.

"Winston! Are they drawing the number?" Mrs.
Egbert asked, hurrying into the room. Winston's father was right behind her. Like the rest of us, they
were amused and curious.

"OK, folks," Ollie said as if he'd been waiting for
Winston's parents to find seats. "Hold on to your tickets!
The winning number is nine-six-five-eight-one-one!"

Winston's jaw dropped so far, I thought it would
hit the carpet.

"Egbert, that's you!" Bruce yelled, jumping to his
feet and snatching the ticket from Winston's hand.
"God, he's done it! I can't believe it! The odds
must've been about a million to one!"

Winston's parents looked stunned. Elizabeth and
Enid and Jeffrey were chattering like crazy. Maria's

209

eyes were huge, and she kept opening her mouth but not saying anything. Regina and Bruce were hugging each other as if they were the ones who had won—not that either of them really needed the money. And Lila and I were trying to get a look at the little green ticket that was suddenly worth more money than I'd ever seen in my life. Everyone else was screaming and jumping up and down and pounding Winston on the back. In other words, the place was about as chaotic as a Sweet Valley High pep rally.

In the middle of it all, Winston grabbed back the ticket and stared at it wordlessly, as if he expected it to jump up and perform a cheer. For someone who just became rich, he sure looked confused.

Money is wasted on the wrong people.

Tuesday night

Elizabeth's Interlochen application arrived today. Yippee. I'm so excited I could just throw up. . . .

"I can't believe it," Elizabeth said, grabbing a thick manila envelope out of the mailbox as soon as we got home from school. I could see about six hundred colorful foreign stamps on it. "It's come, Jessica—the material from the Interlochen School! Look how thick it is! They wouldn't send a letter saying I'm too late to apply in an envelope this size, would they?"

"Who knows?" I said, hoping it was a bizarre Swiss custom to send tons of material with a rejection letter. "Look at all those stamps," I said glumly. "It looks like they sent it from Mars."

Ten minutes later Elizabeth had brochures, applications, and catalogs spread all over the kitchen table.

"I can't believe how perfect this sounds," she said. "Jess, they actually have scholarships for the creative-writing program! Listen—'The Margaret Sterne Memorial Prize for creative writing is presented in memory of Margaret Sterne, who was from California and studied at the Interlochen School in the 1950s. It is to be given to an eligible student for a full year of study in the English department. Included are three months of intensive writing workshops in the summer and nine months of combined creative writing and academic work in the senior year.'"

"I wonder who Margaret Sterne was," I said, hating the unknown woman, even though she had most likely been dead for years. "She was probably some poor girl who abandoned her family and came to a horrible end in the Alps somewhere."

"You happen to be wrong," Elizabeth said. "Margaret Sterne was a talented young writer who died prematurely of a terminal illness. It says right here that the Sterne family set up these scholarships in her name."

I sighed dramatically, but Elizabeth didn't even notice. She began reading aloud from the literature. "'Applicants should have a demonstrated ability for creative writing. They must be female, between the ages of fifteen and seventeen and must be from California. They must show a commitment to scholarship and academic excellence, as well as embody the traits Margaret Sterne was known for: courage, persistence, dedication, and an involvement in community affairs.'"

"Gag," I said, searching the cupboards for something decadent to eat, preferably chocolate. "No wonder this girl didn't make it to maturity. She sounds like she was more of a saint than a human being."

"Come on, Jess," Elizabeth said.

I reminded myself to kill her the next time she began a sentence with "Come on, Jess."

Elizabeth continued, oblivious of the danger she was skirting. "I think the Sterne family has done a wonderful thing setting up this scholarship fund in her memory. Anyway, it's sure worth applying for!"

"That is, if you happen to embody courage, persistence, and dedication and be involved in community affairs," I reminded her.

Elizabeth's face turned pink. "So you think I shouldn't even try?"

I sighed. "Of course you should! What worries me, Liz, is that you're absolutely perfect. I can't think of a better candidate. Which means they're going to interview you, find out that you're even saintlier than this Margaret Sterne was, and whisk you away to Geneva." I tore open a package of Oreos. "And that'll be it," I finished. "No more twin. The next time I see you, you'll have fallen in love with the Lonely

Goatherd, and you'll decide to live in Switzerland for the rest of your life."

I stuffed an Oreo into my mouth, but it didn't make me feel any better.

"Mr. Hummel says I have time to make the deadline for the creative-writing program," Elizabeth said, not even noticing how upset I was. "I'll need to have my records and transcripts sent to the Interlochen School as soon as possible, along with three letters of recommendation. I can ask Mr. Collins, of course. But who else? Do you think I should ask Ms. Dalton? I like French, and that way they'll know I have some language skills."

I twisted the top off a second Oreo and glared down at the sticky white cream. "I'm sure half the faculty at school will be fighting to write you letters. I can just imagine the letters now. They'll all go on and on about the work you've done demonstrating leadership—like the time you helped organize the carnival for the handicapped kids with Mrs. Morrow. Or the way you helped set up the foreign-language festival. And all the stuff you've done on *The Oracle*."

By the time Mr. Hummel finished reading Elizabeth's recommendation letters, he'd be ready to make her the dean of the whole school. "It's hopeless," I said, still staring at the cookie. "Absolutely hopeless."

Elizabeth began agonizing over which of her millions of A-plus assignments she should send in as writing samples. Then she got even more worried as she read about the interview process. Each candidate for the scholarship had to be interviewed by a local alumnus of the Interlochen School and by a member of the Sterne family.

"So what?" I asked, grabbing another Oreo. "Tell me they're not just going to adore you, Liz. I mean, what are you afraid of? Your criminal record? Your terrible behavior in school? You're only totally perfect, that's all. No wonder you're worried about being interviewed."

"I'm supposed to call Patrick Sterne in San Diego," Elizabeth said. "He's the executor of the Sterne Fund. And he'll start the interviewing process right away." She stared at me with her eyes all shiny. "Jess, this is really happening! I can't believe it!"

"You're not the only one," I said. "I just can't see why you're so happy about it. What's wrong, Liz? Are we all so horrible you can't stand the thought of living with us for another second?"

This is an emergency, Diary. I'm calling Steven tonight. Between the two of us we've got to find a way to stop this talk about going to Switzerland. I wonder if Jeffrey and Enid will help, too. Well, maybe not Enid. She'd feel obligated to tell Elizabeth what we were up to.

But Jeffrey gets a pained look on his face every time she brings up Switzerland. I feel sorry for him. I mean, what does it say about him, if she'll run to the Alps at the drop of a hat? A girl who's lucky enough to have a hunk like Jeffrey for her boyfriend has no business leaving the country! But I haven't talked to Jeffrey about it, and he'd probably be too loyal to Elizabeth to tell me what he really thinks. I wish there was a way of learning the real story.

To tell you the truth, I feel a little bad about trying to sabotage something Elizabeth's so excited about. But you've got to understand, Diary. I know in my bones that she shouldn't go. She should stay here with her friends and family, keep writing for the newspaper, and graduate with our class, as we always assumed she would.

Most of all, Elizabeth belongs with me. That's what twins are for. It'll be our senior year, and we should be together. It may be our last chance. After next year she may go off to some big-shot Ivy League college in the East. I couldn't bear to lose her a year early. I just couldn't. There's no way I can make it without Liz. And I can't believe that she thinks she can make it without me.

Elizabeth and I fight a lot, but we've always been there for each other—until now. I remember how scared I was when she was in a motorcycle accident, and I thought she was going to die. That's almost how I feel now— as if my sister is slipping away from me, and there's nothing I can do to stop it.

Elizabeth has always said she loves her

life here. Doesn't it mean anything to her anymore? Don't I mean anything to her? Does she love the idea of studying in Switzerland more than she loves me? Maybe she thinks she does, Diary, but I can't believe she really means it, deep down. If Elizabeth goes to Switzerland, we'll both be miserable for a year. And things will never be the same between us. Never again.

I have to stop her from going. I have to!

Friday night

Something weird happened tonight, Diary. Something disturbing. A lot of the kids decided to go to the Beach Disco, and Jeffrey even managed to convince Elizabeth to forget about her application for an hour or two to go with him.

I had a date with Randy, but he didn't feel well, so he brought home by nine thirty. I slipped into a cotton blouse and jeans, thinking I would hang around the house and watch a movie. But my parents were out, the house was too quiet, and I got bored. So I drove over to the Beach Disco to see what was going on there. . . .

I arrived just in time to see Elizabeth step outside with Enid, heading for the wooden steps down to the beach. Jeffrey was busy talking to Winston,

Bruce, and Regina and didn't see Elizabeth leave. But he did see me a minute later. As usual, my heart skipped a beat when his big green eyes locked on to mine.

"Elizabeth," he said after he weaved through the crowd to reach me. "We've got to talk."

I realized too late that Elizabeth had also been wearing a white blouse and jeans that night. I opened my mouth to tell Jeffrey I wasn't Liz, but then I snapped it shut. Pretending to be my sister might be the best way to find out whether Jeffrey felt as rotten as I did about Switzerland. I let him steer me toward a table in the far corner, where the music wasn't quite as loud.

"How do you honestly feel about my going to Switzerland?" I asked in my best Elizabeth voice, before he had a chance to say anything else. "I really want to know."

Jeffrey looked surprised. "You know, Liz, that's the first time you've asked," he said gently, sounding hurt. "I was beginning to think you didn't care what I thought."

He looked sad and hopeful at the same time. I couldn't believe Elizabeth never even asked him. My sister can be such an idiot.

"I'm sorry, Jeffrey," I said carefully. "I guess I've been so wrapped up in the application process for the scholarship. But tell me now, please. How do you honestly feel about it?"

Jeffrey took a deep breath and laid his hand on mine. At the touch of his fingers, I took a deep

217

breath, too. I hoped he couldn't feel my pulse pounding away, faster and louder than the music.

"Liz," he began, leaning close so I could hear him over the hubbub, "I don't want to hurt you. But I told you once before that I didn't want you to leave, and you acted like you didn't even hear me." The feel of his warm breath against my ear was almost more than I could handle. "Again, to be perfectly honest, I wish you wouldn't go to Switzerland."

Forget about Switzerland! I wanted to scream and throw myself into his arms. *I'll never leave you, Jeffrey French!*

I restrained myself. "Why shouldn't I go?" I asked in as reasonable a voice as I could croak out, with those hypnotic green eyes staring at me, so full of love. Luckily, the place was loud enough so that he couldn't hear how strange I must have sounded.

"I know it's selfish," he said. "But I can't stand the thought of your going so far away. And I don't like what this application process is doing to you. You're obsessed with this school! You talked this afternoon like you didn't even trust me not to louse up in front of the interviewer."

I hadn't been privy to that conversation, but I knew exactly what Jeffrey meant. Elizabeth had done the same thing to my parents and me. This Mr. Sterne would be interviewing friends and family members about Elizabeth's character, and she'd gone totally manic on us, trying to coach everyone on what not to say. She must have given Jeffrey the same treatment.

It was a far cry from the way I'd treat a boyfriend like Jeffrey, I thought, gazing at the little golden hairs on the back of his hand.

"I'm sorry, Jeffrey," I said. "It's not that I don't trust you. I guess I have gone overboard. But studying at the Interlochen School has become the most important thing in the world to me."

Jeffrey looked as if he'd been stricken. "More important than me?" he asked, grasping my hand tighter.

Oh, God. Now I've done it, I thought. I had to get out of this conversation quickly—Elizabeth could return at any minute. But I had to answer him in a way that wouldn't tip her off later that I had impersonated her. That would have made Elizabeth furious, and she'd run away to Switzerland just to get even with me. I also needed to end the conversation without letting Jeffrey know that I was Jessica—and that I was desperately in love with him.

> *There, Diary. I admitted it. I'm desperately in love with my sister's boyfriend. I AM DESPERATELY IN LOVE WITH MY SISTER'S BOYFRIEND!*
>
> *Does that make me a terrible person? Maybe it does. But I don't know how to stop feeling this way. As much as I try to forget about him, it rips me apart to see them together. It isn't Elizabeth's fault. She can't help it if she's perfect. But I want Jeffrey to look at me the way he looks at her. I want*

him to touch me the way he touches her. And I couldn't help pretending tonight, for just a minute, that it was me he was in love with, not her.

But I had to get myself away from Jeffrey and out of the Beach Disco before I brought my relationship with my sister crashing down around my ears.

A lot of things raced through my mind. First, I was horrible enough to speculate that this could be my chance to break up Jeffrey and Liz for good. I could say yes, the Interlochen School was more important than he was. Then I could let Elizabeth go off to Switzerland, leaving me conveniently nearby to help Jeffrey mend his broken heart.

Or I could go on trying to keep Elizabeth in Sweet Valley, knowing I would lose any chance of ever having Jeffrey for myself. If I manipulated the conversation just right, I was sure I could get him to stop hiding his true feelings and tell Elizabeth the truth about how upset he was about her plans to leave. With Jeffrey enlisted to help me and Steven in the Sabotage Switzerland campaign, our chances of success would sky-rocket. (Of course, we don't have a campaign strategy mapped out yet, but Steven assures me he'll think of something.)

But I couldn't try to manipulate Jeffrey into helping. I was pretending to be Elizabeth, and Elizabeth was always diplomatic. Besides, Jeffrey wasn't mine to manipulate and never would be.

"Of course the Interlochen School isn't more important than you," I said, gazing intently into Jeffrey's eyes and trying to sound like Elizabeth. "Nothing is more important than you." Then I felt tears spring to my eyes, and I jumped up from my chair.

"I'm sorry, Liz," Jeffrey said. "I guess I didn't realize just how much this school means to you."

"I'm OK," I said quickly. "I just need a little air and some time alone. I'll be back soon. Please, let's not talk about this conversation again, all right, Jeffrey?"

"All right, Liz, if that's what you want—" Jeffrey began. But I didn't hear the rest. I ran out of the disco, jumped into the Fiat, and sped home, sobbing like a baby the whole way.

Gosh, Diary, when did I turn into such a basket case?

Sunday afternoon

Campaign Sabotage is underway. I'm sorry I was such a dweeb the other night, Diary. Chalk it up to temporary insanity. As long as I'm nowhere near Jeffrey, I'm perfectly sane and normal. Despite my moment of weakness, I have no doubts at all about

221

wanting Elizabeth to stay here in Sweet
Valley, where she belongs.

At least we have a plan now for keeping
Liz here. I talked to Steven on the phone
today, and we got everything set. . . .

"Mom and Dad seem to have caved in completely," I told Steven on the phone. "As far as I can
tell, they think it's all systems go for Liz to take off to
Interlochen. They keep saying that she's old enough
to know what's best for her. It's really awful."

"It figures Mom and Dad would say something
like that," Steven replied, "especially when it comes
to Liz. She's always been so sensible that they probably feel reluctant to stand in her way."

"So why aren't you panicking?" I wailed. "Steve, I
can't bear the thought of her taking off this summer
and staying away for an entire year! Can you imagine
how rotten my senior year would be without Liz?"

"Calm down," Steven said. "I told you—I came
up with a plan. If you'd stop wailing for just a second,
I could even tell it to you."

"OK," I said. "What is it?"

"Look, this guy Sterne is coming to the house to
check Liz out, right?"

"He's coming to the house on Thursday and to
school on Friday," I said. "He called this afternoon."

"Hmmm. Ok, now, here's what we do, then. I'll
come home Wednesday night. I don't have any classes
Thursday, and Friday's tutorials can be skipped for
something this important. That way you and I will be

222

around Thursday to make sure Mr. Sterne gets the right impression of Elizabeth's family."

"What do you mean?"

"I mean that you and I are going to have to make Mr. Sterne realize that Liz isn't the right girl for the Margaret Sterne Memorial Prize. All it'll take is one obnoxious twin sister and a depraved older brother to make him run in the other direction."

There you have it, Diary. We'll sabotage her home interview by acting as if we have so little "moral fiber"—as Steve put it—that Sterne will decide there's no way Liz can be as wholesome as she seems. And we'll find a way to screw up the school interviews as well, maybe with some help from some of my friends.

Steven is a genius when it comes to devious plans. It's easy to see that he's related to me.

Wednesday night

Steven arrived just before dinner tonight. Now we're ready to put our plan into action. And not a moment too soon. Elizabeth is spazzing out. . . .

She started picking on me at the dinner table tonight, warning me not to talk as if I'm boy crazy in front of Mr. Sterne in the interview tomorrow.

"Darling, we all know how to behave ourselves," Mom told her. Even Mom and Dad seemed to think Elizabeth was taking this interview a little too seriously. Personally, I was waiting to see if she would coach Prince Albert on how to bark politely and drool with style.

"I forgot all about Mr. Sterne," Steven said, with a wink at me. "What time is he coming?"

"Four o'clock," Liz said, about as nervous as I've ever seen her. "Jess, I was hoping you could wear that navy-blue skirt and the flowered shirt Aunt Shirley sent you. You know, the one with the little white collar."

She had to be kidding. "You mean that thing that looked straight out of *Peter Pan*? I gave it to the clothing drive at school last month."

After Mom finished reproaching me for that, I stole a sly glance at Steven and turned back to Elizabeth with an innocent expression. "I was thinking that I might wear that black leather miniskirt and my glittery bandeau and my—"

"Jess!" Elizabeth cried, covering her face with her hands.

"Can't you see your sister is under pressure?" Steven asked me gravely. "God, Jess, she might crack up if you keep going on this way. For all you know, this Mr. Sterne will show up and Liz will just faint dead away."

"Stop it, both of you," Mom intervened. "Liz is going to act just like herself, and I'm sure Mr. Sterne will be suitably impressed." She turned to Elizabeth.

"What exactly is your schedule for tomorrow?"

"I have the interview with him at noon in San Diego, so I'll take the bus down there. I got special permission to leave school. Then he's going to drive me to Palisades, where I'll meet Ms. Crawford, the local alumna, and we'll have a group interview. Then I'll bring Mr. Sterne back to the house so he can meet all of you."

"Four o'clock?" Dad asked. "Honey, did you tell me about this before? You know I don't get home before six."

"Dad! He'll think we have a broken family or something."

I smiled sweetly. "Oh, we'll just explain that we all ax-murdered Daddy and buried him in the basement."

"I'll be here," Mom said, patting Elizabeth's hand. "Won't that do?"

Elizabeth looked furious. "Daddy, I told you about this on Monday. And you said you could get away early. Don't you remember?"

"I don't, I'm sorry to say. But I guess I can rearrange some of my meetings. I'm really sorry, Liz. Don't worry—I'll manage to get here. And if I'm a few minutes late, just explain to Mr. Sterne that I'm on my way."

Elizabeth gave us all a disgusted look, as if she couldn't wait to get to Switzerland and be away from the whole family.

But here's a weird note. I arrived home from cheerleading practice today to hear

Mom and Liz involved in one of their heavy-duty mother-daughter bonding sessions. And I could have sworn I heard Elizabeth say she thinks Jeffrey's cheating on her—with Enid! I find that hard to believe. No guy as good-looking as Jeffrey would want to hang out with a drip like Enid! I think Liz's head is already in the Alps—and the altitude is affecting her brain! But come to think of it, Lila said something about seeing them together a lot lately.

Nah, it can't be true.

Thursday night

You should have seen Elizabeth's face this afternoon. If I weren't so sure I'm doing what's best for her (and me), I would almost feel guilty. . . .

A scruffy, unshaven Steven met Elizabeth and a very stern-looking Mr. Sterne as soon as they walked in. I watched from the stairs.

"Mom called to say she had an emergency and would be a little late," Steven said with a shrug. "And you know Dad."

Elizabeth blinked. "Steven means that my father is always punctual, of course. But he had a meeting, and he'll be a minute or two late himself."

"We're very relaxed in our attitude toward time,

to be honest," Steven said. "What's an hour or two when it's sunny outside? That's what my father always says."

Elizabeth's eyebrows shot up to her forehead. "Steven! He never says that!"

"And what do you do?" Mr. Sterne asked Steven. Mr. Sterne had about the coldest-looking stare I've ever seen, and his beady eyes seemed designed for finding fault.

"Me? Oh, I'm a student. I'm in college."

"Ah, I see. Are you on vacation now?"

Steven yawned. "No, not really. I just find that I really can't function without my family around. See, we're really a tight group—aren't we, Liz?—and somehow I just don't seem to be able to *connect* without my family around. We're all that way. We all get lost unless we keep in constant touch. Isn't that true, Liz?"

"I imagine that must make college life rather difficult for you," Mr. Sterne said, looking uncomfortable.

"Oh, yeah," Steven agreed, grinning. "Just ask my professors.

"Where's Jessica?" Elizabeth hissed, obviously understanding Steven's goal and wondering what else we had in store for her.

"Poor Jessica," Steven said. "She just can't stand the thought of losing Elizabeth."

No lie there, I thought.

"See, they're twins," Steven continued. "Did Liz tell you that? And twins just can't deal with being separated. Jessica is totally unbalanced about the thought of Liz taking off for your little school in Austria."

Nice touch.

"Switzerland," Mr. Sterne corrected.

"Switzerland, Austria, wherever," Steven said with a wave of his hand.

Mr. Sterne disappeared into Dad's study to use the phone, and I prepared to make my grand entrance. Just then Dad showed up at the front door.

"Whose motorcycle is out there?" my father asked.

"Daddy!" I hollered. I raced out to the front hall and bumped smack into Mr. Sterne.

"I don't believe we've met," he said, looking astonished. I could understand his expression. I was wearing my black leather miniskirt with the tight, glittery bandeau top. And I had on about an inch of makeup.

"I'm going to die," I heard Elizabeth whisper.

Needless to say, Mr. Sterne practically broke the door down, running out of the house. Mom got home a few minutes later, and Elizabeth dragged us all into the living room to tell us that we'd ruined her life. First she complained about my outfit and the motorcycle I'd borrowed to dress up the driveway. Then she zeroed in on Mom and Dad for being late, even though they had both been unavoidably tied up at work and had done their best to get home. Then she complained that Steven had made the whole family sound batty.

My parents weren't really pleased with Steven and me, even when we pointed out that Mr. Sterne acted like some alien creature out of *Star Trek*.

"You were all unfair—every one of you!" Elizabeth concluded. "Mr. Sterne was only trying to do his job. I just hope the interview tomorrow goes more smoothly. Maybe I can still salvage things. The way it stands now, he just may pity me. He may think I'm a perfectly nice girl who just happens to come from a family of weirdos!"

Despite our success today, Steven and I are scared that it's not enough. Elizabeth is absolutely right. Mr. Sterne might decide Liz is even greater than they thought, because she's managed to pull herself together so well, despite her family full of weirdos.

We've got to do something really drastic tomorrow. Mr. Sterne will be at school most of the day, checking up on Liz. And that alumna interviewer, Ms. Crawford, will join him in the afternoon. We have to prove that Liz is a maniac. We'll make her seem sweet and loyal and helpful one minute, and totally boy crazy and unstable the next. And I know just how to do it! In fact, I've come up with a totally foolproof plan. Stay tuned!

I am so relieved! Elizabeth is staying in Sweet Valley! Here's how we did it. . . .

I dressed exactly like Elizabeth did for school Friday. I wore a navy blazer, a white blouse, and a pleated gray skirt, and I tied my hair back in a ponytail. It was boring and un-Jessica-like, but I kept telling myself it was all for a good cause. Steve knew what he had to do, and we'd also enlisted the help of Randy, Neil Freemount, and Tom McKay.

I almost ran into Elizabeth right after second period. I ducked into an empty classroom in the nick of time as she came walking down the hallway, accompanied by Mr. Sterne. If he saw us together, dressed alike, my plan would be doomed.

Luckily, they hadn't seen me. I knew Elizabeth was supposed to head to her third-period class, while Mr. Sterne proceeded to the principal's office to start collecting character references. After Elizabeth disappeared down the hall alone, I hurried after him.

"Oh, Mr. Sterne!" I sang out. "I forgot to tell you something."

The gray-suited man spun around, a confused look on his face. "I thought you said you were going to class."

"Oh, class. That can wait. I just realized that I've been forgetting to tell you one of the most important

230

things in my entire life." I batted my eyelashes. "Have I mentioned—at all—how very important I think *men* are?"

"Men?"

I tucked my arm through his. "You know," I said. "Men."

He pushed up his glasses and stared at me. "No, you haven't mentioned that."

"Of course, I don't believe in limiting oneself," I said. "One of my goals is to meet a really rich Swiss banker and spend the rest of my life in luxury. I think it's terribly important for a writer to have some independent means of support, don't you?"

Mr. Sterne gasped. But before he had time to answer, Randy came hurrying toward us, right on schedule.

"Liz! Darling!" Randy cried. He leaned over to kiss me.

"Randy," I said in my sexiest voice, "please meet Mr. Sterne. Mr. Sterne is my *friend,* Randy."

Mr. Sterne was shaking his head disapprovingly. "I don't understand, Elizabeth. You seem like a completely different young lady from the one with whom I was just—"

"Look!" I cried, interrupting him. "There's Tom!" Sure enough, Tom McKay was strolling toward us, looking gorgeous. "I have to dash. Randy, sweetheart, be an angel and walk Mr. Sterne to the office, would you? I have to go ask Tom if he still plans on taking me to the Beach Disco tonight."

"Disco?" Mr. Sterne asked weakly, as I wrapped

myself around Tom, calling him "honey buns" in a high-pitched voice.

"How's it going?" Tom asked in a whisper as soon as Mr. Sterne was out of earshot.

"This is a piece of cake. That guy isn't ever going to forgive Liz. And we've only gotten started."

I was alone a few minutes later when Jeffrey caught up with me in the hallway. "Liz, I've just got to talk to you! Do you realize I've been calling you and chasing after you and trying to find you all over this stupid school for the past couple of days? And you're treating me like an absolute stranger!"

Oops. It hadn't occurred to me that people besides Mr. Sterne could also mistake me for my sister. But I had come too far to blow Operation Sabotage Switzerland now. I would just have to continue playing Elizabeth, no matter how much it killed me.

"Uh, you know how it is," I said smoothly. I gave him a quick peck on the cheek—which was pure torture, since I was dying to grab him and kiss him as he'd never been kissed before. But Elizabeth wasn't into public displays of overwhelming affection. Besides, if I allowed myself to get started with Jeffrey, I might never stop. "I've just been preoccupied ever since I started applying for this scholarship," I explained. I gave his arm a suggestive squeeze. *I'll make it up to you tonight.*

I realized too late that I had delivered the last sentence in much too seductive a tone. As usual when Jeffrey was around, I had gotten carried away. Elizabeth would never talk like that. Jeffrey looked shocked—but intrigued, too, I was pleased to see. Once again I was convinced that a hunk like him was wasted on Elizabeth.

Before I had time to pursue the idea, I spotted Mr. Sterne coming out of Mr. Collins's classroom. I chased after him, leaving Jeffrey gaping at me.

"Mr. Sterne!" I squealed, slipping my arm through his and steering him toward the student lounge. "I feel that you and I have *got* to sit down together. *Alone*," I added, with a meaningful stare. "So we can get to know each other better in slightly less *formal* circumstances."

Mr. Sterne snatched his arm away as if I were contaminated. "Miss Wakefield," he said, "you are a complete enigma to me. I've just come from talking to Mr. Collins about you, and I have to admit I have never—in all my days of interviewing students for the Margaret Sterne Memorial Prize—heard such a glowing report. It almost took my breath away."

I'd like to take Mr. Collins's breath away, I thought, silently cursing the English teacher for sabotaging my sabotage. "Mr. Collins is so darling, isn't he?" I said aloud. "I have to confess I've been madly in love with him ever since I first knew him. I mean, he's the most gorgeous teacher I've ever seen!"

Mr. Sterne glared at me. "Please! Remember yourself, young lady! Don't you realize how inappropriate your comments are?"

"Love does not recognize the word 'appropriate,' Mr. Sterne. I would've thought you knew that—being European and everything."

"I'm not European," Mr. Sterne said, looking as stern as his name would indicate. "I happen to represent the family of Miss Margaret Sterne, or have you forgotten?"

"Oh, yes," I said rapturously. "Tell me, Mr. Sterne—what exactly did the poor thing die of? I've heard nothing but the nastiest rumors. But of course—"

Mr. Sterne's face turned ash-white and then beet-red. Then I made an excuse about having to meet Tom before our two-fifteen interview with Ms. Crawford. Mr. Sterne watched me leave, looking confused and horrified.

In other words, my plan worked perfectly. Just perfectly. Until I got caught.

After I scooted away, Elizabeth and Mr. Sterne met with Ms. Crawford in the principal's office. Just in case there was any chance that they still thought Elizabeth had any shred of decency, Steven called and had the meeting interrupted, claiming to be a boyfriend who needed to talk to her immediately.

Well, in the end Mr. Sterne and Ms. Crawford told Elizabeth her behavior (actually my behavior) was totally unacceptable, despite the strength of her references and academic record.

Elizabeth was heartbroken and as mystified as Mr. Sterne—until she caught sight of me leaving school, dressed in a navy blazer, gray skirt, and ponytail. Then she stalked home and gave me and Steven a piece of her mind. Several pieces, in fact . . .

"I don't know what you two did, but I know you did something," Elizabeth said tearfully when she cornered me and Steven in the kitchen. "And I want to hear the entire thing. From the beginning."

Steven tried to say we did it only because we were concerned about her, but Elizabeth crossed her arms and narrowed her eyes. I had never seen her so angry.

"I want to know exactly what you two did," she repeated. "Jessica, let's start with what you said to Mr. Sterne today to give him the impression that I'm some kind of raving lunatic."

"Lunatic?" I repeated. "Is that what he said?"

"No, that isn't what he said. But it's what he implied. Come on, Jessica. You can't stand there wearing an outfit exactly like mine and tell me that you weren't sneaking around today pretending to be me."

"I did not *sneak*!" I retorted. "I may have pretended to be you, but I never sneaked!"

"Jessica, I'm going to count to ten, and when I'm done counting, I want an explanation. Do you hear me?"

I took a deep breath, a little frightened of the look in her eyes. "I—uh, well, Steven and I thought, that is—"

"Let's face it, Jess," Steven broke in. "We owe Liz an apology. But, Liz, we really did mean well. We felt that you'd just kind of lost it about going to

235

Switzerland. We tried talking you out of it, but that didn't work. So we figured we'd try to keep you from going by something a little more indirect."

Elizabeth's lower lip quivered, and I began to feel guilty. "I don't suppose it occurred to either one of you that the reason you couldn't talk me out of it was because I really wanted to go. I happen to have had a dream that could have come true, and you two managed to ruin it for me."

Suddenly I thought I might cry, too. *What had we done?* The one thing in the world I can't stand is to see my twin sister looking truly upset. And I knew that Steven felt the same. "Liz, we were jerks," I confessed, feeling genuinely sorry. "Can you ever forgive us?"

I tried to put my arms around her, but Elizabeth pulled away. "No. I can't!" she vowed, sobbing. "I know you two may have thought this would end up being funny, but the truth is I think what you did today was really, really rotten. I still don't know the details, but I can guess what must have happened. Jessica, you pretended to be me in front of Mr. Sterne, right? Only instead of being me—the real me—you said a bunch of awful things and made me look like a prize idiot. And you"— she turned to Steven—"you were probably behind that phone call that wrecked my last interview this afternoon."

After Elizabeth raced upstairs, crying, Steven and I stood numbly, staring at the floor. Having Elizabeth despise us forever was tons worse than having her move to Switzerland for a year.

"Wow," Steven said in a low voice. "I feel like a criminal."

We spent a few minutes blaming each other, but then I thought of a new plan.

"I've got an idea!" I exclaimed. Steve opened his mouth to protest, but I pressed on before he had a chance to tell me it was my ideas that got us into trouble in the first place. "Look, we got Elizabeth into this whole mess by trying to make her appear to be something she isn't to Mr. Sterne and the committee. Why don't we call him and make an appointment to see him? We can tell him the truth—from the beginning. At least that way he'll know Liz is really everything her teachers and her records say she is. Then maybe she'll forgive us."

"Yeah," Steven said unhappily. "But then won't they turn around and give her the scholarship after all?"

I shrugged, depressed but resigned. "There isn't much we can do about that. Liz is right, Steve. We really have to let her make up her own mind."

I was trying to be mature about it, but when I thought of Elizabeth thousands of miles away in Switzerland, I was sure I'd spend every night of my senior year crying into my pillow—as I knew Elizabeth was doing at that moment. I was so depressed that it never even occurred to me to be upset about being home with my family on a Friday night.

Elizabeth started to explain to our parents that night that Steven and I had spent the last two days destroying her chance for happiness. Then she and Steven started to argue.

"You all need to stop shouting," Mom said as Dad jumped up to answer the door. "Remember, your parents have had a long, hard week. It's Friday night, and I think both your father and I would really like to sit down and put our feet up. Then, and only then, we're going to hear what happened with Mr. Sterne today."

Then my father walked back into the room. And with him was Mr. Sterne himself, as well as Ms. Crawford.

"Oh, no—Mr. Sterne!" Elizabeth screamed. She jumped to her feet and looked down in dismay at her jeans and crewneck sweater. Mr. Sterne, of course, was still in his boring but impeccable gray suit. And it still didn't have a single wrinkle in it.

"I'm not going to keep you all for long," Mr. Sterne announced, rejecting the offer of a seat. "I'm here under what I think are highly unusual circumstances. Ordinarily we don't pay an unannounced visit. But I think there's been some confusion that we'd like to clear up."

"Oh, dear," my mother said, with a suspicious glance at me. "Exactly what happened?"

We suffered through a long, uncomfortably silent moment. Then Mr. Sterne cleared his throat and put the tips of his fingers together. "We all got a little confused today during the interview process. Suffice

238

it to say that we jumped to some pretty harsh conclusions about Elizabeth, here—mostly because of the efforts of her brother and sister."

"Steven! Jessica!" Mom cried. "How could you?"

Mr. Sterne raised his hand like an angry teacher silencing a first-grader. "Please, let me finish. I don't think I've ever encountered a case like this one. Ms. Crawford and I were all set to close Elizabeth's case this afternoon. We believed that she had promise as a writer, and exceptional grades and recommendations. But her behavior seemed to us erratic—in fact, wildly so. Then we learned that this perception was facilitated by her twin's having disguised herself as Elizabeth in order to give us as bad an impression as possible."

My father looked as if he were about to ground me for life. "Jessica Wakefield—" he began in a harsh tone.

Mr. Sterne held up his hand again. "We learned this when Jessica and Steven called my office late this afternoon to confess what they had done."

Now it was Elizabeth's turn to be astonished. "You're kidding!"

"Are you surprised?" Mr. Sterne asked her. "It so happens that your brother and sister love you so much, Miss Wakefield, that they were willing to try anything—even the kind of perverse behavior we saw over the course of the past twenty-four hours—to keep you from leaving home. Now, Ms. Crawford and I have agreed, after much discussion, that this in itself speaks very highly of your character. And thanks to the impassioned case that Steven and Jessica have made, we've decided to offer you the Margaret Sterne Memorial Prize."

Elizabeth hugged me and Steven. We were glad she wasn't mad at us anymore—and that she seemed so happy. But it was totally depressing to know she'd be in Switzerland for a year. I could see in Steven's brown eyes that he felt the same.

Then the doorbell rang.

"Not again!" Mom said, jumping up and nearly tripping over the yelping Prince Albert. "It's like Grand Central Station in here."

"I, uh, thank you," Elizabeth said to Mr. Sterne and Ms. Crawford. "I barely know what to say."

"Of course, we'll give you the weekend to think it over," he said. But I could tell that in his mind Elizabeth was already sitting in a chalet, writing a terrific short story while staring out a window at a mountainside, and at that little girl with blond pigtails with her goats.

"Will you excuse me?" Elizabeth asked suddenly. Enid and Jeffrey had just walked into the room. "These are my friends, and I think we need to say a few things to one another."

The three of them stepped into the front hall, but they were still clearly visible through the living-room doorway, and we could hear every word.

"Liz," Enid said, handing her a leather-covered scrapbook. "We've been spending every spare minute this week working on this for you. It was supposed to be a good-luck present, but from what your mom just told us, it sounds like it'll be a going-away present too. It's to make sure you don't forget about us."

"You mean—all this week you were working on this?" Elizabeth choked out. "Every time I saw you together?"

Aha! I thought. *That explains the Jeffrey-and-Enid rumor. I knew he had better taste than that.*

"We wanted it to be a surprise," Enid said, putting her arm around Elizabeth. "I felt like such a jerk after the way I acted last week. You know how I feel about you, Liz. And if you want to go to Switzerland, I'm behind you one hundred percent."

Jeffrey leaned over and kissed Elizabeth's lucky cheek. "Hey," he said in a sexy voice. "Don't you and I have a date tonight?"

Elizabeth stared at him, confused.

"Whoops!" I said, clapping a hand over my mouth. "Jeffrey, we kind of got our wires crossed. That was me this afternoon, not Liz."

Now Jeffrey looked confused. Elizabeth excused herself from the group and pulled him toward the front porch.

Oh well, I thought. My sister and her boyfriend had been a little distant since this Switzerland thing came up, but I knew they were about to make up. *So much for my chances with Jeffrey, even with Elizabeth moving to the other side of the world.*

A few minutes later they were back, and not a moment too soon. It had been only a few minutes, but it felt as if we'd been sitting for an hour, trying to make conversation with Mr. Sterne as if he were a regular human being and not some sort of android.

"This isn't going to be very easy for me to say," Elizabeth began, standing in front of us all. I realized that this was the big, official farewell speech. "You've all been very patient with me for the past few weeks. And I guess I owe every single person in this room a big thank-you. First, I want to thank Enid for reminding me what a real friend is. I guess a friend is always a reminder of home. And that's what Enid is to me. Her present is an example of that. She's part of what I love most about Sweet Valley."

She turned to the family next. "I don't think I have to tell Jessica and Steven how angry I was at them this afternoon. But what they did also made me feel good. They weren't going to let me leave without a struggle—and even if they embarrassed me more than a little, it was worth it in the end, especially since they made it all turn out OK."

Then she sighed and turned to Mr. Sterne and Ms. Crawford. "And most of all I want to thank you for your time and patience. You have generously chosen me to represent Margaret Sterne with your scholarship."

Then she shocked us all.

"But I'm sorry to tell you that I can't accept."

"Can't accept?" Mr. Sterne exclaimed. "Do you realize that no one has ever turned down this scholarship offer before? Not in twenty years?"

Elizabeth appeased him with some flattery for the school and the saintly Margaret Sterne and her scholarship. Then she got serious. "It's just that I belong here, with my family and friends. I thought Switzerland was the most magical place on earth, but I can see now that this"—she spread out her arms—"is even more magical. I was looking for inspiration, and I discovered it's right here—with the people who love me most."

I'm so relieved, Diary. I can't imagine life without Elizabeth.

Monday night

Remember I told you about Winston winning the lottery? Well, guess what. . . .

Lila and I were sitting on the school lawn this morning, and we caught an amazing headline in the *Sweet Valley News.*

"Lila," I said, pointing to a big picture of Winston on the second page, "listen to this: 'Lottery Winner Claims He Is Not Rightful Owner of Winning Ticket.' And the subtitle says, 'Generous Boy Proclaimed a Hero by Owner.'"

Lila yawned. "Let me see," she said, obviously trying not to appear interested.

"Wow," I said. "Can you believe it? Winston gave this guy back a ticket worth twenty-five thousand dollars! I'm not sure I would've done it!"

"I certainly wouldn't have," Lila said, tilting her nose in the air as if the very thought of a generous act gave off an unpleasant odor.

According to the newspaper, Winston and an old man named Mr. Oliver had their tickets in their coat pockets and got their coats mixed up at a store the day of the lottery drawing. Winston had known as soon as the winning ticket was drawn that he wasn't the rightful owner, but he had waited for several days before he convinced himself to give back the money.

"How is that boy ever going to get anywhere with that kind of confused value system?" Lila continued, wrinkling her nose. "I should have my daddy send him to one of his cutthroat business seminars. That would teach him not to throw out twenty-five thousand dollars. Besides, I thought he was going to buy us all presents and stuff. Now what are we going to get out of the whole thing?"

I had to admit that she had a point. "Look, here comes the local hero now!"

Winston was strolling toward us up the front walk, with an arm around Maria and a big, stupid smirk on his face.

"You see, Maria, my reputation precedes me," he said grandly, when I asked him if the newspaper account was true. "From now on consider me the Moral King of Sweet Valley High. For a modest fee I'll be happy to offer counsel on the thorniest questions. First there was Socrates—then Plato—and now Winston Egbert."

You heard it here first, Diary.

In other news we've got a new transfer student at school—Kirk Anderson. He's way cute! But he's one of the most obnoxious people I've ever met in my entire life. Why does such arrogance have to be wrapped up in such a tall, dark, and handsome body? The first time I met him, he scoped me up and down in the sleaziest way imaginable. Then he told me that he was going to single-handedly lead the tennis team to international stardom, and that his presence would revitalize the social scene at Sweet Valley High, which couldn't possibly have been any fun before he arrived. He even had the arrogance to imply that if I was really lucky, he might deign to take me out sometime.

Have I mentioned that Bruce Patman used to be the most arrogant person in the world before he fell in love with Regina and turned normal? I was wrong. Bruce was only the second-most-arrogant person. A distant second.

Oh, one more thing. Elizabeth and her creepy newspaper friends have decided to add a personals column to The Oracle. *People will submit blurbs describing what they're like and what kind of person they're looking for. Only the editor will know their names. Everyone else will just* respond to a box number. I think it's a very progressive idea, but I'm not sure how many people will want to admit they can't get a date on their own. If it works, it'll sure give everyone some wild stuff to talk about. I can't wait to see what happens!

Part 8

Dear Diary,

I am so-o-o-o sick of the guys at school. I've dated all the cool ones, and a whole lot of the totally uncool ones, too. So this afternoon at the beach Lila and I decided we need to branch out into the college crowd. We came up with this contest. . . .

"Lila, we've got to take some serious action," I said, sitting up on my beach blanket. We had been tanning on the beach for more than an hour, and not a single cute guy had stopped to talk to us—despite my white string bikini.

Maybe it was Lila's new fire-engine-red maillot that was keeping them away, I speculated to myself. It really did wash out her tan. Nah, I decided. Millions in the bank made up for a slightly faded suntan, any day. It must be the quality of the high-school guys that hung out on "our" strip of beach.

"There's got to be some way to meet some guys," I insisted. *"Older* guys."

Lila was still lying on her back with her eyes closed and her expensive sunglasses pushed up over her light-brown hair like a headband, to keep from getting tan lines on her face. She opened one brown eye and looked at me skeptically.

I suppose Lila had a right to be skeptical. We'd had this same conversation at least once a week for our entire junior year.

"Oh, yeah?" she asked. "Like what?"

"Well . . . ," I began, knowing Lila wouldn't like what I was about to propose. *What the heck.* Lila was always throwing fits. One more wouldn't make any difference. "I think we should use the personal ads in *The Oracle.*"

"What?" Lila demanded, sitting up straight. "That is the grossest idea you've ever had, Jessica Wakefield! Only losers take out personal ads, and only losers answer them."

"For your information, Lila, personal ads are not what they used to be. I read this article in *Ingenue* that said more and more singles use them to meet people because of the pressures of life these days. Lots of people don't have time to go cruising around, you know, so they just take out an ad to say exactly what they're looking for and then pick out the best replies."

Lila still had this scornful look on her face, but I

248

pressed on. Time was of the essence. The first personal-ads column would be in Monday's *Oracle*, and I knew the deadline was Friday.

"It's *the* best way to meet people now," I said, trying to remember everything I had read in the magazine article. "They had these testimonials and pictures of couples who had met through the ads. And believe me, these people were not losers."

"Well, if you're so smart," she objected, "how do you expect to meet college boys with ads in a high-school newspaper?"

"I just happen to know someone in college who gets copies of our paper, and that someone always has tons of good-looking friends in his room."

Thank goodness for Steven.

"And you can always say that only college boys should reply," I continued. "You can spell out exactly what kind of guy you want, you know. Just list the requirements, and you'll get good-looking guys falling all over themselves to get to you."

We started to argue then, because Lila thought it made more sense to use an ad to describe herself rather than the guy she was looking for.

"Well," I said, pulling a notebook out of my duffel bag. "Do it your way. And I'll do it my way. And we'll just see which way is best."

"A little competition, huh?" Lila asked. Lila never could resist a battle of wills. And I was her favorite opponent.

"That's right! A contest—but not a bet!" I had to make that part perfectly clear. It wasn't fair for a person on my allowance to have to wager money against someone like Lila, whose supply seemed unlimited. "We'll each take out an ad and see what kind of guys we get," I suggested. "Then we'll have some kind of double date, and we'll each check out the other one and decide who did better. We could all go to the Swing Fling together or something." The Forties-Night Swing Fling was a big dance coming up at school. Everyone important would be there.

Lila raised her eyebrows. "I *have* a date for the Swing Fling," she said smugly.

"Well, so do I. But if you found the man of your dreams, wouldn't you rather go with him?"

"I guess so."

"OK. Then we'll each write our ads and give them to Lynne Henry tomorrow. That's the deadline." Lynne wasn't a regular *Oracle* staff member. But the new personals column had been Lynne's idea, so the *Oracle* editor in chief, Penny Ayala, had asked her to coordinate it.

I handed Lila a sheet of paper and an extra pencil, and we both settled down to compose our ads.

"I think this ought to do it," Lila said a few minutes later. I read over her ad:

> Glamorous, sophisticated, mature high-school girl looking for someone with the right stuff. I like fast cars, caviar, and the Caribbean. Don't talk to me about commit-

ment—I'm looking for excitement, not a bridge partner. If you can keep up with me, I want you. *Kids need not reply.*

"Wow!" I said, impressed. "You sure know how to write an ad. But I think you're approaching it from the wrong angle. Look at this." I handed her my own effort:

Are you devastatingly handsome? Are you romantic and wild? Do you like girls who aren't afraid of danger? Are you the type of guy who goes for what he wants? Are you in college? If you answered yes to *all* the above questions, drop me a line. I've been looking for you.

Lila nodded approvingly. "I think this might just turn out to be the most interesting contest we've ever had, Jess."

Monday night

The Oracle's *first personal-ads column came out today, and everyone's talking about it. Of course, it included ads from a certain pair of extremely popular and attractive junior girls. The ads are anonymous, so nobody knows Lila and I wrote them. I can't wait to see who answers mine! Unfortunately, it'll take a few days* for the guys at the university to see the newspaper and decide they can't live without us. So we probably won't hear anything until next week.

Tuesday, a week later

Everyone at school has been talking about nothing but the personal ads all week, especially since the second installment came out yesterday. Of course, a lot of the guys are making fun of them—especially Kirk Anderson, that jerk who just moved here. That's mean. Poor, desperate people who have to advertise for a date can't help it if they're losers. I'm glad Lila and I aren't desperate.

I don't know what Neil Freemount sees in Kirk, but it looks like they're friends. Neil is too serious, but he's always been a nice guy. I've even gone out with him myself. Kirk is just plain obnoxious.

I don't know if it's the personals that are causing it, but lots of people are going off the deep end. For instance, Amy Sutton is convinced that Bruce Patman likes her. What a joke. Bruce is so hung up on Regina Morrow that he can hardly see straight. I've never seen him actually in love before; it's kind of sickening. Amy's out of luck if she's planning to make a play for him.

Well, I won't keep you in suspense any longer, Diary. (Drumroll, please.) I got seven responses to my ad so far! I'm so totally psyched, I can hardly stand it. Ooops, Mom's calling me to set the table, so I've gotta go. Right after dinner I'm running over to Lila's to show her my letters. I promised her I wouldn't open them until we were together.

"I wanted you to help me go through my first batch of admirers," I said, following Lila up the huge staircase at Fowler Crest. "I'm sure you'll start getting yours soon."

I couldn't resist a smug smile, but that was probably unfair of me. I had received mine already because Elizabeth works at the newspaper and hand-delivered them a day early.

"Well, let's see them," Lila urged as we plopped down on her satin-covered bed. We started ripping open envelopes and reading the letters. Then I read the most promising one aloud.

Dear Miss Excitement:

I'm no stranger to boasting, but I get the feeling you know how to put your money where your mouth is. You definitely sound like dynamite about to go off, and I want to be there for the explosion, even if it means getting a little singed. The girls I've met at college are nothing compared with someone like you.

I like slow dancing and romantic dinners. And I like dessert, too. . . .

Drop me a line. I think we should get together, *mi amore.*

"Doesn't that just give you goose bumps?"

Lila shrugged. Sometimes she can be infuriating, with her Miss Superior act. "Maybe it gives *you* goose bumps, but it gives me a rash! He sounds way too conceited to me."

Look who's talking, I thought. "Conceited? Lila, for your information this guy is obviously incredibly sexy and sophisticated. He's not some shy little dork, you know. And you did notice that he speaks Italian, didn't you?"

Lila rolled her eyes. "Jessica, anybody could learn two words of Italian. Give me a break."

"I'm writing back to him," I declared. "And just you wait. If I date this guy, it's going to turn out to be the biggest romance of the century."

Monday night

I got another letter from my mystery man today. His name is Paolo. I just knew he was European. I knew it!

I bet he's tall and slim and dark-haired, with classy Italian suits and a sexy accent. He's probably some kind of international student—maybe the son of rich, important diplomats. We'll go to foreign films together and dance at the most exclusive clubs in Los Angeles. Then he'll take me to Rome for spring break next year.

Lila is being all secretive about her own replies. It's not fair! I let her read Paolo's letters. Maybe only dweebs answered her ad. When she meets Paolo, she will absolutely die.

So will I. But I'll risk it! I wrote back to him this evening and suggested that we get together.

Not everyone is so lucky in love. I overheard Kirk and Neil and some other guys talking about a rotten trick they're playing on a poor, insecure girl who wrote an ad. They invented a guy named Jamie who responded to her ad and is now sending her love letters. Isn't that the most awful thing you've ever heard? I knew Kirk was a worm. But I'm surprised that Neil would be in on such a nasty joke.

On the other hand, the poor girl left herself open for it. Some people just aren't good enough judges of character to know when a letter is sincere, and when the writer has ulterior motives.

Wednesday afternoon

I can't wait for Friday. Paolo and I will finally meet! He's going to be gorgeous. I just know it.

> *My date with Paolo was a disaster. Paolo was a disaster. The whole evening was such a disaster that it was funny. . . .*

"Wow!" Elizabeth said with a whistle when I posed near the bathroom door. "Jess, you look fantastic!"

"Do I really?" I asked, though I knew she was right. "Are you sure?"

You should have seen me. I was wearing a straight blue linen skirt and a skimpy white tank top in a nubby silk knit. Elizabeth's teal-blue scarf was knotted around my throat—very European. And I had spent an hour, and most of a can of mousse, giving my hair a look of rumpled abandon. I just hoped I could get out the door before Elizabeth noticed that I had blunted her new blue eyeliner pencil to make my eyes huge and sultry.

I dabbed on some perfume and asked Elizabeth to stay upstairs until I was gone. I didn't want her to dilute Paolo's first look at me.

When the doorbell rang, I arranged my face in the most sophisticated expression I could manage. (Thank goodness for years of coaching from Lila!) I envisioned tall, handsome Paolo standing on the front porch in his classy Italian suit. Then I pulled open the door and froze.

Paolo was fat. And he wasn't the least bit handsome.

"Jessica?" he said without even a smidgen of Rome

256

in his voice. "Hi, I'm Paolo. I'm so glad to meet you."

I couldn't bring myself to reciprocate. I accepted the red rose he held out and ran into the kitchen under the guise of putting it in water. I needed to collect myself. Big time.

I had never dated a fat, ugly boy in my life. I didn't think I could go through with it. *What if somebody saw me with him?* My reputation would be ruined forever. Lila would never let me forget it. I had to find a way to get out of the date, but I had no idea how. I couldn't exactly run out the back door and hide. So I threw the rose into the sink, raced back to the foyer, and grabbed Paolo's pudgy arm to get him out of there before Elizabeth saw him. Then I dragged him out to the Camaro that was parked at the curb.

"I guess you really do like to move fast," he said with a chuckle.

I forced myself to smile. "I thought you were Italian."

"Well, my parents are. But I've lived in California all my life."

Great, I thought. *So much for a sophisticated European.*

"And I bet you're wondering about—" He paused. "Well, I'm not exactly a devastatingly handsome guy," he admitted.

Now, that was a blinding flash of the obvious.

I couldn't think of a thing to say.

He said he was taking me to Tiberino's, the most fashionable Italian restaurant in the valley.

Uh-oh, I thought. *What if somebody who knows me is there?* I resolved to find a way to cut this date short—whatever it took.

Paolo didn't seem to notice that I wasn't saying anything on the ride over. He was blabbing on and on about astronomy and black holes, which he said have such a strong gravitational pull that they suck up everything around them. I wished one would suck me up. Better yet, I wished one would suck *him* up.

We were in the restaurant, Diary—at a booth in the back, where it's dark and hard to recognize anyone—when I finally thought of a way to get out of the date. . . .

"So tell me a little about yourself," Paolo said, after he had ordered for both of us in rapid Italian. "I already know you're the prettiest girl in the restaurant."

"Well," I began. Then my brilliant idea hit me. "I . . . actually, I've been sort of an invalid all my life," I lied.

"You're kidding. But you look so healthy."

"Oh? Well, looks can be deceiving, I guess. Anyway, I get these terrible headaches—I had a CAT scan yesterday, in fact. I'll know in a few days whether it's—it's—" I broke off dramatically and tried to look brave.

"Whether it's—" Paolo prompted.

I shrugged. "But I like to ignore the pain when I can. Life is just too short."

"Jessica, I had no idea. What you must go through! But you're OK right now, aren't you?"

I hesitated for the briefest of instants. "Oh. Yes. . . . Yes. I'm OK." I lowered my voice and looked at my napkin.

I've always said that I'm Academy Award material.

"You're so brave," Paolo said. "I can't tell you how much I admire you, Jessica. You're really remarkable."

"You have no idea," I said under my breath. In a few minutes I'd be out of the restaurant and free for the rest of the evening. And Paolo would have no idea what hit him.

"No, I'm not, really," I whispered, allowing a slight flicker of pain to cross my face.

He straightened up in his seat. "Are you sure you're OK?"

"Paolo, I . . ." I shook my head. "I just wanted to have fun like a normal girl! For once! Instead of staying home and taking medicines and—"

Within a minute Paolo was on his feet and offering to drive me home.

"You're wonderful, Jessica," he said as he walked me to my door. "It's been an honor meeting you. I'm only sorry it didn't work out this time. But give me a call when you're feeling better."

He drove away, and I leaned gratefully against the door. I had the feeling this illness was going to turn out to be terminal.

After Paolo left, I vowed to give up dating forever. I mean it, Diary. I seri-

ously considered joining a convent.

But there was this letter waiting for me when I got home. Actually, there were several. Elizabeth had picked up some more responses to my ad at the Oracle *office that day and had forgotten to give them to me earlier. She was out on a date with Jeffrey. (Some people have all the luck, Diary!) But she left the letters on the kitchen table for me. . . .*

"I guess I'd better check these out," I muttered to Prince Albert, who was drooling on my knee.

When I tore open the first envelope, a photograph fell out. I picked it up and gasped. The boy was deeply tanned, with warm brown eyes and thick, wavy blond hair. He was adorable.

His letter said his name was John Karger, and he sounded wonderful—friendly, sincere, and straightforward. He said he was a college freshman who liked adventure, surfing, and tennis. And he suggested getting together.

I was game. I wrote him back right then and there. But I decided to keep John a secret from Lila. I didn't know yet how I would explain Paolo to her. If John turned out to be a loser, too, Lila would never have to know.

Monday afternoon

It's all set. I have a date with John Karger on Wednesday night. I'm trying to stay low-

key, after my last blind date, but I've never been very good at low-key. Besides, this time it isn't really a blind date. After all, I do have a picture of John. Even if he turns out to be a nerd, a date with a guy that cute couldn't be a total waste of time.

Speaking of wastes, Kirk Anderson was at it again at lunchtime today. He was bragging to his friends about the trick they played on the poor girl who wrote the personal ad. It turns out it was Penny Ayala, a good friend of Elizabeth's. OK, so I was wrong about her being a loser. Penny's the editor in chief of The Oracle, *and a straight-A student, so I guess "loser" isn't the word for her. She's just too studious. But even that doesn't make her fair game for Kirk's sick sense of humor.*

Kirk and his friends arranged for her and "Jamie" to meet at the mall on Friday and watched to see who showed up.

Penny doesn't know anything about that. She's just heartbroken that Jamie stood her up—or so I gather from Liz. I guess I should mention that Elizabeth didn't exactly come out and tell me all this about Penny. Liz is the loyal, secret-keeping type. Even with friends like Penny, who's too boring to have any really interesting secrets. I'm just good at keeping my ears open. It's especially helpful to keep my ears open while listening in on telephone extensions. And the rest I heard from Kirk himself, when he was bragging to his friends.

If there's one thing Elizabeth can't take, it's watching somebody hurt one of her friends (or me, I guess). She's determined to teach Kirk a lesson. So she astounded me and Enid and Jeffrey at lunch today by coming up with a plan that's devious and sneaky and underhanded. In other words, she came up with a plan that I wish I had thought of myself.

Wednesday night

I think I'm in love. . . .

John showed up at the front door for our date tonight, looking even better than his photograph.

"Hi, I'm John Karger," he said in a sexy voice that matched his gorgeous face and perfect body. He had long legs, strong hands, honey-gold hair, the world's whitest teeth, and a confident, mature look. He was dressed preppy, in khakis, a tweed jacket, and tortoiseshell glasses. Very collegiate. Very sexy.

I thought I would hyperventilate. Lila would just *die* when she saw this guy. The contest was as good as won.

"I thought we could go to this little Greek place I

262

know and have a nice long talk with no interruptions," John said after we got into his car. "They serve a mean baklava."

"Great," I breathed. "Perfect." I had no idea what baklava was, but I figured I would find out soon enough.

The restaurant was dimly lit and romantic, in an exotic sort of way. Greek folk music played in the background, and the air was fragrant with sweet spices I didn't recognize.

"So tell me about yourself, Jessica," John said. He rested his chin on his hands and stared into my eyes. I felt my insides melting. "I want to know everything about you."

Another point in his favor, I decided. I was one of my favorite subjects. "Well, I like lots of things—like having a good time, doing exciting things." I wanted to bite my tongue. That didn't sound very sophisticated.

But John looked totally absorbed. "Like what?" he pressed.

"I guess you could say I like a dare," I said. *Now, that sounded less high-schoolish,* I thought, more satisfied. "I'll do anything once—and I'll do it again if I like it." I glanced at him suggestively.

"I bet you've got tons of guys asking you out all the time."

That was a tricky one, but I hit on exactly the right approach to responding. "Well, I do. But the problem is, most boys are so immature. I'm hoping to meet someone more adult. . . ."

I gave him a meaningful stare that I hoped was sexy, and I was glad to see that he looked interested. No, enthralled. I asked him to tell me about himself.

"Oh, I'm just another guy. I'm a freshman—a sociology major. That's all."

"Sociology? What's that all about?"

"People. I study people."

"I see." And I certainly did see. At the moment, John was studying *me*. And the intensity in his brown eyes was enough to make me feel warm all over.

"Would you consider yourself an adventure seeker, Jessica?"

When I told him I was, he asked for an example. I guess he wanted proof that I was as adventurous as I claimed in my ad. I couldn't fault him for that. I knew after my experience with Paolo that you could never be sure people were representing themselves honestly. Luckily, I hadn't been exaggerating one bit. I could have cited hundreds of examples.

"Well," I began, laughing, "there was the time I made Jeremy Frank have me on his TV show. And the time I got stuck in a cave with a bear. And once I smuggled a puppy into our house and kept him hidden from my parents for a whole week. I've done all kinds of things like that."

He went on asking me questions about myself, as if I were the most fascinating person in the world. You're right, Diary, if you're thinking that he sounds more serious than most of the guys I go out with. But I think I like the serious type. Especially when it's me they're serious about. Unfortunately, he had to get back to his dorm to study, so he cut the date short—kind of abruptly, I thought. I guess college is like that. And I guess that's one of the pitfalls of being in love with a serious guy. He did say he would call me, though, and maybe take me out this weekend.

I was disappointed that John had to take me home early, but I felt better in the car, when he went on asking me all kinds of questions about myself. It was clear that he couldn't get enough of me. When the car stopped in front of my house, I turned my face to him, waiting for a kiss.

"I had a wonderful time," I said in a husky voice.

But he didn't kiss me. He just smiled his sexy smile. "Me too, Jessica. Good night."

Apparently, John Karger is a gentleman. Now, that's just the opposite of what everyone says about college guys. I guess it's all part of his serious attitude. That's OK, Diary. All in good time.

I can't wait for the Swing Fling dance. And I especially can't wait to see Lila's face when she meets John and sees what a hunk he is. I am definitely in love.

Oh, I almost forgot, Diary. Elizabeth put her plan into action yesterday in the school cafeteria—the plan to get back at Kirk for being such a stinker to Penny. I wasn't there when Elizabeth struck, but she told me all about it afterward. Apparently, her plan worked like a charm. . . .

Elizabeth glanced at Kirk, sitting alone at the next table and intent on an ice-cream sandwich. She slipped a handful of magazine clippings out of her notebook and passed them to Enid.

"Liz!" Enid said in a loud voice. "You never told me your cousin was so gorgeous! I can't believe she's so beautiful."

Almost imperceptibly, Kirk inclined his head to listen.

"Yes," Elizabeth answered. "When she got her modeling contract, none of us were surprised. She's always been the prettiest member of the family."

"And so sophisticated, too," Enid gushed, holding up the pictures for a better view of the stunning, raven-haired model.

Enid wasn't the only one who got a better view. Kirk turned around and stared at the magazine clippings, no longer bothering to hide his interest.

"Well, she does live in New York, after all," Elizabeth explained, pretending not to notice Kirk. "Sixteen in Manhattan is a lot more mature than sixteen in Sweet Valley."

"Boy, I'll say!" Enid answered. "Erica must be one

of the most glamorous girls in the country."

"Well, you'll get to judge for yourself when she gets here. She's got a screen test in L.A., so she'll be coming up to visit us over the weekend."

"This weekend?"

"No, next."

"Hey, that's the weekend of the Swing Fling!"

"Who is that?" asked Kirk, trying to sound casual—which wasn't very convincing, given the way he was hanging over Enid's shoulder.

"That's my cousin, Erica Hall," Elizabeth said. "She's a model."

Kirk's keen blue eyes glittered with excitement. "Did I hear you say she'd be in town next weekend?"

"Yes. Why?"

"I want to take her to the dance, that's why," he announced, tossing his glossy black hair off his forehead. "She's exactly my type."

"Well, sure, but it's just that—well, Erica never goes out on blind dates. There are so many guys asking her out all the time that she's really picky."

"Well, of course she'd pick me if she met me," Kirk said, as if there were no question about it.

"But she won't even get here until that afternoon. She wouldn't have time to meet you. She only likes to go out with really good-looking guys. She never takes a chance."

Kirk looked positively indignant. "Look, Elizabeth. Just send her my picture. That should take care of everything." He pulled out a copy of the previous week's *Oracle*. "See, here I am, getting congratulated by the guy I slaughtered at the Big Mesa tennis tournament. That's my best side."

Elizabeth took the photo from him. "I don't know. I can't promise anything. But I'll send this to Erica. It's totally up to her."

Elizabeth's story wasn't completely a lie. Erica Hall really is a model. She's been in Ingenue, Mademoiselle, *and all the other magazines. And we really do have a cousin. But her name is Jenny, she lives in Dallas, and she's fifteen, fat, and a pain in the neck. And, thank goodness, she's not coming to Sweet Valley anytime soon.*

But besides those teeny little details, Elizabeth's story was totally true. And Kirk fell for it—hook, line, and stinker.

Thursday afternoon

I was hanging out with Lila and Cara at the Dairi Burger after school today. . . .

Cara sat across the table from me and Lila, sipping her diet soda. Suddenly the straw fell right out of her mouth. "Did you see that?" she said, obviously floored.

"What?" I asked.

"Neil Freemount and Penny Ayala over there. They just kissed."

"You're kidding!" I said. Penny had apparently bounced back pretty quickly from being stood up by Kirk's fictional Jamie. I'd hardly ever even seen her *with* a guy, let alone kissing one in public. And a cute one, at that. Knowing Neil, I figured he couldn't stand the trick they were playing on her and confessed it all to Penny. Apparently, she wasn't holding a grudge.

"I swear," Lila drawled, jiggling the ice cubes in her own soda cup. "Sometimes you see the most unbelievable couples."

That gave me the opening I needed. "There just happens to be a new couple," I said mysteriously. "And I'm not talking about Penny and Neil."

Lila shot me a keen glance. "Oh, really? Does this have anything to do with our little wager?"

Cara's eyebrows went up. I guess any contest that pits me and Lila against each other counts as a true spectator sport.

"Lila and I both placed personal ads to see who could come up with the best guys that way. And I won."

"You won?" Lila snapped. "Who says you won?"

"Well, last night I had a date with one of the guys who answered my ad. And let's just say he was—unbelievable."

Cara's eyes lit up. "What was he like, Jess? What was his name?"

I decided to continue being mysterious. "All I'm going to tell you now is that he's gorgeous, and he's crazy about me."

Lila chuckled. "Gorgeous, huh? Well, Jessica, I

just happen to have a date tonight with someone *I* think will win our little contest. So don't speak too soon."

Not so fast, Lila! Just wait until you get one look at John.

Sunday

I met John at the university snack bar today. He was even more gorgeous than he was on Tuesday night.

And I thought of a way to show him off to Lila. John's going to meet me at the big beach party Saturday afternoon. There's a free concert, and everyone will be there. To make sure John notices nobody but me, I'm going to buy this leopard-spotted bikini I saw in Lisette's this week.

Oh, God, Diary. I just had an awesome thought: John Karger in a bathing suit! I can't wait until Saturday.

Speaking of Saturday, John says he can't make it to the Swing Fling that night. I think he'll change his mind after spending the afternoon with me and my leopard bikini.

Monday

Elizabeth called Kirk to tell him Erica wanted to go to the Swing Fling with him.

What a joke! Enid and I were there to hear the fun, and Liz filled us in on Kirk's side of the conversation as soon as she hung up.

Kirk's voice was full of arrogance as he instructed Liz over the phone, "Tell her I'll pick her up at your place at eight, OK?"

"Well, you can't do that," Elizabeth said. "See, she's driving up from L.A. that afternoon and will only be getting here just in time. She'd rather just meet you outside the gym."

"That's fine with me."

"Kirk," Elizabeth said, "I really don't think you should take her."

"Why not?" he snarled, so loudly that Enid and I could hear his voice crackling through the receiver.

"It's just that I don't think you'd like her, Kirk. She's really arrogant and conceited about her looks—she's always bragging about how wonderful she is."

Just like Kirk, I thought. I caught Elizabeth's eye and knew she was thinking the same thing.

Kirk only laughed. "I like a girl with self-confidence. If she's got it, she should flaunt it. I like that."

"She's just impossible to have fun with, Kirk," Elizabeth warned, describing Kirk perfectly. "She's so self-centered, so bossy, so superior—"

"Look, I don't know what your problem is," Kirk said, cutting her off. "All of a sudden you don't want me going out with your cousin. But I'm taking her out, got it?"

"Well, all right. You'd better get her an orchid or something really fancy as a corsage. She's used to being treated well."

Elizabeth hung up the phone, holding it with her fingertips as if she were afraid Kirk's voice had dirtied it. "He was practically drooling into the phone," she said with a shudder. "How can he not have realized I was describing him?"

"Well, he obviously loves himself, right?" Enid said. "So it makes sense that he'd like a girl who's just like him."

"Well, anyway, we've got him right where we want him. Now all we can do is wait until Saturday."

It'll be fun to watch Kirk taken down a few pegs. Of course, I have a much more compelling reason to look forward to Saturday. I can't wait to see Lila's face when she sees John. I love getting the last laugh.

Saturday night

I didn't get the last laugh. John Karger got the last laugh.

The thing that made what happened especially embarrassing was that so many of our friends were watching to see the handsome guys Lila and I were going to show up

272

*with. Did I tell you that Lila was also meet-
ing her new college man at the beach
party? We planned to show them off to
each other during the concert—without
their knowing what we were doing, naturally. Amy and Cara, along with three
other cheerleaders—Maria Santelli, Jean
West, and Sandra Bacon—were going to be
the judges. We had both broken our dates
for the dance; the winner of the contest
would take her college man to the Swing
Fling.*

But Lila and I had a rude awakening. . . .

"Where's your mysterious man?" Cara asked as I
joined her among the crowd on the beach.

I craned my neck to look for him. "He's meeting
me here. Don't worry."

I narrowed my eyes when Lila approached. She
was wearing an oversize designer T-shirt, knotted
above her hip—revealing the bottom half of a leopard-spotted bikini, just like mine.

"Nice suit," Lila said grimly. "I guess after years of
being a twin, it's just natural for you to copy."

"I'm not copying you!" I protested. "You're the
one who's copying me!"

Amy pushed herself between us. "Hold it, you
two! Give me a break! We're not judging your bathing suits, remember. We're here to see who got the
best results from her personal ad. Where's your date,
Lila?"

"John's meeting me here."

I gaped at her. "John? His name is John?"

"Yeah. What's wrong with that? Oh, there he is!" She waved at someone in the crowd and then broke into a run. Amy, Maria, Sandra, and Jean followed her.

"What is it, Jess?" Cara asked me.

"My date's named John, too."

"So what? It's the most common name in the world."

We followed the other girls. I knew Cara was right, but I couldn't help the peculiar sensation that was growing in the pit of my stomach. I spotted a group of girls milling around a tall boy. The sensation got stronger.

Then I saw Lila, standing on the outskirts of the group, her face white with rage. In the middle of the circle was John Karger.

"Hey, Jessica!" he shouted happily. "Hi!"

Standing next to him was a stunning redhead. "Girls, this is Faye, my partner on my sociology project. And my girlfriend."

"Just what is going on here?" a pudgy blond girl demanded. "I thought we had a date, John!"

"What? He has a date with me!" another girl said.

Faye shook her head. "I'm afraid you're both wrong."

"I'm sorry," John said to the group. "I hope I didn't give you the impression—"

"What are you trying to say?" came another indignant voice.

"I was doing research for my sociology project.

274

I wanted to see how people presented themselves in personal ads and what they thought was appealing about themselves, so I answered all of your ads."

Jessica gulped.

"But, John!" wailed the pudgy blond. "I thought you really liked me!"

John's handsome face turned crimson and he began stammering. Apparently, John was a better student of sociology than he was of real people. He had been completely oblivious of the effect his questions—and those gorgeous brown eyes—would have on us all. "Oh, no," he concluded, staring at the angry, humiliated girls all around him.

I groaned. "Oh brother." The girls began slipping away, humiliated.

"Uh, I think I see someone I know," John said, his eyes wide with fear. "Come on, Faye." He grabbed the redhead by the hand, and they melted into the crowd.

Finally Cara, Amy, Sandra, Jean, and Maria couldn't hold in their laughter. It burst out of them like a dam breaking. Lila and I whirled on them.

"I fail to see what's so funny!" she seethed.

"Oh—oh—J-J-Jess—" Cara gasped between giggles. "Lila, you look so funny! You and your matching bikinis!" She screamed again with laughter and actually threw herself onto the sand.

"It's not the least bit funny!" I hissed. But the sight of the five of them, hysterical, began to infect me. And Lila's angry glare only added to the effect. I had to admit it—the whole situation was completely ridiculous. I couldn't help myself. I started laughing, too. A moment later Lila joined in. And we all howled there on the beach until tears came to our eyes, while people stared at us as if we were aliens.

In a way, I guess we got the last laugh, after all. It was the best! And we both ended up at the Swing Fling with dates. College men! We met them at the beach party, and one thing led to another. . . .

Not everyone was so lucky. I'll never forget the sight of Kirk hurling an expensive corsage to the floor when he realized my stunning "cousin" had stood him up. He stomped out of the gym like a maniac. What a trick! My sister is constantly surprising me. I guess hanging out with me for sixteen years is finally rubbing off on her.

Speaking of schemers, Amy wasn't at the dance at all. Neither was Bruce—though Regina showed up alone, saying he had to study. She seems to trust him completely. But I've known Bruce all my life. And he would never miss a big dance in order to study on a Saturday night. And he's always been the love-'em-and-leave-'em type. Could Bruce be reverting to his old ways?

Normally, when it comes to love, my motto is pretty simple: make sure you get what you want (except when what you want is your twin sister's boyfriend). But Regina's so sweet that it seems crummy for a flirt like Amy to grab her boyfriend. On the other hand, if he's willing to be grabbed, then maybe there wasn't much between Regina and Bruce in the first place.

Of course, I don't know for sure that Amy's trying to steal Regina's boyfriend. But I have a feeling that wherever Bruce was tonight, Amy was somewhere close by.

Part 9

> *Wednesday night*
>
> Dear Diary,
>
>   *Amy is out of control. She's got her claws in Bruce Patman and she's not taking them out. It started with this special project on drugs they're doing together for health class.*
>
>   *"What about Regina?" you ask. Amy says Bruce and Regina are through. You should have heard her in the locker room before cheerleading practice today. . . .*

"Jess!" Amy cried, running into the locker room with several other cheerleaders. "You were completely wrong about Bruce Patman. And I mean completely! Just ask these guys." She gestured toward Maria, Cara, and Sandra. "We just bumped into him in the hallway, and you should've seen the way he looked at me. It's obvious, Jessica—the guy's completely flipped over me!" She flipped her long blond hair over her shoulders, for emphasis. "He and Regina Morrow are history!"

I usually defended Amy—especially when Elizabeth complained about how boy crazy Amy had become. But this time I was skeptical. Ever since Amy had gotten it into her head that Bruce was in love with her, she'd been impossible to live with.

Maria pulled her cheerleading skirt out of her locker. "It's true, Jessica," she confirmed. "Believe me, I couldn't have imagined it either. I thought Bruce was as devoted to Regina as a guy could possibly be. But he really was fawning all over Amy. He seems hopelessly in love."

Now that didn't sound like macho, cool Bruce Patman at all. Until he started seeing Regina, he was more the don't-call-me-I'll-call-you (if I feel like it) type. But Maria was about the most levelheaded person on the cheerleading squad. She wasn't one to start imagining romances everywhere, like Cara or Amy.

Was it possible that Bruce's attraction to Amy was more than just wishful thinking on Amy's part? It was hard to believe. Not that Amy wasn't pretty. Some people would say gorgeous. She has ash-blond hair and big gray eyes and perfect legs that go practically up to her armpits. But lately even *I* thought she was too hung up on making herself attractive to boys. When she wasn't blabbing on about Bruce, it seemed all she could talk about was diets, eye-shadow colors, shoulder pads, and tricks for bringing out the highlights in her hair.

"You know how it is," Amy said, grabbing a hair-brush out of Maria's hand. "You start working with someone—especially on an intense project like ours—and one thing kind of leads to another." She stopped brushing her hair long enough to lean forward to admire her reflection in the mirror. "Naturally, Bruce is very attracted to me. I mean, at first I could see how hard he was trying to restrain himself, but it was just too much—for both of us. I really admire Bruce for wanting to let Regina down easily. After all, you know how fragile she is—how temperamental. If he told her how he felt about me right away, who knows what she'd do?"

I'm not sure if "fragile" is a word I'd use to describe Regina. It's true that Regina is shy and always seems sort of, um, gentle. But Regina fought to lead a normal life for sixteen years, despite not being able to hear. Then she traveled all the way to Switzerland for those treatments to give her almost normal hearing. "Fragile" doesn't seem like the right word for someone who's come through all that and now is just like any normal teen-ager—except that Regina's sweeter and friendlier than most of the kids I know. And tons richer. And did I mention her glossy black hair, an ivory complexion, enormous blue eyes, and perfect figure?

On the other hand, Regina is totally in love with Bruce. He's the first guy she's ever dated seriously. I think it would tear her up to lose him. She may not be fragile, but she is sensitive—and inexperienced when it comes to boys.

I crossed my arms and stared at Amy. "You really think things have gone so far that Bruce is going to dump Regina for you?"

"Jessica, please! You make it sound so heartless. It's obvious that their relationship is over, that's all. Bruce has pretty much said so himself. I don't want to push him or anything. After all, they've been together a long time. But I do think it's inevitable that they're going to split up." She smiled knowingly. "And I intend to be right there for Bruce when they do!"

Well, Diary, it would be too bad if poor Regina gets hurt, after everything she's been through. On the other hand, if Bruce really does like Amy better than Regina, why shouldn't he go for it? And if Amy really likes Bruce, why shouldn't she go for it? Besides, if Bruce really is hanging all over Amy, that means he's reverting back to his arrogant, womanizing ways, which means that he's all wrong for Regina—but perfect for Amy, who's kind of a man-eater, herself.

(Is Bruce reverting? Gag. I've been enjoying life without God's Gift to Girls.)

Anyway, no matter who wins, the race is sure to be interesting.

*I told Elizabeth all about it tonight—
while she made dinner and I stood around
letting her think I was helping. (You ought to
try it sometime, Diary. It's a very effective
way of getting out of doing work!) As I predicted, she was horrified by the whole thing.
Elizabeth is not exactly the all's-fair-in-love-
and-war type. . . .*

"I can't believe Amy Sutton," Elizabeth fumed as
she rinsed a head of lettuce in the kitchen sink. "It
sounds to me like she's completely out of line. She's
wrong to be trying to get Bruce to like her, and she's
certainly wrong to be telling all you guys about it!
What if Regina hears about it from someone before
Bruce talks to her? That is, if Amy's right and there
really is something going on. It wouldn't surprise me
if she's just made the whole thing up."

"I don't think it's necessarily such a bad thing," I
said, snatching a slice of avocado she had cut up for
the salad.

Elizabeth, always the big sister, actually slapped
my hand. "Save some of that for dinner, OK?" Then
she gave me this searching look. "Don't you care
about Regina's feelings? I can't believe Bruce, even
the old Bruce, would consider giving up someone as
wonderful as Regina for Amy."

The funny thing was that Amy had originally been
Elizabeth's friend, not mine. In sixth grade she was
more interested in building tree forts with Elizabeth
than swapping fashion magazines with me. But Amy

had moved to Connecticut for five years. When she returned to California in our junior year, she had become cool, like me and Lila and Cara.

"Liz, I can't see why you're so hard on Amy." I gave her a meaningful stare. "Anyway, I don't think it's healthy for couples to stay together so long. I mean, what's the point of being young if you can't have lots of different experiences? Bruce and Regina have been together forever—even longer than you and Jeffrey!"

"I'll try to ignore that. I know you aren't big on serious relationships, but even you have to admit that Regina's done Bruce a lot of good. If he really likes Amy—"

"Amy says it's because they've been thrown together so much on this health-class project. They're supposed to be doing an oral report on drugs in Sweet Valley, and Amy says they're finding out all kinds of stuff. She says it's just natural that she and Bruce would end up feeling really strongly about each other."

"That makes absolutely no sense," Elizabeth objected. For someone who was dating the most attractive boy in the junior class, Elizabeth sure didn't know anything about mutual attractions. "All I can say is that Bruce would be out of his mind to lose a great thing like his relationship with Regina. Let's just hope he realizes that—and that Amy's exaggerating things. It sure wouldn't be the first time."

Elizabeth's wrong, Diary. I know Amy pretty well. And when she wants something as badly as she wants Bruce, she almost always finds a way to get it.

Elizabeth is also wrong to criticize Amy for going after Bruce. Think about it, Diary. Regina isn't Amy's problem. Amy doesn't have any commitment to her. If Amy makes a play for Bruce, it's totally up to him to go along with it or not. Amy can be pretty convincing, but nobody's twisting Bruce's arm. If he chooses Amy in the end, it's his own free will. That's Bruce and Regina's problem, not Amy's.

But I wish I hadn't brought up Elizabeth and Jeffrey's relationship. Thinking about Jeffrey makes me so depressed, Diary. And excited. I don't know what to do about him.

I just had a scary thought. Liz is spazzing out because she doesn't want Regina to hear about Bruce and Amy through the grapevine. What if Liz spills the beans to Regina? She'd better not tell, or I'm dead. And knowing Amy's temper, I'd expect it to be a slow, excruciating death—like being forced to listen to nonstop Winston Egbert jokes for a week. Liz had better keep her mouth shut.

Friday night

Amy gave me the lowdown at lunch today. Last night she went to Bruce's house (mansion) so they could work on their project

285

for health class. They were sitting on the patio overlooking the gardens. First, Amy got Bruce to agree to a meeting tonight with her and her cousin Mimi, to work on their report. Mimi, who's studying to be a social worker, works at a drug-rehabilitation clinic and knows a lot about the local drug scene.

The significant thing about the meeting with Mimi is that Amy finagled it for tonight—Friday night. Date night. That means Bruce will be out with Amy on a Friday night instead of out with Regina!

But Amy didn't stop there. She made up a great story to tell Bruce, about how she had dreamed that they were working together on their report when suddenly he kissed her.

If I were wearing a hat, I'd take it off to Amy. What a brilliant strategy for getting a guy to realize he wants to kiss you. I may use that tactic myself sometime. Naturally, it worked for Amy. With a lead-in like that, the old Bruce resurfaced, and he just couldn't help himself. Amy told me the whole story at lunch in the school cafeteria today. . . .

"You should have seen the stars in Bruce's eyes when he kissed me!"

"So you really think he's going to break up with Regina?"

"Of course he will. And Bruce had better tell her soon. I don't mind being the 'other woman' for a little while, but it'll get boring soon. I want the whole world to know that Bruce and I are in love." Then she got down to her real motivations. "And I want him to take me to the country club and buy me lots of expensive presents and stuff. How can he do that if he's still going out with Regina?"

"You've got a point," I said with a laugh. After all, what's the good of dating a guy whose family owns half the town, if nobody can know about it? Then I remembered something. "Hey! Liz and I were going to invite some people over tomorrow for a cookout. If we invite you *and* Regina, what's Bruce going to do?"

Amy shrugged. "It'll be fun to watch and see. Actually, I think it'll do Bruce a lot of good to see us together. Don't you think I'm lots prettier than Regina is?"

I squinted across the room at the table where Regina was sitting. "I don't know, Amy," I said honestly. "Regina's awfully pretty. Hey! What's she doing eating lunch with Justin Belson? I didn't know they were friends!"

"Who cares who Regina eats with—as long as it isn't Bruce. I think you're wrong about her looks, Jess. She's way too pale. She looks like the sort of girl you'd want to bring home to meet your parents, not the sort of girl who can really make your pulse race."

"I think you've been watching too much TV. You're starting to sound like a perfume commercial." But my eyes were still on Regina and Justin, about as unlikely a pair as I could imagine. "The last I heard, Justin was on academic probation," I said. "He isn't exactly Regina's type. He hangs out with Molly Hecht and Jan Brown and that whole crowd."

"Yeah, Molly Hecht is trouble," Amy agreed. "My cousin Mimi saw her at a party in L.A. last weekend that was busted by the police. Two of the college guys got arrested for having cocaine."

"You think Molly and Justin are on drugs?"

But for once gossip about other people couldn't hold Amy's attention. "I honestly don't know," she said with a shrug. "And to tell you the truth, Jess, I just don't care. All I care about is making sure that Bruce leaves your house tomorrow night with *me* and not with Regina! If you've got any ideas on how to make that happen, promise you'll let me know."

For some reason Regina and Justin together made me uneasy. Justin was kind of cute—a little too thin, but tall, with thick auburn hair and nice, chiseled features. But he had a tough-guy expression. Maybe it was because his father had been stabbed to death a couple years earlier, when the liquor store he owned was held up. And there was no denying that Justin hung out with some rough kids.

Somebody as innocent and sheltered as Regina might not know just how rough, I thought. I hoped she had the sense to stay away from him and his crowd.

Apart from my concerns about Justin's reputation and background, seeing him and Regina together does throw another element of suspense into the whole Bruce-Amy-

Regina triangle. Our cookout tomorrow may be very interesting. I'm getting into the drama of it all.

Saturday night, late

Did I say drama? That was an understatement. . . .

From the moment Amy walked into my backyard Saturday night, everyone at the party knew we were headed for disaster.

The weather was perfect, the late-afternoon sunlight was golden, and the smell of burning charcoal was making us all hungry. Most of the guys were playing some kooky game Winston was making up on the spot—a combination of Frisbee, softball, and badminton, I think. A group of girls, including Regina and me, were sitting around a table on the patio. And Bruce, who had been declared King Coal, was presiding over the grill, looking spiffy in a snow-white polo shirt.

Amy ducked the Frisbee as she hurried across the lawn toward us, looking like a model in a pure-white sundress and cotton espadrilles. She stopped in a pool of golden sunlight, which made her blond hair shine and her dress sparkle. Bruce froze at the grill, captivated. For a second that seemed like an hour, Amy's gaze locked on to Bruce's, and she smiled her smug little smile.

Then the connection was broken. Amy joined us

at the patio table and Bruce's eyes swiveled down to
the grill, where he went back to fiddling with the
charcoal. But in that one second everything had
changed. And everyone in my backyard knew it, including Regina.

I had seen the way every speck of color drained
from Regina's face at the sight of Amy's little smile
and the look of understanding in Bruce's eyes. And a
few minutes later, when Amy offered to help Bruce
flip hamburgers, Regina blinked furiously, as if she
were trying to hold back tears.

> *Elizabeth looked uncomfortable. I knew
> she was chastising herself for listening to me
> when I told her not to tell Regina that Amy
> was after Bruce—and that Bruce wasn't re-
> sisting. But I didn't think it would have made
> a difference if Liz had told Regina earlier. It
> certainly wouldn't have changed anything
> between Bruce and Amy.*
>
> *I know it sounds as if things had hit the boil-
> ing point, but the situation didn't really heat
> up until the charcoal was cooling down. . . .*

Candles were flickering under a dark-gray sky
and everyone was stuffed full of hamburgers and hot
dogs and marshmallows. People were scattered
around the pool and across the yard in groups of two
and three and four, singing songs, telling ghost stories, lying on their backs to watch stars pop out in the
sky, and—well, kissing.

Then Elizabeth noticed Regina sitting alone by the edge of the pool. Elizabeth started looking around for Bruce. Suddenly she grabbed Jeffrey's hand. "Look! Isn't that Bruce over there behind that tree?"

Jeffrey squinted into the dusk. "Uh-oh," he groaned when he realized what Bruce was doing. "He isn't alone, either. He and Amy couldn't resist each other even long enough for him to take Regina home."

Elizabeth went to distract Regina to keep her from noticing that her boyfriend was necking with another girl. And Jeffrey ran over to break up the activity between Bruce and Amy.

But Elizabeth and Jeffrey were too late. Regina's eyes widened as she stared across the lawn at the spot where Jeffrey was emerging from behind a tree. Right behind him were Bruce and Amy, their white clothes gleaming in the dusk. Both had sheepish expressions on their faces.

Unfortunately, Regina wasn't the only one who saw them. Everyone else at the party noticed, too.

Regina whirled on Elizabeth. "You knew where he was all along. You all knew! Why didn't you tell me, Liz? I thought you were my friend!"

Elizabeth patted Regina's arm. "I didn't think it was up to me. Let me take you home. I'm sorry I didn't say anything. I just wanted to keep you from getting hurt."

Regina jerked her arm away. "Let go of me! I thought you were my friend," she repeated in a voice so cold that it sounded like the voice of a stranger. "You all knew! You knew, and you let me come here and make a fool of myself!"

"Regina," Elizabeth said, her eyes brimming with tears, "please let me try to explain—"

Regina stormed across the yard to Bruce, her black hair flying behind her like a raven. "Don't give me that look!" she snapped, trembling with rage. "I want your car keys. I'm taking the Porsche, and I'm going to drive it to my house. Come pick it up whenever you want it. The keys will be in the mailbox." Her face shone ashen in the candlelight. "I never want to speak to you as long as I live!"

The backyard was so quiet that everybody could hear Regina's ragged breathing as she turned to Amy. "I hate you!" she cried. "I hate all of you! You make me feel as if I'm worthless. Worse than worthless!"

Bruce took a deep breath. "Regina—"

"Give me the car keys!" she insisted.

A few minutes later Regina was gone. We all heard the door of Bruce's Porsche slam shut in front of the house. And we all heard the squeal of tires as Regina sped away.

Elizabeth is ready to kill me. In fact, she just spent half an hour complaining to me about pretty much everything I've done, said, or thought in the last two weeks.

It's not fair! Elizabeth has no right to be mad at me. It's not my fault that Regina and

Bruce broke up. That was Regina's decision, and it was because of Bruce and Amy—not me! But Elizabeth is mad at me for everything. She says I ruined her friendship with Regina. She says I encouraged Amy to flirt with Bruce in the first place. And she's mad at me for pressuring her not to tell Regina the truth about Amy and Bruce.

I'm sick of Elizabeth acting as if she's so much better than I am. And I'm sick of her blaming me for things that aren't my fault! Sometimes, Diary, I really want to put my sister in her place.

Monday night

Amy is still impossible. She talks about nothing but her and Bruce. And she talks about Regina. She's not worried about how Regina feels, of course. She's just worried about how Regina's feelings might affect her and Bruce.

Amy was blabbing on and on about Bruce again at lunchtime, and it was becoming even more sickening than the cafeteria food.

"I really do think Bruce should forget all about Regina," she said. "It bothers me the way he keeps bringing up her name all the time. I mean, it seems to me that Regina is *history* as far as he's concerned, don't you agree?"

Until then I had been finding this whole love triangle to be kind of entertaining. But now that Amy had gotten her hooks into Bruce, the only interesting part left was Regina. I pointed across the room with a french fry. Regina and Justin were emerging from the lunch line together, carrying trays. "You know, I've seen Regina and Justin Belson together *three* times today, and it's only lunchtime. What do you think is going on between them?"

Amy dropped her fork. "Oh Lord. I hope Regina doesn't do something stupid like go rushing right into another relationship. It might make Bruce crazy."

I could have reminded Amy that Bruce was the one who had rushed right into another relationship. But I kept my mouth shut.

Elizabeth believes Regina is upset with the world because she thinks everyone has treated her badly. Not just Bruce and Amy, but Elizabeth and everyone else who knew about Amy but didn't tell her. Elizabeth thinks Regina wants revenge. And to a girl like Regina, who's been sheltered all her life—and who's wholesome and brave and pretty and studious and a model citizen—the best way to get revenge is to hang out with a lowlife.

Maybe Justin is the best way Regina can find to show us all that she's different from the old Regina who got taken advantage of. Especially since Justin is about as far away as you can get from rich, spoiled, aristocratic Bruce. Maybe she's trying to show us that she doesn't need any of us— that she's perfectly capable of finding other friends.

I just hope Regina isn't going to do anything stupid.

Wednesday night

Regina has left our crowd completely and found a new one—Justin's crowd. Justin doesn't seem too bad. And as I said, he's really kind of cute, which can make up for a lot, in my book. But he hangs out with freaks.

Molly Hecht is trouble, big time. She's a junior, like us, but she's a teeny little blonde who looks about ten years old. Everyone says she's into hard-core drugs. I think she and Justin used to be a couple, but they broke up and are just friends now. The others are even worse: Jan Brown and her boyfriend Jay Benson. They're mean, they're hardly ever in school, and everyone says they're druggies.

It's hard to imagine what sweet little Regina has in common with them. Today Elizabeth tried to warn her to be careful, but Regina got mad and yelled at her. So naturally Elizabeth blamed me. Elizabeth always blames me.

Wow. My instincts were right about Justin's friends being pond scum. Amy just called to tell me about the meeting she and Bruce had with her cousin Mimi this evening, at the Box Tree Cafe. Mimi told them some pretty scary things about the local drug scene. . . .

Mimi gazed across the table at Amy and Bruce "Do either of you two know a junior named Margaret Hecht?"

"Margaret Hecht?" Bruce repeated. "I don't think so. Why?"

"She's supposedly part of a group of kids at Sweet Valley High who are really heavily into drugs. I've got a few other names—Janice Brown, James Benson— but the reason I'm bringing up Margaret's name is that she's supposed to have a big open party at her mother's house on Saturday night, and it looks like one of the biggest dealers in my college is number one on her guest list."

Bruce's eyes widened in recognition. "Margaret— you mean *Molly!*" He turned to Amy, horrified. "Oh God. That's Justin Belson's old girlfriend. The guy Regina's been hanging around with."

Mimi raised her eyebrows. "So you know Molly Hecht?"

Bruce nodded. "At least by sight, anyway. She's a tiny little blonde."

"Well, from the people I've talked to, she isn't the problem. It's her best friend Jan who is. This girl Janice Brown seems to be incredibly messed up. I don't know how they ever got to know Buzz Jackson, but for their sake they'd be better off without him."

Amy was scribbling notes frantically. "Wait, wait! Who is Buzz Jackson?"

"Buzz happens to be the biggest cocaine dealer at my college right now. He's bad news."

"We're trying hard to get Buzz locked up," Mimi continued a few minutes later. "The people I work for at the clinic really want him put away. We've been working with private detectives for the past month trying to track him down. That's how I know he's been invited to the Hechts' on Saturday."

"What can we do to help?" Bruce asked.

"If you know anyone who's supposed to go to the party, warn them. Buzz is a smooth operator, and he's been known to get kids who have never so much as tasted a sip of beer to try something dangerous."

Bruce paled. "I'd better call Regina."

Amy, of course, wasn't pleased at the prospect of Bruce still being so worried about Regina. And she was even less pleased at the thought of any contact between the two of them. But she would have looked like a witch if she'd objected.

Bruce did call Regina, Diary, just an hour ago. He told Amy about the call. But Regina doesn't want advice from any of her old friends—least of all Bruce. She says she can take care of herself.

I wonder if I should tell Elizabeth all this. Maybe not. Last time I told her something about Regina, I only ended up getting into trouble. On the other hand, if Regina really could get hurt, somebody sensible like Elizabeth might know how to prevent it. Well, Liz is already asleep, so there's no point in worrying about it tonight. I'll decide tomorrow.

Friday night, late

I'm so mixed up. I did something terrible to my sister today, though she doesn't know anything about it. I knew it was wrong. I never should have done it. But at the same time, I'm glad I did. Now I feel so guilty and depressed! As I said, I'm mixed up.

It's all Elizabeth's fault for being so mad at me this week. If I hadn't been mad at her for being mad at me, maybe I wouldn't have done it. But it's not fair, Diary! It's not fair that she gets to be so happy while I'm so lonely and miserable.

There. I said it. I'm lonely. Everybody else has someone. Steven and Cara. Winston and Maria. Penny and Neil. Amy and Bruce now. And even Regina and Justin. But most of all, Elizabeth and Jeffrey!!!

Jeffrey . . .

Elizabeth caught up with me at our lockers before my last-period gym class Friday.

I braced myself to be yelled at. I didn't think I'd done anything wrong, but with the way she'd been acting all week, that didn't seem to matter.

"Jessica, I'm glad I found you," she said in a rushed voice. I breathed a sigh of relief. Whatever she was up to had her in too much of a hurry to spare any time for screaming at me. "I've got to leave school right now," she said, twirling her combination lock. "Penny's out sick today, and there's a problem with *The Oracle*. I have to drive downtown to the printer's and get things straightened out."

"Elizabeth," I said with a sigh of mock martyrdom. "I really don't have time to write another last-minute article for you on bad dating experiences."

Elizabeth yanked her navy sweater out of her locker and turned on me with an impatient glare. Apparently, she was in no mood for joking around. "I just need you to track down Jeffrey to deliver a message for me before school ends today. *Do you think you can handle that?*"

I didn't like her tone, but she'd been so touchy all week that I ignored her sarcasm and tried to be pleasant. "No problem. What do you want me to tell him?"

"Tell him I'm sorry I have to break our dinner date for tonight. I won't be home from the printer's until six o'clock. I had planned to work on my Civil War paper for Mr. Jaworski this afternoon. Now I'll have to finish my rough draft tonight if I want to go

299

to Lila's movie-watching party tomorrow. So I can't go to Tiberino's with Jeffrey."

"You're staying home to study on a Friday night?"

You would think I'd be used to Elizabeth's screwed-up priorities after sixteen years, but she still surprises me. If we didn't look exactly alike, I'd think she was left on our doorstep as an infant, by visiting martians.

"Yes, I'm staying home to study," she said, glaring at me. "But I don't want to wreck Jeffrey's evening. Tell him to go out and have a good time. I'll call him tomorrow to apologize myself and to confirm things for Lila's party."

I shrugged. "Sure. I'll tell him."

She gave me a searching look. "You won't forget?"

"You don't have to treat me like I'm six years old. I *said* I'd do it, didn't I?"

She nodded, satisfied. Then she slammed her locker door and hurried down the hall, tossing the navy sweater over her shoulder.

My intentions were good, Diary. I was going to find Jeffrey after class and deliver Elizabeth's message. As it turned out, I didn't have to look for Jeffrey. He found me first.

I was standing at my locker in the crowded hallway, after the last bell. I had just slipped on my own navy-blue cardigan when I heard a deep, sexy voice behind me and felt a warm, strong hand on my shoulder.

"Elizabeth," Jeffrey said. Then I turned to face him just in time to see his sexy smile fade. "Oh, Jessica!" he said, blushing. "I'm sorry, Jess. Your locker is right next to Liz's, and I know she wore a blue sweater today. . . ."

Normally, I hate being mistaken for Elizabeth, but it was hard to be angry at someone with beautiful dark-green eyes, thick blond hair, and the best body in the junior class. "It's OK, Jeffrey," I said with a smile, wishing he were as happy to see me as he would be to see my sister. "Actually, I'm glad you found me. Elizabeth asked me to give you a message."

I opened my mouth to tell Jeffrey that my sister had to break their date. Honest, Diary! I really did mean to tell him. But then I heard my own voice saying something entirely different. . . .

"She had to go to the printer's for *The Oracle,* but she'll be back for your dinner date. She wants you to pick her up a little early so she can get home in time to put in some work on her history paper."

"No problem," Jeffrey said with another big, sexy grin. "What's good for her? Six o'clock?"

"Make it five thirty."

At five twenty I was ready. I'd left a note on the kitchen table for Elizabeth, saying I had a date. My parents were having dinner in Los Angeles with a prospective client of my mother's, so I knew the identity of my date would remain a secret—as long as Elizabeth didn't arrive home early from the printer's.

Otherwise, I was sure I could make Jeffrey believe I was my twin. My hair was pulled back with her pearl-studded barrettes. I had on the aqua cambric dress that Heather Sanford had designed especially for Elizabeth. In my opinion the dress reached way too high on the neck and low on the legs. But its body-skimming form was flattering, the skirt twirled out nicely when I moved, and the dozens of tiny pearl buttons were more elegant than anything I owned. Also, its aqua shade made my eyes look even bluer, especially with navy mascara and eyeliner—just a tad more than Elizabeth would have worn.

I stared at myself in the mirror, and I could have sworn I saw my sister staring back. All I needed now was Jeffrey on my arm, I told myself. And I'd be magically transformed from the evil twin to the perfect twin.

When the doorbell rang, I had a moment of panic. *This isn't right!* my brain kept screaming at me. I couldn't go through with it. As I rushed down the stairs, I decided I would have to tell Jeffrey the truth.

Then he was standing in the doorway, and my resolve faded, along with the voice of conscience in my head. Jeffrey looked absolutely gorgeous. He was wearing a tweed jacket and navy pants. Through his white cotton shirt I could see a hint of color—a faint reflection of his tanned, well-developed chest. In his hand was an orchid. But it was his face that held my attention. On it was the expression he always reserved for Elizabeth. For months I'd dreamed of his green eyes looking at me that way, so full of love. And I knew I was about to have the greatest night of my life.

"You look incredible," Jeffrey said. Then he leaned forward and kissed me. It was only a quick peck on the lips, but I thought my heart would pound right out of my chest.

"Are you feeling all right?" he asked. "You look a little flushed."

"I'm feeling terrific," I said, careful to sound like my sister. "I guess I was so anxious to see you that I sprinted down the stairs a little too fast."

He pinned the orchid on my dress. Even through the fabric my skin felt as if it were burning up wherever his fingers grazed me.

Dinner was fabulous, Diary. Jeffrey was fabulous. We laughed and talked, and his eyes looked even deeper green by candlelight. Of course, I had to watch what I said very carefully. But I know my sister better than anybody. And I have a lot of practice impersonating her. When Jeffrey hit on a subject I was unsure of, it was easy to steer the conversation around so that he could supply me with the information I needed.

Luckily for me, Elizabeth had been so freaked out about Regina all week that

Jeffrey didn't think it was strange for me to seem distracted.

My sister is the luckiest girl in the universe. I had never been on a date with a guy who listened to me so intently and accepted me so readily.

Jeffrey thought I looked fantastic—he said so over and over again, and I knew from the admiration in his eyes that he was sincere. But he loves Elizabeth for more than what she looks like. He loves her for what she is like. It took me a while to figure it out, but that's what was so different about dinner tonight. I'm used to boys who want to go out with me because I'm pretty and popular. That's all right, I guess. We have fun together. But this was different. This was special. This was what it was like to be with someone who loved me for myself. And I could almost make myself forget that it was Elizabeth he loved.

For a few minutes while we were eating cannoli for dessert, I was afraid Jeffrey was getting suspicious.

"You seem so different, tonight, Liz," Jeffrey said. His green eyes were like pools of warm water, deep enough to drown in.

I concentrated on my last forkful of cannoli. "I'm the same person I always am," I told him. "What seems different?"

He smiled. "I'm not sure. I guess you're more—*intense.*"

"Does it bother you?"

"Let's just say it intrigues me."

I sighed. "I guess it's because I'm so glad to be here with you tonight—after the rotten time we've all had this week. It's all this stuff going on with Regina. I've been so uptight about her thinking I betrayed her and then turning to those awful kids for friendship." I laughed. "You should see how rotten I've been to Jessica all week. By now I think I've blamed her for everything from Regina and Bruce's breakup to the Great Depression, the Civil War, and the food in the school cafeteria!"

"She'll get over it."

"I know."

He was gazing into my eyes with such intensity that I wanted to grab him and start ripping off his clothes, right there in the restaurant. I guess he was thinking along the same lines. "I know you have a paper to write," he said, "but do you have time for a stroll on the beach first?"

Warning sirens began screeching in my head, but I tuned them out. "For you, Jeffrey, I have all the time in the world."

On the beach is where it happened, Diary. I knew we shouldn't have gone there. I knew it was a bad idea. But I couldn't help myself. I've been in love about twice a month for the last five years. But this was different.

305

This was real. And I knew that I had to see it through.

"I love walking on the beach at night," I said, dabbling a bare foot in the cool surf. Low waves rustled endlessly against the softly shining sand. The sky and water were a deep midnight-blue, with a million tiny, twinkling stars mirrored by the golden lights of boats. A seagull flew overhead, a ghostly white blur in the night.

"Me too," Jeffrey said in a husky voice. I realized with a start that he was as breathless as I was. "As long as I'm walking with you, Elizabeth."

I could see his face in the light from the pier, and it was full of love and longing. He pulled me to his warm, strong chest and placed his lips against mine.

Oh, Diary. It was the most incredible kiss I have ever had in my entire life. A romance-novel kiss. The feelings started with my mouth and spread through my whole body so I thought I was on fire with this delirious, uncontrollable happiness. I wish I were a real writer, like Elizabeth, so I could describe it to you better. But suddenly the kiss changed. A shudder went through Jeffrey's body, and his hands tightened on my shoulders.

Jeffrey's eyes opened at the same time as mine. In them I saw the sudden realization that the twin he was kissing was not Elizabeth.

We separated, and Jeffrey looked at me wordlessly.

306

Different emotions flashed through his eyes in that brief instant—recognition, shock, excitement, guilt, and desire. I held his gaze for a second that seemed like an hour. We both knew what we were doing, but in that second we both realized that we didn't want to stop.

Jeffrey pulled me roughly toward him again and kissed me even more passionately. I responded with a moan, feeling as if my heart would explode with a million tiny, twinkling stars of light.

We were wrong. We knew we were wrong, but we did it anyway. And after one delicious, unforgettable minute, the guilt began creeping in until it overshadowed everything else. We pulled apart, overcome with it. Then we stared at each other wordlessly, shaking our heads.

Jeffrey and I didn't say a word to each other as we walked back to the car and drove to my house. Before I opened the car door, I looked at him and he looked at me. We still didn't talk, but we communicated just the same. Our eyes said that we both loved Elizabeth. And that we both knew our kiss this evening was the first and last one we would ever share.

And maybe—just maybe—Jeffrey regretted that fact almost as much as I did.

Friday night, even later

Oh, God, Diary! I just had a horrible thought. Jeffrey and Elizabeth claim that they're always honest with each other! What if he tells her?

He can't. He just can't.

I wish I never had to see Jeffrey again. It would be easier if I could forget about him. But I do have to see him again. I'll have to convince him to keep this secret from Elizabeth. She must never find out. It would just kill her.

Saturday afternoon

Elizabeth was furious with me at break-fast this morning. But, thank goodness, it had nothing to do with last night.

I finally decided to tell her all the stuff Amy told me Thursday night about Molly's party. . . .

Elizabeth pushed away her empty cereal bowl, so hard that I thought it would clatter to the floor. "Jessica, I can't believe you waited until now to tell me about this! Amy told you all this stuff Thursday night about Molly's party?"

I concentrated on my left index finger as if filing the nail to a perfectly smooth edge was the most important task on earth. "I just didn't think it was something Regina couldn't handle, that's all."

Actually, I had decided yesterday to let Elizabeth know about Molly's party. Other events distracted me last night, as you can imagine. But I couldn't exactly explain that to Elizabeth.

"Anyway," I concluded, sounding lame even to myself, "you always get mad at me when I spread rumors."

Elizabeth shook her head, distraught. "It figures. The one time I would've liked to have a little advance warning about something, you decide to get coy about spreading rumors."

Don't you hate it when she uses words like "coy"? No normal person talks that way.

I told myself that, but then I sighed. I was trying to be mad at Elizabeth, to make me feel less guilty for my evening with Jeffrey and that perfect kiss under the twinkling stars. But it wasn't working. I had done a terrible thing to my sister, and nothing could make me forget it.

Anyhow, Diary, Elizabeth ran right upstairs to call Regina. I hurried after her, although telling Regina seemed like a dorky idea to me. After all, Elizabeth had already tried to warn her about Justin's crowd. And Bruce had called her Thursday night to tell her not to go to the party. If I were Regina, I'd be getting sick to death of people my own age acting as if they had the right to run my life. And I'd probably rush right out to Molly's party, just to show them that I could make my own decisions.

But Elizabeth will never understand the teenage mind, never having been a teenager herself.

As usual my instincts were correct. And as usual nobody cared what I thought. . . .

"Regina?" Elizabeth said into the receiver while I listened from the doorway of her bedroom. "It's Elizabeth Wakefield. Regina, I wanted to apologize again for our misunderstanding."

I wasn't sure what Regina said—and Elizabeth never saw fit to enlighten me. But whatever it was, it sure made my sister happy. Elizabeth smiled wider than she had in weeks. "I'm so glad you're not mad at me anymore! That means you won't get mad when I tell you what Jessica just told me about Molly Hecht's party."

It seemed to me as if Regina hadn't had time to answer, but Elizabeth kept talking as if she assumed Regina was willing to listen. Meanwhile I silently cursed my sister for bringing my name into it. If Regina really thought of Molly as a friend, she would now be ticked off to think I was running around town, telling everyone Molly was a juvenile delinquent.

"The thing is, Regina," Elizabeth said, "I'm sure Justin's a nice guy, but what do you really know about Molly? Or Jan Brown? Or any of their friends? Apparently some guy named Buzz is supposed to show up at the Hechts' house with drugs. Real drugs—stuff like cocaine and speed."

She paused while Regina replied, and I watched as Elizabeth's hopeful smile crumbled into a look of dismay. Apparently, Regina had not appreciated the warning.

"Well, I guess you know Justin better than I do," Elizabeth croaked out.

After another second my sister closed her eyes and practically whispered her next words into the receiver: "Please be careful."

I could tell from the way she stared at the receiver that Regina had hung up angry. And I could tell from the way she turned to glare at me in her doorway that I was not welcome in my sister's room just then.

> *Obviously, I'm not the only one who hates it when Elizabeth tries to act like somebody's mother.*
>
> *Well, Diary, Elizabeth finally decided later this afternoon that she's been too hard on me all week. I don't know why it took her so long to see that I didn't cause Regina to lose Bruce or to hate Elizabeth. She said she was too distraught about Regina to think straight. I don't know for sure what changed her mind, but I know she talked to Jeffrey on the phone today. Maybe he put in a good word for me. Obviously, he hasn't mentioned last night to her.*
>
> *How weird. Now that I really do have something to feel guilty about, Elizabeth is no*

*longer mad at me. And somehow that makes
me feel even guiltier, even though she was
mad at me in the first place for things that
weren't my fault. Does that make any sense?
Anyhow, Jeffrey is coming by to pick up both
me and Elizabeth in a few minutes, to go to
Lila's movie-watching party. Me and Jeffrey
and Elizabeth in a car together. Doesn't that
sound cozy?*

    Diary, I feel terrible.

    *So does Elizabeth. But she feels ter-
rible about Regina. In fact, she's throwing
a fit. I'm not used to seeing her in such a
panic. . . .*

"What am I supposed to do?" Elizabeth wailed to
me as we stood in the bathroom getting ready for the
party. "I just can't let Regina go over to the Hechts'. I
can't!"

"I hate to say it, but I don't really see you have
much choice," I told her. *This is a switch,* I thought.
Elizabeth was falling to pieces, while I was the mature voice of reason.

I sprayed my hair with a new spray-on highlighter
I had just bought that day. "Look, this stuff goes on
just like spray paint!" I exclaimed, admiring the red-
dish streaks. "Isn't it fun? I look like a rock star."

"You look like a freak. Help me, Jess! Tell me
what I should do."

"Well, you could call Nicholas," I said, truly hoping to give Elizabeth an idea that would make her

feel better. I figured I owed her that much. "That way at least you'd dump some of the responsibility onto *him*."

Elizabeth's eyes widened as if I'd just announced a cure for cancer or a new design for the space shuttle. "That's not such a bad idea," she admitted.

Why do people always look so surprised when they say things like that about me?

"You know, Jess," she continued, "you may have a point. Why didn't I think of it myself?"

> To tell you the truth, Diary, I wasn't convinced that it would do much good, as far as Regina was concerned. I know from years of annoying experience that an older sibling is the last person whose advice is wanted in situations like these. Especially when an ex-boyfriend and an ex-girlfriend have already taken turns nagging you to do something.
>
> Actually, I can't quite believe that Regina could be in serious trouble. Could she be?
>
> This is going to sound awful, but I even envy Regina a little bit. No, I'm not saying I want to go to parties with sleazy drug dealers. But I've always been a little curious. I know people think of me as a partyer. But I've never done any drugs more serious than aspirin. Not even marijuana. I'm not saying I have any great desire to do drugs. I'm not even saying I would puff on a joint if someone offered it to me. I'd probably be too

scared. But I admit that I have wondered what it's like.

Very late Saturday

Oh God, Diary. OH GOD! Regina Morrow is dead.

Monday night

Did I say I was curious about drugs, Diary? I'm not. I never want to be anywhere near them, ever!

We're all numb. We're walking around in shock. I'm not even sure I can write. But I'll try to explain what I know about what happened at Molly Hecht's house Saturday night. . . .

Regina didn't fit in with Justin's friends, and she knew it. According to what Justin told the police, she was uncomfortable from the moment she arrived. The room was dim and smoky, the stereo was blasting acid rock loud enough to hurt her ears, and the place was packed with people ranging from junior-high kids to college age. Everyone was guzzling beer. Somebody handed one to Regina, and she drank it, even though she never liked beer. A few people were smoking pot, but things were still relatively tame.

Jan began giving Regina a hard time about being a little rich girl and a Goody Two-shoes. And Molly accused her of trying to steal Justin from her, even though Molly and Justin had split up, and Regina and Justin were only friends.

Then somebody yelled, "OK, everyone, let's party!"

Buzz had arrived.

Regina tried to slip out to take a walk in the fresh air, but Jan called her back. That's when Justin realized he had been neglecting Regina.

"Come sit down for a little while," he said, resting a hand on her arm. "Then I'll take a walk with you."

Jan gave Regina a dirty look. "We're having a perfectly good time right here. Why do you have to drag Justin away and ruin it?"

> *I think Regina wanted to fit in with Justin's friends. And she didn't want them to think she was stealing Justin. Mostly, I believe she was sick of being obedient and sheltered. She was sick of having people tell her how to run her life—people like her parents, Nicholas, Bruce, and Elizabeth—even though she must have been beginning to realize that they had reason to be concerned about her welfare.*
>
> *If only she had listened to them!*

So Regina sat down with Jan and the others. When Buzz started pulling out cocaine, Regina asked Justin to take her home. But Justin was afraid that his presence was the only thing keeping Buzz from trying Molly on heroin. So Justin asked Regina to stick it

315

out for half an hour. Neither of them planned on Regina doing any drugs.

Then Jan and Jay began making fun of Regina's inexperience. Buzz told her how wonderful cocaine would make her feel. Suddenly Regina wanted to prove to everyone that she wasn't as predictable as they thought. Just once she wanted to do something wild.

"I'd like to try it," Regina said. Instantly people were smiling at her. She was part of the group.

Regina did only two lines of cocaine. It shouldn't have been enough to hurt her badly. But drugs are unpredictable. A rare reaction to the cocaine caused a heart attack. Regina felt dizzy and sick. Her pulse began to race. Even the hardened drug users at Molly's party began to worry.

Then Regina's brother Nicholas marched in, bringing the police. Buzz managed to slip away from the house before they could catch him. Regina was conscious long enough to tell Nicholas, "It wasn't anyone's fault," and to ask for Elizabeth and Bruce.

She died in the hospital a few hours later.
School today was awful. Everyone was quiet and depressed. Mr. Cooper held an assembly to tell people the real story, because crazy rumors were already spreading like crabgrass. He said that Regina's family didn't want us to blame anyone except Buzz for her death.

"In no instance is anyone to be treated as if he or she had any responsibility in Regina's death," the principal said.

But a lot of people are to blame.

Justin and Molly didn't show up for school today. That was probably smart. Bruce kept muttering all day about wanting to kill them.

"I think they should be locked up for the rest of their lives," Lila said as a group of us talked about it this afternoon. "I can't stand them for what they did to Regina."

Jeffrey said he thought the police would take some kind of action against them.

"Maybe that's why Justin and Molly aren't in school today," I suggested. "Maybe they're already in prison."

I hoped it was true, but I figured it probably wasn't. It didn't seem fair. Justin really liked Regina. He knew she wasn't like the rest of his friends. I didn't understand why he would take her to a party like that. And I didn't understand why he would let her use cocaine.

As angry as we all are with Justin and Molly and their friends, I think we were only focusing on them because we were even angrier with ourselves. Bruce has dark circles under his eyes, as if he hasn't slept in two days. Even Amy has the grace to look guilty.

But Elizabeth is the person I'm the most concerned about. She's been so quiet since I picked her up at the hospital Saturday night. But one thing she did say was that it's our fault. All of us. And I know she blames herself most of all. I wish she would let herself off the hook. She did everything she could to keep Regina from going to that party. I'm afraid she'll never forgive herself.

It's my fault, too. I treated Regina's breakup with Bruce as if it were a spectator sport. And then I waited two days before I told anyone what Amy told me about the party Molly was planning. Sometimes I can't believe what a rotten person I am. Not to mention the horrible thing I did to my own sister this week—though I have to admit that it seems trivial compared to Regina's death. Nothing could be worse than this.

Saturday night, when we came home from the hospital, Elizabeth was crying as if she'd never be happy again. I liked Regina a lot. And I miss her terribly. But she was one of Elizabeth's very best friends. My sister was devastated. She leaned forward over the table, her shoulders wrenching with every sob.

Over Elizabeth's back my eyes locked with Jeffrey's. We didn't say anything, but we both understood. Elizabeth comes first. And we can't hurt her. We won't hurt her. Not for anything. Elizabeth will never know what happened between me and Jeffrey Friday night. Nobody will ever know.

If there's one thing I've learned, Diary, it's this: nothing is more important than the people you're the closest to. I only wish Regina hadn't died thinking her friends had betrayed her. I wish she understood how much we all loved her.

Friday afternoon

Regina understood!
A few days ago I found a letter in our mailbox. It was spooky. . . .

"Liz!" I yelled, hurrying into the house with an envelope in my hand. Elizabeth was in the kitchen, chopping onions for dinner. "Look, it's a letter for you. From Regina."

Elizabeth dropped her knife. "What are you talking about?"

"The return address says Regina Morrow. Open it, Liz."

Elizabeth turned the letter over and over in her hands, as confused as I was. The postmark showed that Regina had mailed the letter the day she died. But seeing her handwriting on the envelope made it seem as though the nightmare of the last few days had never happened at all. I could almost convince myself that Regina was alive and healthy.

Regina dashed off the letter while waiting for Justin to pick her up for Molly's party. In it she apologized for being mad at Elizabeth and told her how much she valued her advice. She said Elizabeth wasn't to blame for what happened at our cookout. The signs had been there for weeks, but Regina had refused to see that she and Bruce were growing apart—long before Amy appeared on the scene.

There was a memorial service for Regina at school today. I'm sorry to be staining you with big, blotchy tears, Diary. But I can't help crying just thinking about it. . . .

The memorial service began with the school choir singing a song from a German mass Regina used to love. Then Mr. Collins spoke. After that it was Elizabeth's turn. Nicholas had asked her to say a few words about Regina.

When my sister stepped onto the stage, she looked sad but composed. "I thought about bringing a prepared speech to read to you about Regina," she began in a clear, natural voice. "But somehow, each time I tried to write something, it seemed wrong to me. Regina would've hated something like that. Everything about Regina was natural, spontaneous, and unpretentious. The things she loved—like spending time with close friends, reading, taking long walks by the beach—were simple things."

Elizabeth's eyes shone with tears, but she blinked them back. "I don't really feel there's anything I can say about Regina's death, which is too tragic and too terrible for me to fathom. What I can say something about is Regina's life. I never knew anyone who faced problems, tough problems, with as much courage and humor. I never knew anyone who so gracefully managed to combine strength and gentleness. Regina was a fine person and a wonderful friend. And I know I'll never ever forget her."

I'll never forget Regina either, Diary. None of us will. If only Regina could have known how much she meant to all of us, how bleak the world seems without her. If she'd known, she never could have done this.

Epilogue

When I looked up from my diary, warm tears were streaming down my face. I lay my head on my cluttered desk and cried—for me and Jack, for me and Jeffrey, and for Elizabeth. But mostly I cried for Regina, who would never again be with her family and friends and know how much they—*we*—loved her.

After the tears stopped, I rose from my chair. Piece by piece, I slowly pulled the clothes from my suitcase, folded them neatly, and placed them in my dresser drawers—handling each item as if it were heavy, and very, very fragile.

Bantam Books in the Sweet Valley High series
Ask your bookseller for the books you have missed

SIGN UP FOR THE SWEET VALLEY HIGH® FAN CLUB!

Hey, girls! Get all the gossip on Sweet Valley High's® most popular teenagers when you join our fantastic Fan Club! As a member, you'll get all of this really cool stuff:

- Membership Card with your own personal Fan Club ID number
- A Sweet Valley High® Secret Treasure Box
- Sweet Valley High® Stationery
- Official Fan Club Pencil (for secret note writing!)
- Three Bookmarks
- A "Members Only" Door Hanger
- Two Skeins of J. & P. Coats® Embroidery Floss with flower barrette instruction leaflet

- Two editions of *The Oracle* newsletter
- Plus exclusive Sweet Valley High® product offers, special savings, contests, and much more!

Be the first to find out what Jessica & Elizabeth Wakefield are up to by joining the Sweet Valley High® Fan Club for the one-year membership fee of only $6.25 each for U.S. residents, $8.25 for Canadian residents (U.S. currency). Includes shipping & handling.

Send a check or money order (do not send cash) made payable to "Sweet Valley High® Fan Club" along with this form to:

SWEET VALLEY HIGH® FAN CLUB, BOX 3919-B, SCHAUMBURG, IL 60168-3919

NAME_____
(Please print clearly)

ADDRESS_____

CITY_____ STATE _____ ZIP_____
(Required)

AGE _____ BIRTHDAY_____ /_____ /_____

Offer good while supplies last. Allow 6-8 weeks after check clearance for delivery. Addresses without ZIP codes cannot be honored. Offer good in USA & Canada only. Void where prohibited by law.
©1993 by Francine Pascal   LCI-1383-193

Life after high school gets even sweeter!

Jessica and Elizabeth are now freshman at Sweet Valley University, where the motto is: Welcome to college – welcome to freedom!

Don't miss any of the books in this fabulous new series.

College Girls #1 ....56308-4 $3.50/4.50 Can.

Love, Lies and Jessica Wakefield #2........56306-8 $3.50/4.50 Can.

Bantam Doubleday Dell
Books for Young Readers

Bantam Doubleday Dell
Dept. SVH 11
2451 South Wolf Road
Des Plaines, IL 60018

Please send the items I have checked above. I am enclosing _____ (please add $2.50 to cover postage and handling). Send check or money order, no cash or C.O.D.s please.

Name _____

Address _____

City _____ State _____ Zip _____

SVH 11 2/94

Please allow four to six weeks for delivery.
Prices and availability subject to change without notice.

Life after high school gets even *Sweeter!*

Francine Pascal's
SWEET VALLEY
SVU
UNIVERSITY
Life after high school gets even sweeter

ssica and Elizabeth are now freshmen at Sweet Valley iversity, where the motto is: Welcome to college — ●lcome to freedom!

n't miss any of the books in this fabulous new series.